By JJ Knight

USA Today bestselling author of

Single Dad on Top

The Accidental Harem

Big Pickle

Hot Pickle

Spicy Pickle

Royal Pickle

Tasty Mango

Second Chance Santa

Uncaged Love

Fight for Her

Reckless Attraction

Want to make sure you don't miss a release?
Join JJ's email or text list.

Royal Pickle

He's a prince on the run. She's a deli worker with a dream. Their spontaneous royal wedding is a match made in *mayhem*.

I have to find a wife.

And not just any wife.

A love match.

My parents gave me ten years to find a princess on my own, and the deadline has arrived.

I've outrun the palace guards for months, but due to a rooster Speedo incident that went viral, they have tracked me to America.

I'm not known for my stellar taste in the opposite sex. The last one put my naked pictures on Instagram.

But there is this one girl.

I saw her in a New York deli making sandwiches. She helped me escape the photographers.

Smart. Beautiful. Quick-witted.

Yes. I choose her.

Now all I have to do is convince her to marry me.

The wedding is in *seven days*.

—

Royal Pickle is a standalone romantic comedy about a prince who can't keep his pants on, a poet who writes naughty limericks, and a made-up European country where everyone likes to sing and dance. With donkeys.

Casey Shay Press
PO Box 160116
Austin, TX 78716
www.jjknight.com

Also available in paperback: ISBN 9781938150951

CHAPTER 1

Sunny

Day One

I've just refilled the cheese on the sandwich line when the glass door to our Brooklyn deli flies open and a blur of a man launches past the entrance.

Rachel and I glance at each other, leaning over the sneeze guard to get a better look.

The small dining area is empty of customers. It's midafternoon and well after the lunch rush.

I hold up my hands to Rachel in a *stay there* gesture. I'm the owner's granddaughter. Rachel is high school help. If something bad is going down, I should be the responsible one.

I walk cautiously around the counter. The man is army-crawling beneath the tables like it's World War III, and Grammy's deli is the front line.

"Can I help you?" I only get a look at his legs and butt in form-fitting jeans before he disappears again.

I push aside a chair. "Hey! What's going on?"

A face pops above the table, and I almost stumble back. He's *gorgeous*.

"Shhh!"

"Shhh for what? It's only me and Rachel."

He peers around. His eyes are green and mischievous beneath a shock of wild brown-gold hair. He doesn't look like a criminal on the run. He's closer to a magazine model.

"Do you have a bathroom?" Now that he's said actual words, I get a load of his accent. I've served people from all kinds of places in my years of working with Grammy. But I've never heard anyone talk like this.

"Yes. In the back."

"Great." He leaps to his feet and dashes through the room, dodging tables like a hockey player skirting opponents.

Rachel slides up beside me, her long brown ponytail swinging in an artful curl. She's adorable, all magnetic lashes and killer nails. She's a senior in high school and way more put together than I am, despite my being almost ten years older. "What's all that about?"

"I guess some bathroom emergency. Did you hear him talk?"

She nods. "Dreamy. Did you see his butt?"

"Totally."

Rachel examines her manicure. "I hope he's not getting sick in there. It's my turn to clean."

There's a commotion on the sidewalk. A half-dozen men with cameras rush by the windows, nearly knocking a lady with a stroller into the street.

"Cripes!" Rachel says. "What's all that?"

I tuck a chair into place. "I have a feeling it has to do with the man who crawled through the deli."

"I bet you're right." Rachel chomps on her gum at an accelerated rate, like she always does when she thinks she's onto something exciting.

The door opens and one of the camera guys looks in, two long lenses strung around his neck. "Not in here!" he calls. He sees us standing there. "Hey, you girls see a man go by, yay tall, kind of a looker?"

Rachel cocks her hip. "What's it to you?"

The man's eyes light up. "We're trying to catch him! Is he here?" He steps inside. "Don't tell anybody else. If I get an exclusive, it's worth ten grand."

"Ten grand!" Rachel's jaw starts working a mile a minute. "What's so great about him that his picture is worth ten grand?"

"He's the Prince of Avalonia!" the man says. He twists the lock on the door. "Where is he?"

Rachel watches him. "What's in it for me?"

I'm seething. I don't like that these two are brokering a deal in my grandmother's deli. It's not right. Clearly, the prince is in distress.

"She's screwing with you," I tell the photographer. "He's not here."

"What?" He turns to Rachel. "Are you serious?"

Rachel catches my eye, and I give her a glare that would peel paint.

She sighs. "Yeah, I was yankin' your chain."

"Damn it! Now I'm behind." He curses more as he races

to the door, yelping as he fights to untwist the lock. Yeah, it sticks.

When he's out of sight, I move closer to the back wall. "They're gone," I call.

It takes a minute, but finally, that perfect face peers around the corner. "Thanks for getting rid of him."

Now that he's out here, my knees shake. Could he really be a prince?

Rachel is the one who asks. "So you're the Prince of Avalonia, huh? Where's that?"

"Europe," he says. "And it's small. It's not England. Or even Monaco."

"Then how does it sustain itself?" I realize too late that I've nerded out, but I blindly keep going. "What do you export?"

He grins at me. "A smart one. I like that."

But he doesn't answer the question.

"I always wanted to be a princess," Rachel says, then lets out an *oof* when I elbow her.

"Any special reason they're chasing you?" I ask.

He straightens his blue-striped shirt, which fits his chest and shoulders the way a lock hugs a key. "I'm supposed to go home to choose a bride, but I've decided to extend my bachelorhood."

"I'll marry you!" Rachel volunteers. I spare her the elbow this time.

He grins at her. "That's a tempting offer. But I better go before they find me."

"There's a back door," I tell him. "The alley will take you to a street that leads straight to the subway." Then I want to smack myself. The Prince of Avalonia would never take the subway.

"That's smart." He gives me a wink that makes my belly flip. "They'll never suspect I'd ride a public train."

Okay, then. "This way." I gesture to the swinging doors that lead to the kitchen. "And take this." I grab a Manhattan Pickle hat that Uncle Sherman insists we stock even though this deli isn't part of the Pickle chain. "It will keep them from recognizing you as easily."

"I like the sneaky workings of your brilliant mind." He tugs the hat low on his head, almost obscuring those devilish eyes.

We cross the kitchen to the back door, Rachel trailing behind.

He tugs it open and peers out. "Which way?"

I point down the alley. "Head to that street, then to the right two blocks. The photographers are headed the other way."

He turns to grin at me. "You're saving me here. Can I kiss you?"

I take a step back. "Uh. No."

"Damn. I never like to leave a beautiful girl unkissed. Handshake then?"

I hold mine out. "Sure."

He grips my palm and my whole body feels electrified, like he carries a charge. I stare at my hand after he lets it go.

He touches the hat brim, and then he's gone.

Rachel peers out the door. "Awww, Sunny, why didn't you kiss him?" She crosses her arms over her green deli apron. "I could have been your waiting lady or something."

I push the door closed. "If he kisses every girl he sees, he doesn't sound like happily-ever-after material."

Rachel kicks out her hip. "He didn't ask to kiss *me*."

I head to the walk-in fridge. "I'll start chopping the pickles for the dinner rush. You watch the front."

"What if those photographers come back?"

"You don't have to say a thing."

"All right." She twists her ponytail around her finger as she heads to the sandwich line.

When she's gone, I take a breath and lean against the wall. A prince in the deli! What a wild and strange thing to happen.

I glance down. My rainbow-striped pants don't quite match my polka-dot sweatshirt. I swipe my fingers across a big smear of mayo on my apron. I didn't know *that* was there.

But he asked to kiss me! Me! And not Rachel!

That's certainly not an everyday thing.

I'm nobody's first choice. Everyone says I'm odd.

And not *princess* odd, like Belle with her head stuck in a book or Rapunzel in her tower. I don't have a perfect soprano voice or cascading waves of sunshine hair.

My only contributions to the world are my mixed expressions.

A penny for your head in the clouds.

The apple doesn't fall far from the chopping block.

But my favorite has always been *birds of a feather bark up the wrong tree.*

Because that's how everybody looks at me. The staff. The customers. Even my own sister. They all have opinions about what I should do with my life. They don't see who I am, just who they think I ought to be.

It doesn't matter. I'm too busy writing my odd little sayings in beautiful notebooks. I've given up hope that one day I'll make the pages of *A Universe of Poetry*, the biggest and most prestigious poetry magazine in, well, the universe.

I'm fine with working in a deli. I can ignore everyone's sidelong glances and unhelpful advice about my clothes, my hobbies, and my future.

I do have one person on my side, though. Grammy gets me. She's the great matriarch of the Packwood clan, or the Pickles, if you look at Uncle Sherman's side of the family.

She has a clear-eyed view of each of her grandkids. I'm the youngest, and I've worked beside her in this tiny walk-up deli in Brooklyn since I was old enough to press my face against the glass case.

I'm not the odd one, she tells me, it's that the world is too full of straight lines and hard edges for a colorful, ever-changing creature like me.

She's the only one I tell my dirty limericks. I can create them spontaneously, but I almost never write them down.

I already have one for the prince. I start chopping pickles as I repeat the lines again in my head.

A prince once ran into my store
His butt wiggled over the floor
He dampened my panties
Like a sex vigilante
Turning nice girls like me into whores

CHAPTER 2

Prince Leopold

Gave 'em the ol' slipperoo.

That was close, though. The paparazzi in America are nothing compared to the British version I encountered in London, but they have plenty of bite.

I'd hoped to fly under the radar for a while. After a party in Amsterdam got live-broadcast and my father's security detail showed up, I had to leave the country.

Then in London, I spent the night with exactly the wrong woman, who had an Instagram following in the millions and posted very compromising photos.

Father's old flunky Grisholm damn near caught up with me there, but I booked a chartered flight with my cash on hand. I landed in New York a week ago and kept my identity under wraps until someone uploaded a photo to Facebook and the facial recognition outed me. Damn that platform.

Now the photographers *and* my father's men are on my heels. I can't return to the Ritz. No doubt there's an Avalonian contingent waiting to nab me. I'll have to find a new spot to crash.

All this to avoid all of my family's chosen brides waiting for me back home.

I spy the concrete stairs to the subway. I recognize them from American movies. When I get down in the pit filled with machines, there are revolving mechanisms that several passersby push through.

No problem.

I race toward one, ready to dash to my freedom.

And a steel bar nails me in the crotch.

I stumble back, arms crossed over the royal jewels. What in the devil?

No one seems to notice or care about my plight. I lean against the wall, trying to clear the stars from my vision.

Everyone else is going through them fine, including the one that stopped me cold.

What does that bar have against an Avalonian prince?

A pair of men hurry down the stairs and don't even break their conversation as they pass through the bars. I watch more closely and realize there is some sort of card they use to gain access.

Maybe I can procure one from these machines.

Loud voices on the street level above catch my attention. I swear I hear the word *prince*. Great. I have to act.

Two boys crash down the stairs on skateboards. I plan to ask them if there are men with cameras up there, but they grasp their boards and leap over the rotating bars without bothering with cards.

Good enough for me. One good jump, and I'm inside.

I follow the young chaps into a maze of wide hallways.

There's a press of people, so I feel more secure that I won't be spotted. Still, I pull the hat low on my brow.

Another set of stairs leads to concrete platforms with tracks on either side.

A monstrous train approaches, stopping and opening its doors.

People pour out.

This is the subway. I've seen it a million times on screen.

I follow a group onto one of the cars and only let out a breath when the doors close, and we're careening into a tunnel to another part of the city.

I made it clean away, thanks to that dark-haired woman in the apron.

Perhaps I will purchase her place of employment and end her servitude. She seems far too cunning for such a position.

As I sail into the oblivion of safety, I plot my next move. I know I can't run forever. Marriage will be required of me, eventually. Avalonia needs an heir.

My parents married for love, not political advantage. My whole life they preached they wanted the same for me.

They gave me ten years to find my great love. I filled my time with actresses, models, and flings. I focused on life over wife.

And now, on the eve of my thirtieth birthday, time has run out. The wedding will be for political gain after all. The cultural director has selected three brides for me to choose from upon my return.

But I don't plan to pick any of them.

I will find my own bride, and I will avoid my father's

men until the deed is done. I have plenty of cash and New Yorkers so far have been fabulous about helping a bloke out.

Like that woman in the deli.

As the walls whiz by outside the windows, I keep touching on the memory of her sharp gaze and the long hair flowing down her back.

I'd asked to kiss her, and she'd refused.

That was new.

And her interest in Avalonia was not its royalty, but its exports. How it sustained itself.

So interesting.

I've run from country to country for a decade, and I've never met someone like her.

The penthouse pool party is in full swing when I exit the elevator to the roof. I'm glad for the diversion, seeing as I don't have a place to stay nor a stitch to my wardrobe beyond what I'm wearing.

I was invited by Claude, an ambassador's son I met a year ago on a diplomatic trip. He assured me no one would know me, and even if they did, everyone there was a celebrity of some sort and prized their privacy. I'd be plenty incognito and could meet more potential princesses.

A band plays under a pavilion on the far end of the pool. The New York summer day is sublime and dozens of gorgeous women in bikinis decorate the place. This is definitely my kind of scene.

Claude breaks away from a small group to greet me. "Leopold, you made it!"

I frown at the name, sure I'll be outed.

He claps my back. "Don't worry, my friend. You're safe here."

He's right. In mere moments, I'm dunking my feet in the pool, drinking a whiskey and feeling fine. Two girls splash their way over to me.

"Where's your swimsuit?" one asks. Her concoction of strings can scarcely qualify as a complete garment.

"Didn't bring one." More like, no longer own one. I'll have to find a personal shopper to replenish my wardrobe since I can't return to my suite.

"I've got something," the other says. She pulls herself out of the pool with a cascade of water.

"Don't bother on my account," I say, although I could use a dip.

"No bother at all," she says, leaving wet footprints on the concrete as she heads to a lounge chair.

"I like your accent," the other says. "Where are you from?"

"Europe." I should engage a coach, learn to speak less formally and clipped. It gives me away.

"Nice." She is only making conversation, not truly pressing for my origin of birth. I relax.

"Here you go." The other woman has returned, a pair of swim trunks in her hand. "I was going to give them to my boyfriend, but I think I've just decided he's my ex."

"I'm so sorry to hear that." I accept the trunks. "Thank you."

"There's a cabana with a changing room." She points at

a structure at the head of the pool. "I could help if you like."

I know an invitation when I hear one, but if my last year has proven anything, it's that I'm a terrible sucker for beautiful women who are bad for my image. "I think I can manage, but thank you for the offer."

Inside the small room, I shuck the jeans and shirt I've worn all day and put on the trunks. They are quite fitted, not the loose shorts some of the other men are wearing. But I've seen this style at swim competitions, so they must be all right.

The pattern is odd, but I pick up a towel from a stack and head out into the sunshine of late afternoon.

The two women let out a whoop at the sight of me. The outfit makes quite a stir among the partygoers nearby.

"Come over here!" The woman who brought me the garment gestures her way.

I oblige her, standing at the edge of the pool. Only now in the full light of the sun do I recognize the image on the front of the tight swimsuit.

A rooster.

"Is this a common prank in America?" I ask them.

"Totally," the one woman says. "Jeannie's done it twice this summer. But that cock looks good on you."

I suppose I should have immediately changed, wrapped in the towel, or something.

But I did not.

And that is how a photo of me with the words "Prince of Avalonia, King of Cock" goes viral on all forms of social media.

I've made my final mistake as a free man. Everyone will

know I am here. What I look like. The pursuit will increase tenfold. There will be no more flying under the radar.

With the whole world knowing my face (and my cock), I'm as good as caught.

No more bachelorhood.

My parents will haul me back to marry.

It will be some bride they've found "suitable" since I've been unable to form a love match.

Unless.

Unless I beat them, as Americans like to say, to the punch.

Do they mean the refreshing drink?

Or a boxing glove?

No matter.

I have precisely the right woman in mind.

Smart.

Friendly.

And living in servitude.

She'll be grateful to be released.

Turned into a princess.

Yes! A quick fairy-godmother transformation, and I'll have my very own Cinderella.

Buoyed by the idea, I escape the cursed party that has turned a prank into my doom. Such a brilliant solution.

I just have to get to her in time.

CHAPTER 3

Sunny

Grammy and I are stacking chairs, the 'closed' sign long since turned, when there's a rap on the glass.

"I'll look." I wind through the tables, avoiding the freshly mopped spots.

My stomach flips when I recognize the prince through the glass. He's still wearing the pickle hat. I quickly twist the lock and gesture him inside.

"Thank goodness you're here," he says, breathless. The bits of hair sticking out from under the cap are curlier than before, and he smells faintly of chlorine.

"Are you in trouble again?"

"The worst. The biggest. I climbed two fire escapes and hopped three buildings to get to you."

Grammy leans on her mop, peering over her glasses. "That's commitment. Who is this young man?"

"Let me introduce myself." The prince bows with a flourish of arm movements. "I am Leopold the Second, Prince of Avalonia, and heir apparent to the throne."

Grammy cuts her eyes at me. "Should I call the police?"

I shake my head. "We met earlier. Photographers chased him into the deli, and I helped him get away."

"Oh." Grammy smoothes her apron self-consciously. "I'm so sorry. We don't get much royalty in Brooklyn."

He turns to me in a rigid, formal gesture, his heels practically clicking together. "Milady, I don't believe I caught your name when we last met."

"Sunny," I say. "Sunny Packwood." My fingers reach for my head self-consciously. I've twisted my hair into a messy topknot to clean. There's way more than a mayo smear on me now. I smell of bleach.

Leopold tugs on his shirt, looking almost nervous. His eyes dart back and forth. He touches the cap, then jerks it off, holding it at his side as if it's an affront to be wearing it.

"Are you okay?" I ask.

"Do you have a father I could approach?" His gaze won't meet mine.

"He's in Florida right now." Why would Leopold want my father? "I'm not following what you're getting at."

But Grammy is ahead of me. "If you're looking for family, I'm her grandmother."

Leopold exhales. "Oh, good. Sunny, I need your help one more time, I'm afraid. You're the only woman I've met since leaving Avalonia that I think could take this on."

I take a step back. "Take what on?"

He fumbles with his pants. "In my country, it is customary to empty our pockets at this moment, so please indulge me in this exercise."

I glance over at Grammy, who shrugs. She has a smudge of something black on her cheek and her gray curls are chaos. I probably look about the same. We're in no shape to be standing here talking to a prince. At least her apron is more or less clean. I dumped soda on mine trying to clear a clog in the fountain reservoir.

Leopold sets a leather wallet on a table, then a roll of bills that looks like something you might take to a strip club. There's a smooth, vibrant green stone. Then a bit of twine tied around what appears to be a hound's tooth.

And a condom.

He winces when he sees it. "Sorry about that."

Like it matters to me.

"Why are you emptying your pockets?" He's low-key freaking me out.

"It is an Avalonian ritual. I understand that there is a custom here as well." He gets down on one knee, and I can't do anything but stare.

"Grandmother of Sunny, please inspect the betrothal ring of Avalonia, intended for its future sovereign queen." He tugs a carved ring from his finger and holds it out.

Grammy takes it, holding it close to her nose. "It's very impressive. Am I looking for something in particular?"

"In a moment, you will bestow the blessing of your family by passing the ring to your granddaughter, if she consents." Leopold is deathly serious, his face taut with anxiety.

What is he talking about? If I consent? Future sovereign queen?

He gazes up at me. "Sunny Packwood, might I hold your right hand?"

I glance over at Grammy, and she's practically glowing. She clearly thinks this bizarre ritual is fascinating. I hold out my hand, then take it back and wipe it on my apron before extending it again.

Leopold takes it in his. His skin is warm on mine, and the thrilling zip I felt earlier darts through me once more. He's stupidly handsome. *Pretty as a panther.* Particularly right now.

"Sunny Packwood, by the sworn authority of the crown of Avalonia, the jewel of Europa, and its heir apparent, I wish to bequeath upon you the title of Princess, as my bride. Or, as you would put it in the country of your birth, will you marry me?"

What.

The.

Ever-loving.

Hell.

Surely I heard him wrong. Or misunderstood. "What did you say?"

Grammy nudges me. "You really going to make him repeat it?"

Leopold swallows, his Adam's apple lurching. "If you consent to our marriage, your grandmother will convey her blessing upon our union by placing the betrothal ring on the center finger of your right hand. We will also, as is custom in your country, procure a proper diamond for the fourth finger to signify our engagement to your fellow Americans."

I stare at his face. Is this some sort of prank? "I barely know you."

He nods. "I assure you, I know you more than the brides already chosen and waiting for me when I am hauled back to Avalonia."

So, he's using me as an out. I get it now.

Breaks squeal on the street. My focus shifts past him. Two black cars, both emblazoned with strange flags, pull up in front of the door.

"Grammy, twist the lock," I say. I won't let them interrupt until I figure out what's going on.

She moves faster than a woman a quarter of her age to secure the door. Men appear at the glass, but Leopold ignores them.

I draw in a deep breath. "How do you know I'm not already married?"

He glances at my hand. "You are not wearing the customary ring signifying a preexisting union. Am I incorrect?"

"No. I'm not married."

"Nor betrothed? Or intended?"

"No, none of that."

Leopold's grin is disarming. "Good. Fate has brought us together. But I must tell you one thing. Avalonian law requires that we perform the wedding ceremony in seven days."

Grammy turns at that. "Seven days?"

"What if I change my mind?" I ask.

For the first time, Leopold grins. "So the answer is yes?"

"I don't know!"

Bang, bang, bang. The men pound their fist on the glass. Grammy faces them, hands on her hips. "Don't you go breaking my window!"

"I promise to ensure your happiness," Leopold says.

"We have seven days to figure things out before, as you say here, the knot is tied."

He's serious. "Is there divorce in Avalonia?"

He frowns. "It's not illegal. However, no crown price has ever divorced in our history."

"How long is that history?"

"Seven generations."

Oh, geez.

I press the back of my hand to my forehead. "How did you get to the point that you need to ask a random woman to marry you?" I'm vaguely aware that the standoff between Grammy and the men is continuing, but they seem to be at a stalemate.

"I am almost thirty, and my parents already extended my time of bachelorhood."

"Isn't there anybody else you can ask?"

He runs his thumb along my palm. "I have met many women. I could have chosen any of them at any point. But now that I am at this juncture, I choose you."

He chooses me. After only talking to him once.

"I need more than that. Why would you pick me?"

"You are smart. You already knew that a small country like mine needs proper exports to survive. You are kind. Despite not knowing me, you helped me escape the photographers. You sacrificed a tidy sum of money that might have helped you to instead let me escape. You are exactly what my country needs. What I need. Fate has played its hand."

"Oh." Maybe he does see me. I've never had such an ardent declaration of liking me for who I am in my whole life. "Grammy? What should I do here?"

She turns to me. "I won't put this ring on you if you aren't interested in giving it a shot. But I don't want you working in this deli all your life. It's like he said. Sometimes fate draws a card. You still have seven days to decide if he's worthy of you."

I try to keep the tremor out of my voice. "What would we do in those seven days?"

"We would talk! And get to know each other." His face is animated, glowing with happiness. He practically buzzes with energy.

Is all this for me? This optimism? How?

A million thoughts blur through my head. High school. Two years of junior college that never led to a degree like I planned. I lost my confidence and gave up. Since then, I've kept my head in the clouds, and my hands in the dishwater in Grammy's deli.

I could leave it, right now. Go with this beautiful man. Not worry about rent. How to support myself. And all those nasty judgmental people could go stuff themselves. I would be a damn *princess*.

Even so, this is crazy. "What if we hate each other?"

His hand grips mine, warm and loose. "Then you abandon me and I take a pre-chosen bride. But I urge you, unless we despise each other, please consider my proposal. I can give you a life you desire. You could study. Travel. Pursue an art."

"I could do nothing but write poetry?" My heart speeds up. I'd always set that desire aside as futile. Nobody makes a living writing verses and I definitely won't do it for professors anymore.

"That sounds like a beautiful pursuit. We can declare a

month of poetry around your birthday. Establish a poetic council." His eyes shine. He's excited for me. We've only met two times, and yet, he's on my side.

"I could make my whole life about poetry?" I want to cry. The future I've always dreamed of could actually happen. My hope sprouts all over again, as if it had never been crushed.

"Absolutely. My mother's pursuit has been watercolors. My grandmother's was pottery. Avalonia is known for its arts."

I can scarcely breathe, thinking of how I might spend my days, writing, thinking, experiencing the world to put into verse. And not just dirty limericks. Real poems.

"Yes," I say. "I would like very much to be the Princess of Avalonia, pursue poetry, and establish a Council of the Poetic Arts in your country." It sounds amazing, perfect, like I've been waiting all my life to say the words.

Grammy hustles over. "Here goes the ring." She takes my hand so that both she and Leopold are holding it.

"Let them see," Leopold says. "They can bear witness to the transfer of the betrothal ring."

We shift so that the men in suits can see what we do. As the ring slips onto my finger, heavy and loose, one of the men's eyes go wide. He shoves a phone next to his ear.

"It is done," Leopold says. "Blessed and witnessed." He pulls me close to him, and the smell of chlorine mingles with my bleach. His lips press into my hair. "Now to prepare for the wedding."

I step back. "What happens next?"

"Pack your things. We should be close these seven days. My security detail will send a car for you. You are now the most precious jewel of my country, and you will need to be protected. I will turn myself in." He tilts his head toward the men. "I'm staying at the Ritz. We will secure a suite for you. Your grandmother is welcome."

Leopold strides to the door and turns the lock. The men surge inside. One in a bold blue suit with a gold sash beneath the jacket looks like he's about to have a heart attack. His face is mottled red.

"Did you perform the ritual and pass the betrothal ring?" He stares at the contents of Leopold's pockets laid out on the table.

"I did. You can inform Father and Mother that I have already chosen my intended."

"But we must have the wedding in seven days." He pockets all of Leopold's items, frowning at the condom.

"Yes, we will." Leopold grins at me. "A wedding in seven days."

Grammy passes me the mop so I can hold on to something solid. I've completely changed my life for a complete stranger.

What have I done?

I think I might have jumped *out of the frying pan and off my rocker.*

CHAPTER 4

Prince Leopold

Grisholm tries to grill me in the car, but I have yet to speak. We're stopped by traffic on the bridge to Manhattan, and I stare out over the city, hoping I've done the right thing.

I was so sure as I dashed through the subway back to the woman's deli that she was the one. But her questions make sense. How have I gotten here? How do I know this is the right path?

The machine has been set in motion. With the call that Grisholm placed the moment I got in the car, the wedding preparations began.

The seven-day decree is normally no issue, because the betrothal ring is held until the prenuptial party, even though the bride and groom have planned to marry for a year or more.

The groom's pockets are ordinarily filled with ceremonial items to be displayed, not cash and condoms. At least I had the signet stone given to me by my grandfather and an ancestral war tooth I keep for luck. It's not gems and ancient coins, but it's something.

The original decree was intended to ensure the family, who often was creating a trade or land agreement with the marriage, did not change their mind before the ceremony could take place. Once the ring was placed, the bride was confined to the palace's nuptial sanctuary in the east tower.

It has been at least a hundred years since the bridal selection and the ceremony have been in such proximity. I'm not entirely sure how it will unfold, since there has been much speculation on the nature of a twenty-first century royal wedding. My parents' own nuptials were broadcast on television in 1986, following the trend set by other European royals.

I'm not sure I want that. There isn't time, anyway. Perhaps I have done us all a great favor. I will allow one of my younger sisters to luxuriate in all the pomp and festivity.

For me, I will have Sunny Packwood, a food service worker in Brooklyn, New York.

If I can convince her to keep me. I have seven days. I've had entire relationships rise and fall in that time.

Most of them, actually.

The car moves forward and Grisholm answers another call. I listen in to see what fates are being decided.

"Yes, I understand. Of course. We will collect her immediately. Yes, we have the location of her domicile. No, the inquiries are being made."

The squeaky, indistinct voice coming through the speaker sounds like Rosenthal, the cultural director in charge of finding me a bride. Since it is not my father, their conversation is of no consequence. I tune Grisholm out, watching the brake lights on the unyielding river of cars when I hear him say, "Virginity uncertain."

Oh, hell no. "You will not inquire about that, nor will there be any physical examinations. Do you understand?"

Grisholm's grizzly eyebrows draw together.

I move swiftly, knocking the phone from his hand. "Is that understood?"

He sighs, leaning down to pick up the phone. "There hasn't been a physical exam since 1840," he says. "Good grief, did you stop paying attention to cultural rules and standards in level four?"

He's right. I'm remembering the old standards. I don't want Sunny to be put through anything demeaning. She's an intellectual. I could see that from the moment we met. A dreamer, too. I caught that gleam in her eye when she talked of poetry.

I will not be the cause of her feeling anything but anticipation and joy. I have dragged her into the unknown with only a promise and a dream. I will owe her.

Since she and her grandmother appear to be the proprietors of their establishment, there is no need to rescue her from servitude. I am pleased she is a hard worker. She can now apply that rigor to pursuits she loves. A smile flirts with my lips that we both smelled of chemicals during our betrothal ceremony. It will be a story to tell our children.

Should that occur. I have no idea if we will be a match. I will be true to my word that I won't force her to go through with the nuptials.

Until my parents, Avalonian royal weddings were for political, financial, or social gain. Certainly, the women chosen for me were enlisted with that in mind. But after the papers are signed, often the heart goes where it chooses. My grandmother's lovers were legendary and of great despair for my grandfather. My parents changed the rules in hopes that the future royal couples could find happiness.

Still, I like what I see with Sunny. Should she feel the same, we can hopefully make something work.

At least I got to make the choice myself.

For better. Hopefully not for worse.

CHAPTER 5

Sunny

The gleaming car waits at the curb when we finally put away the cleaning supplies, and Grammy locks up the deli.

I slipped the ring in my pocket while I finished up, warily watching two men stand on either side of the door as we completed our work.

"I'll go with you, child," Grammy says. "I think we will close shop while this is settled. I want to make sure with my own eyes you are taken care of."

I'm relieved. I don't even know who else to tell. Mom and Dad are on vacation in Florida. My sister Greta would freak out. And Uncle Sherman? He might give these bodyguards something to worry about.

The night air feels good after the work and the stress of the evening. Honestly, if the men hadn't been standing outside the door, I might have assumed I dreamed the whole thing.

One guard turns to me as Grammy pockets her keys. "Do you have an automobile that needs moving?"

Grammy shakes her head. "No, I live up the road. Sunny walks me then takes the subway home."

"Not today." He opens the back door to the car.

Inside is luxurious, smelling of leather and expensive alcohol, like a private club I visited once or twice with Uncle Sherman and my cousins.

Grammy and I sit close together on a seat that faces another. One of the men slides across from us.

"Where are we going?" I ask.

"Our instructions are to help you pack and deliver you to the hotel."

"It can't wait until morning?" Grammy asks.

"We only have a week," the man says. "We need as much time as possible for preparation. We are awaiting instructions from the King about when we will fly to Avalonia."

"We can't close the deli that long!" I protest.

Grammy squeezes my hand. "We'll work it out."

The man nods in understanding. "You will be compensated for the period your establishment will be unable to provide income."

"Oh, that isn't necessary," Grammy says, but the man shakes his head.

"These procedures are written in Avalonian law as a preparation for a new princess."

"Well, we wouldn't want to break Avalonian law," I say, but hush when the man's eyes narrow.

Grammy and I steal a glance, both biting back a laugh.

The car moves forward, and Grammy tells the man her address. "I'll pack a few things," she says.

The neighbors standing by the stoop to her walk-up stare at the official-looking car as we scoot out of the back seat. The man who rode with us follows us to the door, but remains outside to stand watch when we go inside.

Grammy closes the door and plops onto the sofa. "What craziness is this?"

I lift my hand, and the heavy ring spins on my middle finger. I move it to my thumb, then wonder if *that* breaks Avalonian law, and move it back. "Do you have some string? Or tape? This is terribly loose."

Grammy tugs some knitting out of the bag by the end table. "What color?"

"Any is good."

While she pulls on a skein, I sit beside her to look up Avalonia on my phone.

At first I only get the micro-continent from the Paleozoic Era, but eventually I'm routed to the small sovereign principality tucked on a narrow strip of land between Luxembourg and Belgium.

They *are* tiny. How can a country that small even support a royal family? My first question to Prince Leopold stands. What is their export?

But the land is beautiful. Rolling hills and green valleys. There are ancient castles and long stone walls. I type in "Avalonian Palace" and nearly fall off the sofa.

Grammy looks up. "Everything okay?"

I turn the phone to her. She peers at it and drops her reading glasses down. "Is this his house?"

"Yes." The gray stone castle looks straight out of *Cinderella*. Flags fly on high turrets. There are tall towers on each end. Out in front is a long plaza surrounded by shops, like in the movie *Frozen*. I half expect to zoom in and see singing, dancing townsfolk.

Grammy whistles low. "That's something."

I set down the phone. "Why are you encouraging this?"

"I told you. Something has to knock you out of your safety zone."

"I'm getting *married*."

Grammy presses her lips together, like she always does when one of us is arguing with her. "Only if you like him. You have a week to figure that out."

"A week is nothing!" I jump from the cushion and pace the small living room. "What was I thinking? I don't know this guy! What if it's a big con? What if I'm getting sacrificed to some volcano god?" My chest goes tight, and I clutch it, trying to draw a breath.

Grammy is instantly at my side. "Breathe, girl, breathe. If it's some sort of racket, you'll bail. You know all we have to do is call those three cousins of yours and nobody's making off with you anywhere you don't want to go."

"They're not even here." My voice wavers. Jason is in Texas. Max lives in California. Anthony is sometimes in Manhattan but mainly stays near his deli in Colorado.

"You don't have to do this," Grammy says. "Go give this ring to the man outside the door and say it's been a big mistake."

I make a fist to hold the heavy ring on my finger. I haven't looked at it closely. We raced to finish the deli work, then we left in the car.

I pull it off to examine it. The stone on top is a multi-faceted gold gem. All around the face are carved symbols, like a high school ring. On one side, there is the word peace. On the other, family.

Nothing ominous there.

I pick up my phone, which fell to the carpet during my leap. The page on Avalonia is still up. I read aloud.

"There have been seven kings over Avalonia, dating back to 1695. Currently, the reigning sovereign is King Francisco with Queen Pulmaria. The heir apparent is Prince Leopold, followed by his sisters Princesses Octavia and Lilianne."

Grammy squeezes my arm. "That all sounds good. Is there more on your prince?"

I head back to Google and type in "Prince Leopold of Avalonia."

The first hit is an image of him, taken earlier today, standing on the side of a pool in a Speedo with a rooster printed on the front. I sink back down on the sofa to read the headline.

Avalonian prince runs from marital demands and lives it up on a three-country party spree.

I don't show Grammy. Two women wearing so little that I have to zoom to see the existence of their swimwear sit at Leopold's feet, each holding a leg. I wonder what he needs me for. A wife at home so he can continue his wild lifestyle?

A lot of skin in a set of photos catches my eye next. I click through to the Instagram feed of a makeup influencer. She's posted dozens of pictures of Leopold, sometimes wrapped in red satin sheets, sometimes totally naked with "WOW" stickers over his crotch.

Whoa.

That was just a week ago.

My stomach falls to my shoes. It's not very flattering to be chosen by a prince when he's clearly on a vagina spree.

There once was a princely man-whore
With more pussy than he could
    account for
He might have proposed
And lied through his nose
But his ass will get kicked out my door

My traitorous brain is already thinking ahead. One of these women is not like the other. I could never wear a swimsuit like that, and I'm more likely to get mascara in my eye than on my lashes.

Grammy's TV sits opposite us, the flat screen dark and reflective. There I am, hair on top of my head, wearing a deli apron in need of a wash. My shirt sleeves are rolled up haphazardly but still got stained.

Does he think I'm so pathetic that his offer is something I can't refuse? Does he plan to shove me at his parents so they'll stop trying to drag him home from his pool parties and naked photographs with hot women?

I press my hand to my belly, trying not to throw up. This is worse than being chosen. It's like being picked first for dodgeball because everyone wants to see you get hit in the face.

"I don't need a week to decide." I pull the ring off my finger. "This is too crazy, even for me."

"I'll go with you," Grammy says.

I untie the apron and set it aside, wanting to look less pathetic when I face the guard. When I open the door, he turns. "All packed?"

I thrust the ring at him. "I'm not going. I looked up

your prince, and he's been banging every chick from Amsterdam to Manhattan. Not really marriage material."

The man's eyes narrow. "I'm afraid I can't allow that. I'm under strict orders to bring you to the Ritz."

Grammy pushes her way between us. "And she says she's not going. So take the ring back to your prince and tell him to shove it."

The man looks between the two of us. For a moment, I think he's going to let us go. Then he picks Grammy up by the waist and sets her aside. "Hey, you!" she cries, but the words are barely out when I'm scooped up and thrown over the man's shoulder.

And he can run. Before I even blink, I'm thrust into the car and the door is closed. Grammy hurries down her steps, but she's been long left behind.

The car takes off, and I press against the window. Grammy is standing on the sidewalk, her arms in the air, waving frantically.

I guess kidnapping is all well and good in Avalonia.

I never did learn to *look before I weep*.

CHAPTER 6

Prince Leopold

I'm catching up on all the Internet hits on my name, feeling deep chagrin at how naïve I've been about my popularity on social media, when my bodyguards James and Rubin enter the hotel suite.

I sit up from where I've been draped over a chair. "Is she here already?"

"Yes, sire," Rubin says. "She's in the suite next door."

"Did she bring many things?"

The two men glance at each other. "No, sir."

My suspicion rises. "Will she see me?"

Another glance. "I doubt it, sire."

Now I'm alarmed. "What happened?"

Rubin stands tall. He's a huge brute of a man and the closest thing I have to a friend on the security staff. "I apologize, sire, I should have gone. I'm afraid the situation was not handled with delicacy by James here."

I leap from the chair. "What situation?"

James has the wherewithal to stare at the floor. "The Princess, my sire, she tried to return the ring. I knew my orders were to bring her to you, so I may have brought her unwillingly."

Good Lord. I smooth back my hair, still damp from my shower. "Take me to her."

Rubin holds out his hands as if to stop me. "You might want to let her calm down. She's in a state."

I'm pissed at myself. I should have stayed with her. I thought to give her some time to herself before my position consumed her life.

"There's no time for that," I say. "The wedding is too close. I need to be wooing her, not pissing her off."

"Pissing, sire?" Rubin looks alarmed. He only knows the version of the word used in Avalonia, the bodily fluid sort.

"Making her mad, Rubin, keep up." I storm to the door. "Show me her suite."

Rubin opens the door and leads me down the hall. It's a great length before we arrive at another entrance. Outside of it, Scorsese stands, his face pulled into a frown. "Sire."

"Let me inside."

His eyes cast toward the door. Inside, I hear a crash. "Now."

He pulls a keycard from his pocket and disengages the lock.

When the door opens, I spot Pace, another member of the security detail, ducking behind a chair.

A ceramic jar hurtles toward the wall. I reach out and pluck it from the air. "Princess Sunny," I say. "Please allow me to correct any errors made by my incompetent staff."

Sunny stands in the center of the room, her chest heaving with anger, tendrils of long, dark hair spilling from a loose knot to frame her flushed face. She is fierce and incredibly beautiful, all fire and power and passion. I might fall a little in love with her right here.

"So kidnapping is legal in Avalonia?" she shrieks. "Because I was thrown into a car, dragged through the back halls of this hotel, and locked in a room!"

I sit on the sofa and set the jar on the coffee table. "Pace, Scorsese, please leave us."

"But sire," Pace says.

"Leave!"

They both give a quick nod of acknowledgment and close the door behind them.

Sunny picks up a lamp from the side table and holds it out like a broadsword. I sense an erection rising at the sight of her ferociousness and will it down.

"Can we talk this over?" I ask. "I can call down for some tea. Or wine? What would help you?"

She doesn't alter her stance, holding the lamp out in front of her. "I gave the ring back to your guard. I saw the video of you. And the pictures. I'm just some ploy to let you live a playboy life. I won't be used like that."

Everything falls into place. Of course she looked me up at first opportunity. And she saw it all.

"Those events were before our betrothal. I am now yours."

"Bullshit."

I hesitate. "I understand that the word is an expletive, but I'm not sure what you mean. Are you calling me manure? Or is it a threat to throw manure at me?"

"It means I don't believe you. Your words are manure."

"Oh! I get it. Thank you. I've heard it used so many ways."

She lets out a long gust of air, making the wild, loose parts of her hair fly around her face. I want to kiss her, feel her, do everything, but of course I cannot. We have this huge misunderstanding.

"Let me order us some food. A few drinks. I'm mad to kiss you."

I think this will help, but she raises the lamp again. "I'm not one of your models who thinks you're some hot number to post naked on their profiles! And what the hell was with the cock shot?"

I lean forward to brace my elbows on my knees. "I travel a lot, see much of the world, but I'm afraid that I'm never anywhere long enough to understand the subtleties of a prank, the inside of a joke."

"Bullshit."

I shrug. "This is why you are so important to me. You are smart. You understand these things. With you, I will be untouchable. Except by you. You can touch me all you want, when it is time, and if you are consenting. I am patient."

She stares at me as if I'm a goat rather than a man, and I realize I haven't expressed myself perfectly. But something in my words has helped, because she sets down the lamp and falls into a chair.

"I didn't get a chance to pack, and Grammy was going to come with me, but your people forcibly removed her and threw me in a car."

"It is their job to bring you to me if there is a problem. Let me call them to bring your Grammy."

She holds up her phone. "She's already in the city. And you're paying the taxi fare."

"Gladly." I glance around the room. Her suite is like mine, two bedrooms, a living area, and a small kitchen. "Tomorrow we can return to your homes. I will go with you, and you can pack."

She seems to deflate, like a child's balloon. "What is going on, Leopold? I can work with a lot of things, but I don't think I can bear the humiliation of being engaged while you run around taking naked photos with Instagram models."

I quickly close the space between us and kneel at her feet. "Sunny, that is past. I have enjoyed my time as a bachelor. I have certainly bedded many women, and for that sordid history, I apologize. I did not think ahead to my betrothed and how she might compare herself to the women who used me to feel important."

"Oh." Her brow creases, but I know it is too soon to wipe the concern from her skin. I merely sit near her.

"I will not lie about my past. Nor will I downplay my love of sexual relations. But until you and I sort who we are to be to each other, I pledge you my faithfulness."

"Oh." She says again. "Me, too."

"Good. Since I currently can think of nothing more than getting you naked in my arms, I say you will lead all the moves."

"Oh. Gosh. Oh." Her face is pink again, and not the same color as before. This is a good thing. I will get to her after all.

"Might I hold your hand, like I did during our betrothal ceremony?" I reach out, but do not touch her.

She swallows, and this is an even better sign. I might not know cultural subtleties outside of Avalonia, but I do know women.

"Of course." She lifts her arm, and when my fingers close around hers, a shiver runs through her body. Yes, this is very good.

"Our path is set," I tell her. "We will not have a customary courtship, but there is time. I think you will find Avalonia a lovely place and a life big enough for dreams, but small enough that you are not hounded in your home like an American celebrity."

"Or a British royal?" She rests our joined hands on her knee.

"That is the worst. Never marry a British royal if you want a shred of privacy."

She smiles, and the moment has passed. The misunderstanding is rectified.

It is not often I see in myself the qualities necessary for my future role as leader of Avalonia, but already, my future queen has shown me the way. Gratitude fills me, and despite my promise to myself to take it slow with her, I lift our joined hands to my lips and graze her knuckles.

When my gaze lifts, she's watching me. "Okay," she says. "This is crazy, but I'm going to take you at your word."

"My word is the law," I say. "Literally."

She laughs, and the sound is music to me.

I smile as well. "Did I get it right? Literally? Or is it misused?"

She laughs again. "You're literally the definition of literally."

"I take that this is good?"

Her eyes take in my face. I like it. "It is."

As her perusal of me continues, I must ask, "Do you have tomatoes on your eyes?"

"What?" The word is like an explosion. "Is this an Avalonian saying?"

"Very common. You know, tomatoes on your eyes." I make a circle with my fingers and lift it to my face.

"I have no idea what you mean. We put cucumbers on our eyes as a spa treatment."

"No, no. When someone asks if you have tomatoes on your eyes, it means, are you seeing the same thing I am seeing?"

"Ohhh. I see. Or are you looking through tomatoes?"

"Yes! So do you? Have tomatoes on your eyes?"

She continues to watch me. "I think the perfect tomato is in the eye of the beholder."

"And what do you behold?" I can scarcely await her answer. Does our match have potential? Will I have made my own choice in the end?

"I behold you," she says. "*Fitting like a glove at first sight.*"

CHAPTER 7

Sunny

Grammy arrives at the suite armed with an umbrella and a rolling pin.

When the guard opens the door, she rushes into the suite, both weapons outstretched. "Where is she?" she yells like an ancient warrior. Ivan the Terrible has nothing on her.

But Leopold and I are sitting on the sofa, holding hands.

She lowers her arms. "I guess you're all right, then."

I hurry over to her. "Thank you for coming."

Leopold stands and bows before her. "I think Princess Sunny and I have come to an understanding."

Grammy sets her weapons on the white carpet and places her hands on my cheeks. "Are you sure, my dear?"

I nod. "Yes. We're going to pack tomorrow. Leopold will come with us so that there are no more rogue guards."

Grammy sinks into a chair. "Good. I'm exhausted. And we never ate dinner."

"Excellent," Leopold says. "Let's order a feast."

Grammy and I share a glance and a smile. We're living in some warped fairy tale.

While Grammy and Leopold pore over the room service menu, I head to the bathroom for a shower. I'm tired of smelling of bleach and stale root beer. Leopold has cleaned up since we parted and wears a smart formal jacket that buttons down one side of his chest, and fitted gray pants that are hard to tear my gaze from.

I wish I had a change of clothes, but at least there's a big fluffy robe hanging on the back of the bathroom door. It's not ideal to wander around a hotel room wearing only a robe in front of a strange man, but then I guess he is only a week away from being my husband.

What *am* I doing? I can barely think straight as shower jets hit me from several angles. I stand for a long time in the spray, thinking over all the dominoes in my life that will fall if I actually do this thing.

First, Grammy will have to run the deli without me. That will be a burden on her. I'll have to call Uncle Sherman and get him to send people from his deli to help.

Will I need a maid of honor? I can ask my sister Greta, if she gets over herself after hearing the news. I don't even know if Avalonian royal weddings have a bridal party. It's so quick. There won't be time for dresses or anything else.

Gosh. This is hands-down the wildest thing I've ever done. Or could ever do.

I don't have so much as a comb to work through my hair. I twist it in a towel and reach for the robe. It's long and soft and covers me neck to ankles. I remember the TikTok hack for tying them to be more flattering and cross the belt over my belly to cinch the two loops rather than circling my waist.

It's not bad.

The bathroom opens to the bedroom. I peek out, but the room is empty. Then I tiptoe to the door to the living area. There are voices, but none of them belong to Grammy or Leopold. Uh oh. Are there guests? Maybe a bellboy with the food. It's been forty minutes. I took too long.

I peer out. Grammy sits on the sofa, lights blazing on her face. What is that? A woman applies a makeup base to her skin. Who is she?

Another woman rolls a long rack of clothing close to Grammy. She holds up gown after gown, all tiny like Grammy, until Grammy points to a lovely dove-gray one with beadwork around the neck.

I gasp, and the makeup woman spots me peering out. "She's ready, everyone!" Four women line up on the backside of the sofa, all bowing their heads to me.

Oh, boy.

I stare through the crack in the door, dumbfounded, until Grammy finally says, "Sunny, are you coming out or what?"

The first woman in the line lifts her head. She's tall and deeply brown, an odd flat circle of a hat topping a shower of tiny braids. "Prince Leopold has returned to his room to await us for dinner. It's only the ladies."

I step out. The room is crowded with racks of clothes, two tables of makeup and hair products, and a large metal box, split open in front to reveal dozens of pairs of shoes.

The first woman steps forward, her friendly eyes

watching me. "Princess Sunny, we were summoned the moment you performed the betrothal ceremony. I am Aisha, head stylist for the royal family. It is always my duty when the entourage travels to identify proper professionals to accompany us."

She gestures to the other women. "These ladies are all New Yorkers, and they will work to create a look for you that will befit your future reign but honors your city. The way you present yourself tomorrow morning with the announcement of your betrothal will influence Avalonian fashion and beauty for many years to come."

Me, influencing fashion and beauty? I feel light-headed, and my knees turn to mayonnaise.

Grammy stands. "Get her to sit. She's been working all day and no supper to boot. It's been a lot."

Two women lead me to a chair. Soon I have a cup of hot chamomile tea and a small tray of cheese and grapes.

My stomach is in knots. They want to change me. Turn me into someone I'm not.

But isn't that what I wanted? To change everything?

A rack is rolled before me. The dresses are stately and sophisticated, all in muted tones of silver, pale gold, and subdued pastels. They're the complete opposite of my bright, colorful wardrobe at home.

As a woman holds up dress after dress, another one slides my feet into a basin of warm water. Then a third one dips my fingers into a bowl of warm gel.

"Are any of the gowns to your liking?" Aisha asks.

"The silver one is okay," I say.

"Perfect." Aisha moves it to the front.

The woman at my side chooses a silvery iridescent nail

polish to complement the gown. She lifts the bottle. "Does this color meet your approval?"

"I'm sure you know better than I do."

The woman nods and begins adding a coat to my nails.

Aisha pushes the first rack out of the way and brings forward a second. "Now for the ensemble to wear during the press announcement."

"What will Leopold be wearing?"

Aisha withdraws a cell phone and swipes through screens, turning it to me. "This is the betrothal uniform," she says. "It was fitted for him on his twenty-ninth birthday and travels with the entourage."

I suck in a breath. Leopold in full prince regalia is too beautiful for words. The uniform is silver-gray with a heather-blue sash across the chest. Bright buttons line both sides from his chest to his waist. A funny flat-topped cap covers most of his hair, which is short and straight in the image, no hint of the roguish curls he has now. It must have grown out since then.

He's going to be my *husband*.

His words from earlier come back to me. *I currently can think of nothing more than getting you naked in my arms.*

My belly warms over. Did he mean that? He'd been so earnest. Every time I'm around him, I'm convinced he says nothing but the truth. But when I'm away, it all feels impossible, like I'm part of some bizarre improv performance.

It's hard to know what to trust, what to believe, what to think.

"I think the blue dress will complement it perfectly." Aisha tugs a subdued knee-length sheath from the rack.

"I guess so," I say. "I feel very unsure about everything."

"It's natural, my dear," Grammy says. "When I met your grandfather, I was convinced he was a conman of the highest order."

I know this story. Theirs had been a whirlwind love affair, leading to a wedding only a few weeks after they met. Grammy never remarried after he died, saying she was wedded to her work.

And she loves that walk-up deli more than anything. She knows the history of every nick in the counter, each framed photo on the walls. She sewed the curtains and cut the plastic tablecloths fitted under the glass tops.

Sometimes I wondered if I'd be with her for always, and if I'd take over after she was gone.

Not now.

This crazy thing I've done has changed everything.

Another woman combs through my hair. "Updo tonight?" she asks Aisha.

"The Prince likes it long," Aisha says. "So down tonight, updo tomorrow for the announcement."

The Prince already has opinions about my hair?

It seems impossible. We've spent less than an hour together total, including his proposal.

But tonight, there will be more time.

Princess Sunny.

It doesn't sound quite right, more like a children's story book character than a real person.

The process of changing me from a sandwich maker to a princess takes time. And pain. My eyes widen when warmed wax strips are laid down my shin.

"I'm not sure I'm ready for — son of a biscuit!" The

adhesive is ripped away, taking all the hair I haven't shaved for a few days — okay, a week — with it.

"Pardon, milady," the woman says. "Only a few more."

Lies. There are so many, many more.

They wax more things. My brows. My chin. Really? Over my lip.

When one woman tries diving into bushy pastures, I lock my knees. "No."

Aisha nods and the woman lets it go.

Then the creams, the blusher, the mascara, the lipstick.

I'm given panties, a bra, and a middle bit that looks an awful lot like a modern corset even if it only hooks into place.

The silver gown is zipped up and shoes are slid over my polished, shining toes. For the last touch, satin gloves cover my manicured hands up past my elbow.

I look like a princess, but I feel like a fraud.

"You are a vision," Aisha says, seeming pleased with herself. "Let's go see your groom."

The Prince stands when I enter the room, eyes alight at my new look. There are servers, staff, and guards. a table set with dozens of silver-domed dishes.

It's a spread fit for royalty.

But as I sit, allowing the Prince to adjust my chair, I seem to only be able to take stock of my discomfort. I shift my feet to take the pressure off my toes in the pinching shoes. High heels are the devil.

The dress, while gorgeous, makes me itch. The sequins lining the edges cut into my skin. More torture.

The gloves are ridiculous. I have no idea if I'm

supposed to take them off before I eat. What if I get gravy on them?

Grammy isn't wearing any gloves, so I can't take a cue from her. I don't know if she knows the answer, and even if she did, I can't easily ask her at this enormous table where we're separated by several feet.

Despite all the food in front of us, I'm afraid to take a single bite until I solve the glove problem.

I look to the left and the right, heat rising in my face. At least the way my cheeks get blotchy when I'm nervous won't show beneath all this makeup.

"Is the meal not to your liking?" Leopold points his spoon at my untouched plate. "We can bring you additional items."

Aisha is watching us, and she steps behind Prince Leopold to meet my gaze without him noticing. I tap my gloves.

Her eyebrows lift in understanding. "Rubin, where are your manners? Please get a tray for milady's gloves."

I try to let out my breath slowly so it's not obvious that I'm relieved to have an answer. A big brute of a guard, looking like he should star in a Paul Bunyan retelling, dashes for a sideboard and selects a silver tray, dumping a pile of letters onto the wood surface to hustle it over to our table.

"My apologies, milady. Grisholm usually acts as butler."

I rest the ring on the table while I pull off the satin gloves. "That's fine. I didn't want to get anything on them."

I don't know if that's the wrong thing to say. Princesses probably don't admit to messes. I lay the gloves on the silver tray and slide the ring back on my finger.

My brain keeps going and going in circles, coming up with more evidence that I have zero understanding of etiquette and manners.

Grammy pipes up. "So, Prince Leo, tell us about the castle."

Leopold swallows his soup and rests the spoon gently on the plate below the bowl. "It's a rather modest structure, as far as castles go. It will not, in fact, hold the entirety of the wedding guests."

I lean forward. "How many people do you expect to attend?"

"We haven't had a royal wedding in over thirty years, so I imagine the abbey will be full. For the ceremony, eight hundred, give or take."

My belly shakes. Eight hundred?

"Additionally, I expect much of Avalonia will travel to the city center to celebrate in the square. So probably another thirty thousand will cram in the open spaces between the abbey and the castle. There will be a splendid party, of course."

"Will they be able to see the wedding?" Grammy asks.

"We haven't worked out the details yet. Perhaps it will be broadcast on screens in the square. I'm not in direct communication with the cultural director. Grisholm will have more of those details, probably tomorrow. He's busily making preparations."

Grammy stirs her soup, nodding. "So, how many of the guests *will* the castle fit?"

"There are ninety bedrooms organized in about sixty suites. Additionally, there is the wing for my parents, their staff, and guards. And then there's the wing for myself and my two sisters."

I sit up at that. This is at least something I know. "Octavia and Lilianne?"

He grins, and the pure charisma in his face makes me want to write a poem about it. "Lili and O," he says. "You will love them. Quite a free-spirited pair, like yourself."

I'm free-spirited? Well, of course I am. But how could he know that? The only times he's ever seen me is when I helped him escape photographers, then his proposal.

Oh wait. I did throw vases at his guards and try to attack him with a lamp. Yeah. He's gotten a good idea.

"Will you stay in the wing with your sisters after the wedding?" Grammy asks.

He shakes his head. "I will be moved to a currently unused wing of the castle, one meant for the heir. Getting married changes my status. I am no longer merely a prince. I am the *Crown* Prince." He glances down at that, and I wonder if perhaps this isn't what he wants. Leadership. Pressure. Responsibility. Earlier today, he was going viral with a rooster Speedo.

Moreover, it's probably only been twenty-four hours since he last slept with another woman.

> *A prince once banged many a girl*
> *There were none he'd pass up for a whirl*
> *But he had to be King*
> *Wear a wedding ring*
> *To evolve from a swine to a pearl*

My belly quivers again. What have I done?

"Aisha mentioned something about an engagement announcement in the morning," I say.

Leopold lifts his head. "Can we clear the room except for the dinner company?"

Aisha, the chef, the servers, and the guards all move through the door.

I grimace. "Sorry. Should I not have said anything?"

"No, no. It's fine. It's only the staff don't know about our agreement."

"The seven-day test?"

He nods. "We must act as though we are a love match. A happy couple."

"But I was throwing vases." Chagrin washes over me.

"A simple spat easily solved." Leopold lifts his wine and takes a sip.

"But should we do a public announcement?" I lean forward to whisper. "What if it doesn't work out?"

Leopold's face is grim. "Then you leave me at the altar. It is fine. I will accept the consequences of my failure."

"Oh!" How could I do that?

"Don't fret. I have every confidence that we will work."

That makes one of us. What happens when he realizes how odd I am? How clumsy? How not-princess?

Grammy reaches out to squeeze my wrist. "You're overthinking. Enjoy the ride."

She knows me. But that's easy for her to say. She's a total believe-in-your-heart kind of person. I like to write about these extravagant feelings. But that doesn't mean I know for a fact that they're true.

Leo has explained to me how he got in this position,

and why it's important to him to choose his own bride, even if he scarcely knows me.

And if these seven days work out, I can spend my time reading and writing poetry. This man says he can make it so, if I marry him.

I guess I'll have to *fake it till I break it.*

CHAPTER 8

Prince Leopold

Day Two

The morning of the engagement announcement comes early.

Grisholm opens the curtains to my bedroom. "Awaken, Prince Leopold." His voice booms as I shield my eyes from the bright sunlight. "The press is already assembling below. We must fit you into your betrothal suit."

I sit up on the bed, the silk pajamas cool against my skin. I haven't awakened alone in many a month. I will have to get used to it, I fear. Sunny is not easily swayed. She practically ran from my table after dinner.

"Did you like her?" I ask the old man, who waves the particles of dust dancing in the light from the window.

"Of course I like her. She is my future queen."

"No, beyond that. Do you think my parents will be glad she is an American?"

"Given that she has no political ties, I'm not sure of the advantage."

"It doesn't matter. She is my choice."

Grisholm's lips pinch beneath his bushy mustache. He is not pleased.

"Out with it," I say.

He stands very tall, the window light shining on his stiff silvery gray uniform. "There were many lovely women already chosen for you back home. My concern is that this young lady will feel out of place. She may not adapt to our lifestyle or the customs of the people of our country."

It's true. None of us know how Sunny will respond to an entirely new environment. "She helped me escape from you all. That's good enough for me."

Grisholm's disapproving *harrumph* propels me from the bed to the bathroom. He really is a morose old beast.

During my shower and preparations, my thoughts often turn to Sunny. I like that she's a hard worker coming from common stock. My parents may very well have picked out future princesses for me, but I can almost guarantee that they were raised to believe that they were meant for something better. And that sort of attitude only leads to disillusionment and bitterness.

I know that sentiment well. It is my daily baggage.

Sunny, for all the risk, is going into this of her own accord. She has no airs about her.

Grisholm brings in the betrothal suit. Despite being almost a year since I first donned it, it fits well.

Grisholm nods in approval. "I thought you might have

packed on a few extraneous pounds in your travels, what with all the drinking and extravagant food."

I punch his arm. "I also hit the gym every time I can, old man. Don't worry about me."

"That's all I do." He turns on his heel.

Aisha is waiting in the outer chamber when I emerge from the bedroom. "Lady Sunny is prepared. I have let her know the order of the events and some appropriate remarks for the press."

"How did she take it?"

Aisha smooths the silvery gray satin that matches Grisholm, completing our silver and blue color palette that will harmonize the photographs of our announcement. "She seems quite nervous. I think she was glad to be given specific instructions on what to say."

Grisholm rubs his hands together. "Excellent. That is exactly the quality we seek in our princess."

I snap my head around. "Really? How about thinking for herself?"

He shakes his head. "Not ideal for the royal meetings that are coming."

I return his *harrumph*. "Let us fetch my bride. Will her grandmother also be in attendance at the betrothal announcement?"

Aisha falls into step behind me. "Given that your family will not be present, I have recommended that she remain off-camera."

"I will check with Sunny. If she feels the need for reassurance and proximity, let them be together."

Aisha bows. "An astute observation, sire. Your new bride's comfort is paramount in these circumstances."

Our party of Aisha, Grisholm, Rubin, and I head down the hall. I am eager to see Sunny again. With her dress and style last night absolutely befitting her station, my parents cannot question my decision to take an American bride and reject whatever lambs to the slaughter they had prepared for me.

All is well.

Rubin knocks, and after a tremulous, "Come in," from inside, opens the door.

But when we enter, Aisha gasps.

"What's wrong?" I barrel into the room.

Ah, I see.

Sunny sits on the sofa, not wearing the pale blue gown Aisha showed me as her selection, but instead, an interesting skirt, split like pants but full around her knees, made of colorful patchwork squares. Red boots, scuffed at the toe. And a bright yellow shirt that accents a green deli apron like the one from yesterday. This one is clean, at least.

Aisha's voice is full of shock. "Where is your dress?"

The grandmother steps in front of Sunny. "We decided it's best to present ourselves as we are, not the way you think we ought to be."

Grisholm stumbles with his words for a full ten seconds before spitting out, "This is no time for your overzealous capitalistic intention."

The grandmother narrows her eyes. She wears a simple gray flowered dress, not a sparkling gown either. "Now that you mention it, it is a rather amazing product placement opportunity." She turns to her granddaughter. "Make sure the pickle logo shows."

Sunny says nothing, watching me. And I understand. This is a test. Do I accept my bride as she is? Or am I trying to change her?

Grisholm draws in a breath to make another ugly pronouncement, but I slash my arm through the air. "Enough from you. This is my bride, and I shall present her as she wishes to be known."

I hold out my elbow. "Sunny, might I escort you to the press conference?"

She stands and accepts my arm.

"But, sire," Aisha insists. "The whole point was to signal to your family that you are making a proper choice."

I open the door to the hall. "If my family does not accept my choice, then it tells me all I need to know about my standing in the kingdom."

"Amen," the grandmother says. Our party heads down the hall to the private elevator. Rubin and Scorsese wait there to escort us down.

"Are the other guards at the bottom of the elevator?" I ask them.

"Yes," Rubin says.

"Then I would like to escort my bride down the elevator alone. I think we should have a moment to gather our thoughts."

"I forbid it," Grisholm says.

I punch the down arrow. "Rubin, my command takes precedence over his." I turn to the grandmother. "Is this amenable to you?"

She nods. "I think that's a fine idea."

"And you, Sunny?"

She nods.

"I will speak to the King about your malfeasance!" Grisholm shouts.

The door slides open, and the two of us enter. "This is the least of my transgressions," I tell him. "And you know it."

Once we are alone, Sunny sticks out her chin. "Are you upset at my outfit?"

"Not at all. I thought you were unable to pack."

"Grammy went back to my apartment after dinner. She gathered a few things for me, and after Aisha dressed me this morning, I couldn't do it. I'm not a princess. I'm a regular girl who works in a deli."

"The title of princess is yours to accept. You don't feel it?"

The elevator descends quickly. I realize we will have very little time to speak, so I punch every floor number to slow us down.

"I want to earn it," she says, pausing as the door opens to an empty private space. Most of the floors will have no access to the locked compartment that houses this secret back elevator, so we should have these moments alone.

"I don't know how things are in Avalonia. But I was raised to believe that you work to show you earned your position in life. And if you rise on the ladder to success, you remain true to the values that got you there."

She stares at the floor for a moment. Despite the odd outfit, her hair and makeup were prepped by Aisha this morning. In fact, she brings to mind other royalty, dressed in common clothes as they volunteer in shelters or build homes for the less fortunate. Despite my staff's overreaction, I think Sunny might be exactly right on this choice of attire.

"That's quite a speech," I say. "I love that, and your clothes. Are you camera shy? Do you think you can say this again to the press?"

The elevator door opens and closes again. "When I was in college—well, junior college, I did a lot of poetry slams."

"Poetry slams?"

"They're usually in coffee shops. You go on stage and read your poetry."

"I can see you in front of a crowd, captivating them with your witty lines."

She smiles at that. "Maybe not exactly. But I did do it."

"So you are familiar with speaking in front of people."

She nods. "I am."

The doors part for the second floor. The next opening will be to the guards and the frenzy. Our private time is at an end.

"Thank you for speaking. While it doesn't matter to me who accepts or rejects you, because my choice is the one that matters, it will be easier for you if we find some common ground to build and nurture."

"I understand."

"Might I hold you closer? Every gesture, every glance will be examined in excruciating detail."

Her laugh is shy and quiet. "Yes. And I will do my best to give them nothing to question."

I pull her against my side so that our bodies fit together. The doors open again, and James and Pace turn to face us.

"The others will be down shortly," I tell them.

"Will Rubin and Scorsese accompany them?" Pace asks. The guards, too, have changed into betrothal finery, gray and blue.

"Yes."

"Good," Pace says. "When we open the door to the corridor, you will be visible to the press who couldn't fit into the room. The hall is quite crowded."

"There are that many?"

Sunny squeezes my hand. "You did go viral in a cock Speedo. Everyone will want to know who you are and what you're doing here."

Of course. "I'm ready."

Pace opens the door. The cacophony rises as people realize I have stepped out of the private corridor. The questions crash over us like a tidal wave.

"Prince Leopold, who are the women you were with yesterday?"

"Prince Leopold, where did you get that cock Speedo?"

"Leo, does your bride know you were hanging out at a party without her yesterday afternoon?"

"How long have you known this woman?"

"Is she pregnant?"

"Will you live in New York?"

Soon, the individual voices are consumed by the noise. James pushes the people back as Pace leads us to a side door.

It's one of the hotel ballrooms, a stage set up with a long table and microphones. It's packed. The moment we enter, all the chairs are abandoned and the reporters crush forward.

Hotel staff hold the line to keep them from approaching the stage.

This is madness, even for a prince. I started my two years as an ambassador in my early twenties, and none of my visits ever got a response like this. I don't even remember my father as King commanding a crowd of this size.

I glance over at Sunny, eyes saucer-like at the madness. They shout questions, same as the hallway spectators.

We sit in the two chairs behind the table.

I realize Sunny's outfit doesn't matter all that much. The only things visible are the top of the apron and her bright yellow sleeves. It's a good lesson that the things we fuss about are often insignificant in the end.

I'm uncertain how to quiet the crowd. Grisholm was supposed to introduce us, but I left him behind. It will be several minutes before he arrives, as the elevator must rise and come down again.

But Sunny knows what to do. She leans into the microphone. "If you can hear me, clap once."

There are only a few claps.

"If you can hear me, clap twice."

More people clap this time.

"If you can hear me, clap three times."

Half the room is involved now.

She smiles at the room. "It's good to know that at least some of you are smarter than a preschooler."

The room erupts in laughter, then quiets down.

I look at her in amazement. "That was brilliant."

She gives me a sidelong glance. "I know."

I feel as though my chest will burst. This woman, this

amazing person I only met yesterday, has so much more to her than I knew.

"I think you all agree I've made the perfect choice," I say.

The room is about to launch into questions again, when Grisholm pushes through the door. "I will direct the questions," he shouts.

The room settles. Sunny glances at me, and we share a conspiratorial look. "You did it better," I say. The room laughs again.

And that is the way of the whole press conference. Sunny is clever and witty, handling the American reporters in ways I could not have managed myself. When my answers for how we met and why we chose each other are only, "She is perfect for my country," she has the more poetic answers.

"What girl doesn't want to be Cinderella at the ball?" she says, quieting the room. "Given the opportunity to build a life with someone as courteous and charismatic as Prince Leopold, wouldn't you take that shot?"

Even questions about my recent foibles in France and Amsterdam and at the pool party are handled with clever bits that halt further poking.

Sunny stares intently at the reporter in the front row who brazenly asks if I cheated on her. "How many of you have misleading photos on someone's Instagram feed?" she asks. "Let those of you without poor decisions caught on social media cast the first stone."

And amazingly, they shut the hell up.

I am the luckiest person alive.

CHAPTER 9

Sunny

After the press conference, Leopold goes to change and I sit on the sofa with Grammy. Apparently the private plane taking us to Avalonia is leaving this afternoon.

Grammy takes both of my hands in hers. "I need to stay behind for a few days to figure out what I'm doing with the deli before I join you. But if you need me, I will come right now, deli be damned. I can lock the doors and not look back."

I shake my head. "I'll be fine. Prince Leopold seems to have my best interests at heart."

"I don't like the idea of you getting stuck with people who may not be who we think."

I settle back against the sofa cushion. "I just had a press conference. They're obviously not doing anything in secret."

Grammy nods. "That's true."

"But you will be there for the wedding, I assume?" I fiddle with the hem of my apron. It was quite a move to wear it.

"Of course. When are you going to call your mother and father?"

I've been putting it off. "I'll do that before the plane leaves."

"Sooner rather than later. I'm sure the press conference is already hitting the news sites. They don't need to learn about it from the television."

I nod.

She patters off to her room to gather her things. I pick up my cell phone. I might as well get this over with.

Mom answers on the second ring. "Sunny, darling. You're actually calling us. With your voice."

"Mom. Millennials know how to talk on the phone." It's her favorite joke.

"I know, I know. We're having a lovely time here in Florida. Is everything okay?"

I don't even know how to say this. With Grammy at my side, I had this feeling that my family already approved of everything. It didn't occur to me that my parents might flip out.

"At some point today, you're going to see some news about me."

"What do you mean, news? Like on the television?"

"Yes. And the Internet."

"Are you all right?"

"Oh, I'm perfect."

"It's about your poetry, then?"

If only. "No. Something crazy has happened, Mom. I'm flying to a small country in Europe tonight."

"You're finally taking a vacation? How delightful. Do you need money? Have you saved up enough?"

"Actually, my fiancé is taking me."

Silence.

I wait a few seconds.

Still silence.

Finally, she says, "Did I hear you right? Fiancé? Do you mean you're engaged?"

"Yes. I'm engaged. And because of his prominence, there was a press conference about it this morning."

"A press conference!" More silence. Then, "Martin, get in here. Sunny, I'm putting you on speakerphone. I'm completely discombobulated. Martin, Sunny's gotten engaged!"

I recognize that strident tone in her voice. She did the same thing when I told her I wasn't going to pursue a four-year college degree and instead work with Grammy Alma in the deli. My dad had purposely stepped away from the family business, letting his brother Sherman take over. And here I had jumped back in.

Dad's voice is gruff. "Sunny, we didn't know you were seeing anyone."

I better nuance this part. "It might be quicker than usual. But he's amazing, and I think you'll like him."

"Still, you got engaged without us even meeting this fellow? Has Grammy met him?"

"Yes, and she gave her blessing. He talked to her first. She was the one to put the ring on my finger."

"Oh, thank goodness," Mom says. "I knew you were getting closer to your grandmother than you were to us. But this is very surprising."

"I hate that it happened while you guys were away. But the decision was sudden. And, well…" Gosh, this is going to throw them. I'll just have to say it. "The wedding is in a week."

Both of them speak at the same time. "A week!"

"He's a prominent figure in his country. It has to be quick. There's a law about it." This sounds so crazy I can barely believe it myself.

"This is highly irregular," Dad says. "Highly irregular. Who is this boy?"

"His name is Prince Leopold." I suddenly realize I don't know his last name. Does he have a last name? "His father is the King of Avalonia. It's in Europe. You can look it up. It's very small. It's not a huge deal. But there is this weird rule about marriage. So the wedding will be in Avalonia."

"Where the hell is Avalonia?" Dad bellows.

"She said it's in Europe, Martin," Mom says.

There's a knock at the door. "Mom, Dad, I think that's the Prince and his guards coming to see me. I'll keep you up to date. Go look at the press conference. I think it will answer some of your questions. I love you both. I'll figure out how to get you tickets to Avalonia. Probably he has a plane that can fetch you, but I don't know. I'll be in touch, okay?"

I end the call. Whew.

Leopold strides in behind the guard. "Are we ready?"

"I guess. I told my parents."

His face brightens. "How did that go?"

"They're confused. It's come from nowhere."

"I bet. Do you need more time to talk to them?"

I shake my head. "I told them to watch the press conference."

"That's a good idea. Is your grandmother going to come while you pack?"

Grammy drags a rolling suitcase from her room. "I think you better call me Grammy like the rest," she says. "And of course I'll come. I need to take all these things home."

Leopold hurries over to take the suitcase. "You're not coming with us to Avalonia?"

She grins up at him. "I'll let the lovebirds have a few days before I get in the way."

"We'll need to get her to the wedding," I say.

"That will be arranged," Leopold says. "Rubin, take a message to Grisholm to plan for a plane to take Grammy to Avalonia at her discretion."

On the ride to Brooklyn, I point out the sights to Leopold. He holds my hand, and his fingers feel good threaded through mine. This is easy.

When we arrive at my tiny apartment, I look around, not sure what I should bring. Grammy and I head to my bedroom. Clothes, mainly. And my books.

Leopold sends Rubin to find my landlord and prepay my rent for a year so I can come back as I choose, regardless of whether our seven days work out. That's one benefit of meeting him.

A packing team arrives, and I instruct them to box up my closet and bookshelves, but most everything else can simply stay.

While they do that, we stop by the deli so I can stay goodbye. I look around the space, the counter where I have worked for so many years, and before that, my favorite place to be as a child.

Grammy seems to understand what I'm feeling. She holds onto my arm. "You'll be back to visit all you want, dear. The deli won't be quite the same without you, but it did go along for a good forty years before you started working here, and it will continue."

"I hate that it's closed today," I say, my voice raspy.

"It will be open again tomorrow. Sherman will send me some help. We've done this before. And I need to prep the family for this big event. There's quite a lot to do in the next few days."

"I'll probably be back."

"You think it won't work out?"

I straighten a photo of Grammy and her husband, the grandfather I never knew. "I'm not sure how it could. How can two people know each other in seven days?"

"Some people figure it out with only a glance."

I slide my arm through hers. "Oh, you and your love at first sight. I don't think I'm in love. He's courteous. And handsome. But I've been catching up on his history online. That boy can't keep his pants on."

"That sounds like a lot of fun to me."

"Oh, Grammy. What if he cheats on me? What if it's after we're married?"

She turns me toward her, cupping my chin in her hands. "Sunny, deciding to love someone is always a risk. You have to go into it with all the hope in your heart. Otherwise, you don't stand a chance."

Grammy holds my gaze. "And if he does swing that schnitzel around, we'll lop it off!"

"Grammy!"

She flips off the lights. "He better watch his schnitzel!"

We walk outside where Prince Leopold and the entourage wait in the car. I pause to look back at the green and white awning. It's been home for me all my life. I can't know if I'll be back in a week, or if I'll make a new life in Avalonia.

And certainly, I can't predict if I'd be happier either place, or happy at all.

But I'm going.

As Grammy waves from the sidewalk, her expression tender, I think to myself, *don't cry over spilt history.*

CHAPTER 10

Prince Leopold

I am unsure how to comfort my sniffling bride as we pull away from the deli where we met. Clearly, despite the difficult, messy labor of food service, she is quite attached to the place.

We are not at a stage yet where I feel comfortable doing much more than holding her hand. So I merely sit beside her in the back of the car as we speed toward a private airstrip where the royal plane waits to take us to Avalonia.

For most of the drive, Sunny stares out the window, pressing a soggy Kleenex to her nose. I pass her a more serviceable cotton handkerchief from my interior pocket. "Holds up better than tissue."

She accepts it, running a finger over the monogram. "Thank you. It only occurred to me when we drove away that I was leaving New York. I've never lived anywhere else."

"You can visit whenever you like. There are very few constraints, nothing like the social calendar of the British royals, for example. We're too small and little-known to be inundated with requests."

She grins at that. "I doubt anyone who saw the rooster picture thinks you are small or little-known."

I can only grunt back at her. "Oh, the folly of that."

"That's what brought us together, though, right?"

"You have a very good point there. Perhaps I shall be eternally grateful for the prank. And perhaps it will become the official swimsuit of Avalonia."

She makes a full-on laugh despite her sad state. That's better.

"Is there already an official swimsuit of Avalonia?"

"Swimming isn't much of a pastime, I'm afraid. Our summer temperatures tend to top out at about twenty-five degrees." When she looks at me in shock, I quickly add, "Celsius. Seventy-five in Fahrenheit. For those who like a hot summer afternoon to take a dip, you won't quite get there."

"Seventy-five seems warm enough."

"If you are acclimated, certainly. It was much warmer yesterday for the pool." I should stop speaking of the matter. I dislike her conjuring the image that proved so popular, the swimsuit and the women so close to it.

I have such a long way to go to woo her. I must double my efforts.

We arrive at the airfield, a long red carpet rolled out at the base of the stairs to the plane.

Sunny watches the preparations. "Is there always this much ceremony, even when there's no one to see it?"

"You mean the red carpet?"

"Yes. Is it so terrible for your shoes to touch the ground?" Her voice has a teasing quality.

"It *is* funny, isn't it? My father explained to me that it's important to keep up the rigor of our customs, no matter who is watching. People treat you the way you present yourself. Look the part of royalty, and you'll *be* royalty."

The driver opens the door, taking Sunny's hand as she steps out. I'm bemused by the colorful, loose pants billowing around her like a skirt, the various colors of the patchwork bright and mismatched.

I follow her up the steps to the main compartment of the plane, which has three rows of seats backed by an open space with a table and chairs. Aisha immediately takes her aside to show her the various rooms. I settle into one of the leather chairs near the front.

Grisholm sits next to me. "Aisha and I have agreed that we should attempt to convince milady to wear something more appropriate to meet your family."

"No. I will not have anyone pressuring her to be someone she is not."

Grisholm holds up his palms. "My prince, the meeting affects not only how your parents will view your future wife, but also the job that I have done in leading you to finding her. Aisha's ability to style the future royal family is also in question. We only wish to ensure that this is what the future princess wishes to portray in these circumstances. We want her first impression not to be a whim, but a choice."

I sit back in my seat. "How can I be sure you will not force her hand?"

"Ask her yourself."

"You can be certain I will."

Grisholm's lips pinch. I swear it's the only expression he knows. "I do wish you had remained in your betrothal suit. Your parents would've liked to see it."

"We were too big of a mismatch. Jeans and a sport coat will have to do."

He *harrumphs*, but turns his attention to his tablet and whatever it is he does. I check my watch. My concern for Sunny is high. But Aisha did work magic the first night. Surely there is a middle ground, one that respects Sunny's desire for eclectic clothing, and Aisha's eye toward traditional royal appearances.

The plane takes off. I must fall asleep, because a short time later, I am awakened by a push on my shoulder.

When I open my eyes, I'm graced with a lovely vision of my bride. She stands in the aisle next to my seat. "What do you think?" She turns in a circle.

She still wears her bright yellow shirt, this time paired with a long, pale gold skirt interwoven with silver threads. She looks like the sun itself.

Her hair has been curled into long dark spirals.

"You are a vision. And your outfit lives up to your name."

She smoothes her hands down her hips. "Perhaps compromise is in order."

I slide down a seat to open one for her.

She drops into it. "How long is the flight?"

"Twelve hours."

"So, a long way to go."

"Plenty of time for us to have all the discussions you would like."

She straightens the skirt around her knees. "It has been a whirlwind, hasn't it?"

"It has. And only six days until the wedding."

Aisha sits across the aisle from us. "I'm so glad you mentioned that. Rosenthal has questions regarding the ceremony. The preparations are well underway. He began the moment he heard last night. But you threw him for a loop."

I shrug. "They were forcing my hand. They should have been ready."

Aisha glances down at her tablet. "Sunny, how many guests will fly in from the States?"

"Oh. I haven't thought about it. How accurate does my number need to be?"

"Not perfectly. The section reserved for your family and friends is made of benches. Therefore, there's a certain amount of flexibility in how many people can sit there."

"How much can it hold?"

"It should seat about a hundred."

Sunny sits up straight. "Oh, I don't think I will invite near that many. It's such short notice. I don't know if people will travel to Avalonia."

"Just start naming names, and I'll tally."

"Certainly my father and mother, Martin and Fran. Grammy Alma. There's my sister Greta and her husband Jude and their son Caden. Uncle Sherman. He's dating someone. I'm not sure she'll be coming but leave a place for her. My three male cousins, Max, Andrew, and Jason. Then Camryn, Magnolia, and Nova, who go with them. I expect we might also have Magnolia's sister Havannah and

Donovan and Rebel, plus Dell, his wife, and their daughter. And, of course, the new Pickle."

Both Aisha and I swivel our heads toward her at that.

"Pickle?" Aisha asks.

Sunny's giggle is nervous. "My uncle and his children refer to themselves with the last name of Pickle due to their delicatessen chain. They recently discovered there was another sister in the family. She's lovely. She spends half her time in New York. She might want to attend, along with her Santa."

Our heads whip her direction again.

"Santa?" Aisha asks. "As in Santa Claus?"

"Yes, he works as a Santa. He isn't the actual Santa. Of course." Sunny stares down at her hands. "You think I'm crazy."

"No!" We both say it at the same time.

"My new cousin is Rory. If she comes, Mack will come. He's the Santa volunteer."

"Got it," Aisha says. "For a royal wedding, we don't have bridesmaids per se, but you certainly might have ladies-in-waiting who are friends. Do you have someone you wish to fill that role?"

Sunny stares at her hands. As the silence lengthens, I gently ask, "Sunny? Are you okay?"

She slowly nods. "My sister might do it. Otherwise, I don't have a female friend for that. I've been working at the deli for a long time. My interests are, well, unique. I don't share them with many people."

Wild thoughts run through my head. Is she a dominatrix? Does she collect frog skeletons? So many things to learn.

"All is well," Aisha says. "Naturally, Prince Leopold's two sisters will serve as ladies-in-waiting for you. The Queen's brother Alistair has a sweet granddaughter about the age of four. She will serve as a lovely flower girl."

"Oh, are there ring bearers? My nephew Caden can fill that role."

Aisha jots this down. "Perfect. We'll get his measurements so an outfit can be created for him."

I sense that we have overwhelmed Sunny, so I meet Aisha's eyes and dismiss her with a nod.

When we are alone, Sunny relaxes more fully into her chair. "That was a lot."

"It was. I apologize that everyone assumes the wedding will come off. You have a choice."

"I know. The closer it gets, the more pressure I'll feel to do it no matter what."

"Please don't. Let us pretend these preparations are merely a party of no consequence. Can you do that? To ease the pressure?"

She clasps her hands in her lap, her gaze focused on the wall in front of our seats. "Maybe. I can try."

Once again, I wish I could touch her in some way. But I suspect I will have to let her come to me.

If I can hold out.

She turns to me, her amber eyes holding my gaze. My body stirs. She really does get to me.

"Tell me about your family at the palace. I just learned that you have an uncle. And I would like to know more about your parents. And particularly your sisters." She reaches across the armrest to squeeze my arm, and the touch of her fills me with an assurance that this mad choice we have made will be all right.

I take her hand and tuck it in my elbow. "I'll tell you everything. First, of Avalonia. It's filled with rolling hillsides and ancient castles."

"Ohhhh," Sunny sighs. "Do you have pictures?"

"I do." I pull out my phone. "So many pictures."

As the plane leaves America far behind and the window view is nothing but ocean, I set out to tell her all she longs to know.

CHAPTER 11

Sunny

Day Three

I awake in a bizarre position, my head resting on something oddly lumpy.

I open my eyes, the gentle vibration of the plane feeling different than it did when I drifted off. Are we descending?

The lump is Leopold's shoulder. He also slumbers, his temple pressed against an out-turned head rest. They were too high for me, so I landed on him. Our fingers are inter-twined. I take him in a moment. For a second, I truly think — am I in a coma? Or some extended dream? This man surely isn't about to be my husband. I can't possibly be heading to a country I've never heard of to become its princess.

There once was a girl from New York
Who never ate with the right fork
She met a hot prince

> *Saved him from a pinch*
> *And now worries she'll be Princess Dork*

"Milady." I realize this soft voice awakened me. I make out Aisha in the dim light.

"Yes?"

"We will land in fifteen minutes. It's our last chance to freshen you up. The car ride to the Avalonian castle will be only a few minutes. The airstrip is in the fields just beyond the gates."

Oh. It's time.

I carefully shift away from Leopold. He grunts when I withdraw my hand. I catch Aisha looking down at where we had been joined. "It is going well, I take it?"

"I guess so."

"Good. You will want to display plenty of that if you want to convince the King and Queen of your suitability."

I want to ask her *what if I don't?* I didn't realize I could be rejected. Then Leopold would have to marry one of those other women anyway.

My belly trembles as I unfold myself from the seat and follow her to the back room of the plane. She flips on the light. "Let me look at you and make adjustments."

I turn in a circle.

She fingers the length of my hair, spinning the curls back into coils. "Just a quick refresh of makeup. I know you do not like it heavy."

I'm glad we've come to an understanding in so short a time. I feel that eventually Aisha can be someone to befriend. She's practical and doesn't get too caught up in the royal protocols.

Her skin is a warm brown, darker than Prince Leopold, but not quite as dark as Grisholm and the friendly guard Rubin.

"Avalonians seem to be a diverse people," I say to her. "At least from what I've observed."

Aisha leads me to the small cushioned chair by a lighted mirror and lifts my chin. "We are. I think it is paradise."

My ears pop. We're descending quickly. "Are the King and Queen hard to get to know?"

Aisha steps back to assess my look, then pins a lock of hair away from my forehead. "They come from a more traditional time. But they remember the changes they forced the King's father, King Montero, to make for their wedding. Queen Pulmaria is like you, not of Avalonia. A love match."

"Oh."

"You are perfect. A look to rival your name. There should be a light meal for you in the main cabin. Eat now. The castle has already breakfasted and it will be a long morning until lunch."

I do as she says, passing Leopold in the sitting room. He's shirtless, and a warmth rises to my cheeks. He reaches out a hand and snares my fingers. "Sunny, might I ask a very forward question?"

I stop. "Sure."

The belt of his jeans rides low on his belly. I could count each muscle of his abs, tan and perfect in the bright light of the room. I can barely swallow.

His fingers squeeze mine.

My voice catches. "What is it?"

"Our conversation was lovely, don't you think?"

I nod. "I'm glad I got to know more about your family. Aisha has filled me in more."

"Good. Excellent. She is one of the best members of the staff."

"But not Grisholm."

Leopold grunts. "Thankfully, he will revert to my father once we are at the castle."

"That's good."

"Only to be replaced by the insufferable Rosenthal. He makes Grisholm look like Santa Claus."

"Oh, dear."

"He believes himself to be the sole line of defense between the old traditions and anarchy. But never mind that." He draws me to him until we are only a breath away from each other.

Heat comes off his skin. His eyes watch me with quiet contemplation, like a lion deciding whether to pounce.

"Yes?"

"We do not yet know if we are a chemical fit."

"Do you mean chemistry?"

"Yes, if that is how you say it."

"I see."

"I suspect we are. But it is untested. And yet, my parents will look for signs. To deny their choices means I must present you as a love match. I know we aren't sure yet, but can we play the part?"

"I think so." My temperature rises by the second, so close to his skin. "Aisha mentioned that your grandfather changed the rules so that your parents could marry."

"He did. He was unhappy that my grandmother took so

many lovers and wanted his son to have a happier marriage."

"And your parents want that for you as well."

He grunts, and I suspect there is more to this story. His thumb slides over my knuckles, making my legs feel rubbery, like they won't hold me up much longer.

"Do you want me to tell them I love you?" I'm a horrible liar, but I suppose I could try.

"No. I want to see if there is anything there, or if I should take care."

"Take care how—" I'm silenced by his mouth on mine.

And I understand. He doesn't want our first kiss to be an unknown element. He'll either kiss me in front of his family, or not, based on… this.

I'm melting.

His mouth moves over mine, gently, as if asking a question. I lean into him, my arms connecting with his bare chest.

The two sensations are wildly at odds. The careful kiss. The sizzle of our skin. I'm overwhelmed with a crazed need to take it deeper, to fall into him.

And he knows it, somehow. His hand slides under my hair and lifts my head so that he might part my lips, delving into my mouth.

It's been years since my last kiss, since dating, since any love at all. I push those thoughts away, as they will sully this perfect moment. I hold on to him, letting everything fall away. No resistance, nothing but his lips, his tongue, the warmth of his body.

He holds me tightly against him, his hand massaging my neck. I want to stay here forever, to endlessly indulge in his attention, his warmth, his care.

"Sire?" The voice is tremulous and unsure. Not Aisha. Definitely not Grisholm.

We pull apart. Leopold's head turns. "Yes?"

It's a woman in a gray uniform, like a flight attendant. "Ten minutes until we land."

He holds me tightly. "Thank you." His eyes take in my face. "That is a good start, yes?"

I nod, not trusting my voice. After another long moment, he releases me and slides a shirt from a hanger over the door. "I look forward to exploring more of this feeling without interruption." He slips on the shirt. "It was okay? We're okay?"

I'm more than okay, which fills me with emotions I can't express right now. "Yes," I manage to get out.

He drops one last, brief kiss on my mouth before turning to the bathroom. "I'll be up to join you shortly. Eat without me. We're short on time."

Then he's gone.

I press my hand to my lips as I head to the main cabin. The table is set with a soft yellow linen, pastries, juice, and coffee. I realize I'm ravenous and take heed of Aisha's warning to eat.

When I try to butter my toast, I realize my hand is shaking. Is it Leopold's kiss or the prospect of meeting his parents?

Both.

I force myself to eat. Eggs. Toast. A danish. I gulp coffee to snap myself out of my daze.

Leopold arrives, a fresh jacket over his shirt and jeans.

He grins as he moves a croissant to his plate. "Am I presentable?"

He's ungodly beautiful, the first light of the sunrise striking his cheek through the window.

"You are."

He aims his fork at the sky. "You can see the hills of Avalonia. Take your first look."

I lean toward the small round glass. Across the landscape, undulating waves of long grasses fill the slopes and valleys below. The gray ruins of an old castle disappear into a copse of trees, merely an outline of what was once a grand stronghold.

Leopold peers down. "That's on the Belgium side. Our boundary is just beyond that peak." He points at a blue-gray mountain topped in snow.

Highways snake along the ridges, the only proof that we've not traveled to some long-ago age. I can barely make out the tiny movement of cars and trucks along the winding gray roads.

"We're close," he says. "See that cluster of buildings fanning out from the stone citadel? That's the palace and the township at the heart of Avalonia."

I see it. The sun casts orange-gold light across the green fields. There are other ruins, and now that we are descending, great flocks of animals clustered between fence lines.

Words fill my head in a way they haven't in a long time.

> *A peak, a valley*
> *a land of grass and gold.*
> *A wayward flock*

> *and a lonely girl*
> *converge in the shadow*
> *of a plane*
> *that flies between*
> *its beauty and the sun.*

Only when Leopold says, "That's beautiful," do I realize I've said it out loud. He reaches across the table to take my hand. "There's the poetry you told me about. Sounds like it should be in the pages of — what was the name of the magazine you mentioned last night?"

"*A Universe of Poetry.*"

"That's right. It would be home within those pages."

My throat goes tight. This is why I came. Not just for the man. I came here for a new future. Uninterrupted time, stretching out in front of me like the winding roads. For the words. The lines. The verses.

For poetry.

CHAPTER 12

Prince Leopold

As the long black car leads us away from the plane toward the palace, I hold Sunny's arm close to my body. I'm not sure if it's for her nerves or mine.

This is the moment. This is the introduction that alters my future. My parents once assured me choosing my own bride was the best course for a happy life. But then they decided I was taking too long.

There is nothing magical about the age of thirty. Sure, they expected a marriage to at least be in the works by now, but there is no Avalonian law or custom that the Crown Prince should take a wife by this age.

And yet, we had a troubling conversation a year ago. Father's personal tailor arrived to measure me. I asked him what we were making, since of late I had bought most of my clothes, as they say, off the rack.

It was only when he said, "For your betrothal suit, of course," that I learned of my impending engagement. I stormed my way to my father's quarters, pins falling in my wake, to ask why the suit was being prepared.

"It's due time!" my father roared, showing his infamous temper.

I pushed back at him with an equally uproarious, "There is no expiration date on my bachelorhood!"

My mother stepped in and said that I'd had plenty of time to locate a suitable princess on my own.

I pushed back again and was treated to a long-winded litany of my errors, women who sold pictures of me in their beds, parties, drunken escapades that made the news.

"I don't think you're going to find royal material via your methods," Mother said.

The more correct they were, the angrier I got. I left the unfinished suit behind, but they sewed it anyway. Unbeknownst to me, it had been carted around by the entourage as they chased me across the globe.

And here we are, ready to convince them I have made a love match with a proper girl who can carry the title.

"You seem nervous," Sunny says.

"How so?"

She lays her hand on my knee, which is bouncing like an electric yo-yo.

"I hope this meeting goes well, that's all."

"You mean you hope we can convince them we are in love."

"We don't have to be overtly demonstrative."

She scoots closer, our bodies pressed together, arms, hips, and thighs. I recall that desire I felt when she was holding the lamp, and again during the long kiss on the plane.

I wind my fingers through hers. We are so completely unpracticed, yet the time has come for a test nonetheless.

"We could practice more," she says.

She doesn't have to ask me twice.

I pull her close, my lips meeting hers. She smells of jasmine and springtime. Her hair tickles my cheek.

My thumb caresses her neck, finding each tender spot from throat to ear. I note when she shivers, when she sighs. I keep the kiss easy and light. This is no time for passion, not with the entire staff awaiting our arrival in mere minutes.

The back side of the palace is private, away from the balconies, grand entrances, and courtyards of the front. I feel the bump of passing through the outer gate and know our time is at hand.

I release Sunny, caressing her cheek with my thumb. "I could kiss you all day."

Her lashes frame those amber eyes and she gazes up at me. "That sounds nice."

"It's a date, then?"

"Of course." Her smile fills me with hope that this will work.

She moves closer to her window. "Oh! We're here! I like the guard uniforms! They're different from the ones at the hotel."

"These guards wear ceremonial garb." I lean down to take in her view. "We called those hats Q-Tips when we were kids."

Sunny laughs. "They do look like the ends of Q-Tips, all fuzzy and white."

"It's a terrible knock-off of the ones at Buckingham. Embarrassing, really. I think we'll abolish them."

"Such are the lofty decisions of a monarch?" She's teasing, her expression light.

"Indeed."

The car circles inside the broad columns of the porte-cochère. More guards stand there, some in ceremonial dress, the others hatless in the standard blue and gray. Rubin is there, along with Pace.

We pull to a stop in front of the broad doors, which are thrown wide for our arrival. A whole host of palace staff line either side.

"They're all waiting for you?" Sunny asks.

"Yes. And to get a look at their future queen."

Sunny's hand covers her mouth, as if she hasn't given this much thought. "But it seems inappropriate for them to meet me before your parents."

"I think that's the way it usually goes, right? Even in America, your friends meet your new boyfriend. The waiter at your favorite place knows you're a couple. Probably your neighbors. Parents only learn once it's established that the relationship is certain."

"I see your point."

"They will bow to you, and you nod in recognition. As the bride of the Crown Prince, the only stations you bow to yourself will be the King and Queen."

"Oh, Lord. What does the bow look like? A curtsy? From the waist? That crazy move debutantes learn where they crumple to the floor and manage to get back up?"

"Oh, I'd like to see that."

She pushes on my arm. "Leopold!"

She almost makes me laugh. "Men bend slightly at the

waist, and women dip straight down by bending their knees. Not far. Not to the floor. You'll see it. The staff will do it."

"And what do I call your parents?"

"Your Majesty to either one."

Sunny lets out a long breath. "All right."

Rubin opens the door. "Sire," he says.

I step out of the car. Ordinarily, a guard would retrieve the princess, but given our recent exchange, I decide to do it myself. We need each other at this moment.

I reach out my hand. Sunny takes it with a small smile. She is understandably nervous, although the way she handled the press yesterday tells me she is smashing at stressful situations.

I tuck her hand inside my elbow and lead her up the red carpet to the apex of the two lines of staff. They all bow, and I give a quick nod. Sunny does the same.

So far, so good.

Grisholm, who went ahead of us in a separate car, awaits inside the doors. He looks harried, his wiry gray hair not quite in place, his cheeks flushed.

"Grisholm, did you run all the way to the King's quarters and back?" I tease.

"Never mind that." His voice is its usual bluster. "The King and Queen request your presence in the main gallery."

The throne room. Interesting. Sounds like they want this to be as formal as it gets.

"Thank you, we'll take it from here."

More staff bows as we pass through the long sitting

room full of paintings that extends along the back wall of the palace's main wing. Sunny can't stop looking at everything, so I slow my step. It is her first view of her new home.

"It's so big. The walls are three stories high!"

"It feels rather cavernous after the cramped nature of modern American architecture."

"The heating bill must be outrageous."

I barely contain a laugh a second time. "Astute observation. Good thing we can manage the cost."

She turns to me. "You never have said your major export. How does Avalonia make its money?"

"I'll explain it all during our week." I lead her to a side hall, passing the great ballroom, quiet and dark. Then the large dining room, used for feasts. Then the smaller, more intimate one, with a table that seats a mere twenty guests.

"We take breakfast here," I tell her, gesturing to the room. Several staff members clear the table. "It has just passed, which is why we had our repast on the plane."

Guards wait outside the towering entryway to the main gallery. They bow to us, then open the white and gold doors.

We enter a broad sitting room filled with paintings of the previous kings and queens of Avalonia, plus many colorful chairs and sofas. This is where guests wait to meet the royal family when summoned. It is empty at the moment.

A second set of tall doors is guarded by Fleece and Johnson, two brutes of men that make Rubin look small.

"Sire," one says. "The King and Queen await."

A tremor goes through Sunny, and I grip her arm more tightly.

"Ready?" I ask her.

"Let's do this," she says.

The guards pull on the handles.

It's showtime.

CHAPTER 13

Sunny

The only thrones I've ever seen are on television. There's the famous *Game of Thrones* one made of the mangled swords from fallen enemies.

Gosh, I hope they're nothing like that.

I can picture Queen Elizabeth's golden chairs. And Catherine the Great sits behind a table for her visitations on *The Great*.

The doors swing open, and I feel like Dorothy in *The Wizard of Oz*.

Now *that* was a throne.

The room is bigger than our deli. The floor is a mosaic of white, gold, and silver diamonds. Tapestries line the walls, and the columns on either side of a low stage are gilded.

Leopold holds me tightly as we walk toward the riser. Two guards stand on either side of two large chairs uphol-stered in red.

And in them, the King and Queen.

Leopold's father is broad-shouldered and lean. He

wears a gray suit with a bright red sash across the shirt front. No crown. I assume those are for more important occasions than meeting me.

The Queen wears a green silk dress. She is slender and stiff, her ankles crossed, hands on the arms of the chair. I'm sure the emerald on her throat cost more than I make in a year. Or ten. Her dark hair is piled on her head in an artful arrangement of curls.

Leopold bows at the waist, so I quickly bend my knees and drop my chin. We rise together, and I'm glad he's holding me so tightly.

For a moment, no one speaks, the four of us sizing each other up.

I'm quite sure I won't be the one who talks first.

"Leopold!" The King's voice is like a cannon firing, and I flinch. "What on God's green earth do you think you're doing, choosing such a last-minute bride? I wasn't born yesterday."

Uh oh. We're busted already? I picture getting shoved on a commercial flight home. I shouldn't have told my parents yet.

"You have so little faith in me," Leopold says. "And here you embarrass my bride at her first meeting." He turns to me. "Come, Sunny. You are too good for the King, apparently. He has no manners."

His mother's voice is firm, but not unkind. "You are right. Sunny, please forgive the King for his unflattering introduction. I am Pulmaria. I understand you are American."

I wait a moment, wondering if I'm supposed to be given permission to speak. Leopold squeezes my elbow.

"Yes, Your Highness, I mean, Your Majesty. I'm from New York."

The King snorts. "American. Leopold, really?"

"Francisco, hush," the Queen says. "Let the girl speak."

Me, speak. I can do this.

"Your Majesty, I met Leopold when he was trying to evade a pack of ridiculous hungry dogs with cameras, chasing him down the street."

"Oh, I like that. Hungry dogs, indeed," the King says.

That's a start.

I gaze up at Leopold. "He asked to kiss me on the very first meeting. He's quite fresh, your prince. Of course I told him no."

"Very good," the Queen says. "He should know that someone is immune to his charms."

"I don't know about that," I say. "By the time he did kiss me, I felt I had been waiting a year." Damn, I'm good.

"Did you, now?" Leopold asks. His face tells me I'm acing it.

"But was it," the Queen asks, "a year?"

"Oh, no," I say. "But it felt like forever."

"So you met before," the King says. "Then circled back around."

I pull my gaze from Leopold. "It was that nasty bit with the unfortunate swimwear that did it," I say. "Leo needs someone who understands popular culture more thoroughly to keep him out of trouble."

"That was my first proposal to her," Leopold says. "To guide me in the ways of double entendres."

"And only later did I get the actual one." I mean, it was like five minutes later. But still.

The King and Queen exchange a glance. I don't know if we're fooling anyone. Even if you could shrug off the party pictures as misleading, the Instagram photos were a mere week ago.

"All right, Leopold," Queen Pulmaria says. "Rosenthal is quite eager to meet with you both. While you were flying, he worked all through the night, arranging the dressmaker for the gown and engaging the bakers and florists. There is much to do. I do wish you'd held off on the betrothal ring."

Leopold bows to her again, and I try to catch up with a quick curtsy. "Thank you, Mother. We're happy to help. There is no need for too much pomp. Save the big guns for my sister."

"Don't be ridiculous," King Francisco booms. "You're the next sovereign. Your wedding is a grand opportunity for visibility and outreach."

Leopold bows to his father, and this time I match him more fluidly. I'm catching on. "I'll keep that in mind, sir."

He spins me with him as we turn around for the door.

"Take the side hall," the Queen says. "There is far too much traffic in the main hall due to the dozens of extra help we've brought in to prepare the palace for the wedding feast."

"Can't have me mingling with the riffraff," Leopold mutters, and I stifle a giggle. "Yes, Mother!"

We spin again toward a set of doors to the right of the thrones. I feel the King and Queen watching us as we cross the room, so I press an impulsive kiss to his cheek.

When we're on the other side of the exit, Leopold lifts me by the waist to spin me around. "You were brilliant! By God, you put the King in his place."

My heart swells with the compliment. No one has ever thought I did much of anything brilliantly.

Leopold lowers me close to him, sliding me down his body. When I land, his mouth is on mine again. The kiss differs from the others, joyful, happy, spirited. He breaks it off to spin me again. "We've done it!"

"So far." The ominous voice of Grisholm sobers us both. "Do not forget that I am very much aware of your story and the timeline."

"Whatever, you old goat," Leopold says. "I want to show Sunny her room before we meet with Rosenthal. Has it been prepared?"

"Of course. Take no more than a half-hour. There is much to do."

CHAPTER 14

Prince Leopold

I kiss Sunny no less than fifteen times on the way to the bridal tower. Traditionally, the groom is kept from his intended during the seven-day wait, but naturally, I will need every minute to ensure Sunny is convinced to go through with it.

"That's the hall to my parent's wing," I tell her, waving toward a wide corridor. "There are several secret channels that connect us, in case of a problem."

"You mean like an attack?"

"I don't think there's much likelihood of anyone sacking the castle." I plant a kiss on her head. "But a fire. Or maybe a crying royal baby."

I slow down as we approach the bridal tower. I haven't been here since I was a child, dashing through the castle with my sisters. "I think I know the way."

"There's rooms here you don't go to often?" Her chin is upturned, taking everything in. Her long hair trails down her back, and I long to bury my face in it.

As well as other places.

"I'm sure there are rooms I've never stepped foot in. The primary guest wing has nearly one hundred rooms. Many are closed off other than for big events."

"Like ours."

I squeeze her hand. "Like ours. It's the biggest."

I want to ask her if she's feeling it, if this is something she can do. But it's too soon. We've barely shown her the palace, or Avalonia. I must be patient.

"This way." I lead her to a set of spiraling stairs.

She takes the first few, peering up. "Is this a damsel in a tower situation? Am I going to get locked in?"

"I'll be the first to knot the bedsheets if so."

Her fingers trail along the stone walls as we ascend. Eventually we reach a landing, which opens to a series of three doors in a half-circle.

"What are these?" she asks.

"The first door is for your maid. The second door is yours. The third one is an antechamber for you to receive guests."

"I hope I have a bathroom because it's a long haul down those stairs."

I could merrily listen to her all day. "I think you'll find you have everything you need." I open the door.

"Oooooh." She pauses at the threshold of the center door. Inside is a room painted pale gold with auburn accents. The large bed has four posts, a canopy, and long sheer fabric enclosing it.

There is a sitting area with a sofa and two chairs. The door to a wardrobe is thrown open, already filled with her gowns.

She steps inside. "It's beautiful." She opens the drawers

of a bureau, filled with frilly things, as well as her clothes from her apartment.

Then she opens a heavy wood door. "The bathroom is bigger than my old bedroom!" She walks the length of it, running her hands along the marble counter and touching the gold handles of the oversized bathtub.

"The toilet is gold!" Her laugh is infectious, and I join in.

"A strange perk, I am sure."

"Totally." She heads back to the bedroom to test the second door. It leads to a short hall and the antechamber, where another set of sofas and chairs furnish a sunny room filled with windows. Along one wall is a sink, a small refrigerator, and painted cabinets.

She hurries to the window. The glass panes are thrown open, and a breeze ruffles the sheer curtains. "It's so beautiful!"

I stand beside her. The view is of the town square, many stories above it. Below, the townspeople wander about the central park, stopping to speak to each other, visiting carts, or carrying packages.

"It's market day." I check my watch. "And it's almost time for the morning ritual. It will be extra boisterous today."

"Are we in *Beauty and the Beast?*" she asks. "I can practically hear that one woman asking for baguettes."

"Do you mean the fairy tale?"

"I do."

"Oh, the resemblance is about to get even stronger."

She sits on the padded bench and braces her elbows on the ledge. "What do you mean?"

The clock tower in the center of the square chimes nine, and the townspeople hurry into their positions. Some move to the roadside, and others fill the space around the tower.

A group of women join hands. They aren't dressed in any particular way. Some wear shorts and T-shirts. Others are in their work dresses or pants and blouses.

Another contingent forms a circle around them, all men.

Then the miniature donkeys arrive.

"What are they doing?" Sunny asks.

"It's a tradition going back hundreds of years to set off the workday. Quite lovely." I don't add *other than the donkeys*.

The bells of the clock tower take up another set of tones.

"Is it playing a tune?" Sunny asks.

The sound rises.

"Are they singing?"

The two circles move in opposite directions. Their voices grow stronger.

"They *are* singing!"

She leans out to get a better look. For a moment, I feel a panic, fearing her falling to her death. I move beside her, my arm tight on her waist. "It's the national anthem of Avalonia."

"Is it in English?"

"Mostly, but with the dialect of the farmers and herd-tenders. Some words are unique to our culture."

She tips her head to listen more carefully. The men and

women cross to each other, making patterns as they swing from one partner to another.

"It's so lovely from up here!"

"A view only for those in the towers. Everyone else sees it from the street."

"Then I'm a lucky one."

"I think that's me." I press my lips to her hair once more.

"Are those baby donkeys?" She points down to the square, where the donkeys are being led into the circle, children on their backs.

"Miniature."

"There's so many!"

The sound reaches its zenith, everyone throwing their arms in the air on the final beat. The circles disperse. Gradually, the townspeople all mingle again, and the moment is over.

"Thank you for showing me this," Sunny says. "I guess when we move to your wing, it won't be above it anymore?"

"No. We'll be at the back of the castle. It's meant to charm the bride into loving her country."

She shifts on the bench to face me. "Well, it's working. That was something out of a fairy tale."

"It's the only period of your life you'll see it, unless you sneak up here later."

"And in a few days, we'll be married."

"That's right." I reach out to slide my thumb over her cheek. "Everyone in New York must constantly tell you how lovely you are."

"Nope, not a one," she says. "Well, other than Harold,

who thinks I should marry him and make him sandwiches at home so he doesn't have to get out."

"Harold?"

"He's eighty-seven."

I chuckle. "Well, he'll have to be disappointed."

Her gaze lingers on mine, and I know a woman who wants to be kissed when I see one. I lean in, and our lips meet softly, emotions colored by the old-fashioned display of pageantry we just witnessed.

But then she scoots closer, and her breasts brush against my chest.

The kiss becomes a frenzy. I want to devour her, take in everything I have yet to explore. I slide my hands down her back, dragging her to me, lifting her so she sits on my lap.

Her satin shirt is slippery and cool. I run my hand over her ribcage, then up to cup that succulent breast I've been keen to touch.

She sucks in a breath, but leans in even more. I take that as an agreement to keep pushing forward. I pass my thumb over the nipple, but the shirt and bra are in my way.

I pull the shirt from the waistband of her skirt. Soon my hand is beneath it, my fingers spreading across the warmth of her skin.

Her arms link around my neck, pushing her breasts more firmly against my chest. I reach for them again, sliding under the bra. Her soft flesh shifts in my hand, her nipple pebbling with my touch.

A groan escapes her mouth, and elation overcomes me. I want her. She's with me. We work.

I turn her to face me, dragging the miles of skirt

around and pushing it out of our way. She seems unsure, but I shift her position on my lap, connecting us so that she can feel my ardor for her.

We move together, bodies straining, eager for closer contact. I slide a hand beneath the skirt. My palm slips up her thigh until it rests at her hip.

When my thumb grazes her panties, she lurches against me with a small cry.

I pause out of concern. She's trembling. "Is this too fast?"

She doesn't answer, holding on to me.

"Sunny?"

"I'm okay."

"We can stop."

"No. I want to keep going. I feel it. I'm just… shy."

I see.

I take my time running my hands along her thighs, only occasionally bumping against those tender parts until she no longer seems timid about my touch.

She whispers, "Yes."

I need no more encouragement. My fingers tug the silk out of the way so that I might slip inside her.

Her moan in my ear is more musical than the song of the town. I want to know how she sounds, what it takes to make her cry out.

"Leopold," she whispers, her body moving against mine.

"Yes, my love." The endearment escapes, one I've been careful never to use, lest some wayward woman get her hopes up. And yet, it seems fitting here.

Her flesh gives way to my touch, warm and pliant. A

shudder runs through her. It is so close, this first delicious moment between us.

Someone clears his throat. "Sire?"

Fuck.

Sunny yelps and leaps off me like I'm on fire. She rapidly tucks in her shirt. I step in front of her.

"Yes, Grisholm."

He looks between us. "You are late. Your appointment with Rosenthal was to commence a quarter hour ago."

"Understood. I didn't want Sunny to miss the morning marketplace display."

"Right."

Sunny continues to stare out the window, and I worry she has been so thoroughly shamed that it will be a setback for us.

"Grisholm, we shall come along in your wake. Let us have a moment."

"I will return immediately if I don't hear your steps."

God, he's insufferable. "Please leave us!"

Then he is gone.

I turn to Sunny, hoping to calm and placate her.

"Sunny, I'm so sorry—" I turn her to me, and realize she is laughing.

"Did you see his face?" Her cheeks are pink with mirth. "Oh, Leopold, somewhere down the line, we have to let him catch us in the real act."

Oh. My. "That sounds like a perfect prank." My heart hammers. This woman. She surprises me every hour. I lean into her. "And we will finish what we started at first opportunity."

She shakes her skirts to make sure they have all fallen evenly. "I guess we better go plan this wedding."

As we descend the bridal tower, I'm not walking on stone at all.

It's air. Pure air.

CHAPTER 15

Sunny

Well, that moved quickly.

Never have I ever met somebody and gotten that wild with them after two days.

Of course, I've never been engaged on day one.

He took his time with me, and that helped. I see I will have to get past my fears, my reservations, my concerns, as soon as possible.

It's time to *get a taste of my silver lining.*

Leopold and I purposely take our time going down the stairs just to make Grisholm traipse back up them. I feel positively five years old as the two of us pass the blustering man who couldn't smile if a fairy gave him a blow job.

I could write a poem about that.

Oh, I shouldn't.

Perhaps a limerick.

There once was a fairy named Kat.
She liked her men surly and fat.
She flitted to Grisholm

And let her small mouth roam
But he wouldn't smile even for that!

Oh, that was terrible.

But so fun!

I can't remember the last time I wrote so many verses in a day.

Even if they aren't any good.

Leopold leads us through a maze of hallways. I have no idea how I'll ever learn my way around. We pass many tall carved wood doors, mostly closed, but a few stand open to reveal a library, a room full of sofas, a billiards parlor. They have everything here. I half expect a bowling alley and a movie theater.

"Is there a pool?" I ask.

Leopold grins at me. "You thinking of skinny dipping? Because I'm game."

He's always so fresh! "So there's a pool?"

"Three. One outdoor, two indoor."

We slow down as we approach a hall where the doors are much closer together. Leopold examines each one. "I can never remember which one is which." He peers at a gold plate. "Ah, here he is. Brace yourself. Rosenthal makes Grisholm look like a peach."

I make sure my shirt is properly tucked and spin the curls in my hair like Aisha did on the plane. Leopold raps on the door.

It opens, and a squat little man appears, looking like he is in costume. His pants are striped blue and gray, oddly coordinating with a long red jacket. He could easily be at home in a circus.

"Sire," he says, executing the most abbreviated bow imaginable. His gaze takes me in. "Now I see what Aisha's had to work with."

Leopold looks mad enough to snort fire. "Rosenthal doesn't believe in pandering to royalty. Father thinks it's a good thing."

"Ah, yes," Rosenthal says. "And you are not exactly in his good graces at the moment."

My anger is brewing at all the people who don't seem happy for Leopold. "Mr. Rosenthal."

The man turns with a heavy sigh. "Yes?"

"If you're not into pandering, then I hope you are quite good at your job. Because I certainly would not have any trouble, as your future queen, replacing you."

He narrows his eyes at me, then stands straighter. "I like her. Americans and their idealized meritocracy are so fascinating."

"I can very well imagine that your family is immortalized in some law providing this position whether you're any good at it or not," I say, feeling heady that I'm challenging someone I barely know. "But you can certainly spend your days in some outbuilding in the hills with the word 'palace' painted over the door. Americans are also pretty good at creatively re-interpreting a law."

"Ho, ho!" Rosenthal turns to Leo. "You picked a fine time to choose one with brains in her head." He toddles around an oversized desk with steps leading to his chair. In this arrangement, he sits taller than Leo or me as we take the seats across from him.

Rosenthal slides a pair of black-framed glasses down his nose to peer at a tablet. "I will update you on the status of the wedding. We have a tailor putting together the Prince's suit. There will be a preliminary fitting this afternoon." His gaze lifts to pierce Leopold. "And you will not run out with pins flying this time. There was a pucker on your betrothal suit that has already been dissected by fashion critics from here to Milan."

Leopold shrugs. "Fine."

"As for the gown, Aisha has determined the style that will be most flattering for the lady's unusual proportions."

I glance down at my skirt. Unusual? Okay, maybe my hips are wider than my boobs are big.

"I like her proportions fine," Leopold says.

"I'm sure." Rosenthal flicks to a new screen. "We have a cake being designed. The local bakers are preparing the sweets for the revelers. Because your wedding is not in the right season, we cannot feature our national flower, but we will create looks with white roses and hyacinth."

"Oh, I'm allergic to hyacinth." I wiggle in my seat, unhappy to have to admit it.

"Then take a nasal spray," Rosenthal says.

"I don't think so," Leopold says. "If there is a single hyacinth in her vicinity, we're flying to Vegas to get married."

"Such divas." Rosenthal slashes dramatically across the screen. "I assume pansies are safe?"

I grip the armrest. "Yes. Pansies will be fine."

"An entire design element up in smoke," Rosenthal mutters. "Also, there is the matter of your bride's name."

Leopold leans forward in his chair. "What about her name?"

"It's too common for our future queen. I suggest Sunholia."

Oh, God. No. "Do we have to do that?" I ask.

Leopold takes my hand. "Surely we don't have to change her name. A common name will make her more relatable. I think Sunny wants that, right?"

"Yes. Definitely." Sunholia makes me think of Beavis and Butthead. CORNHOLIO! Actually, it makes me want to giggle.

"This is not my idea. You will have to take it up with the Queen." Rosenthal grins as he exaggerates a "check" motion on the screen. "Honestly, I don't think I need you for anything. The decisions are all mine. Have you chosen a ring from the vault?"

"Not yet. We've only been here an hour," Leopold says.

"Enough time to get busy in the bridal tower, I hear."

My face burns, but I have nothing to say to that.

"My ardor for my bride will soon be apparent to all," Leopold says.

"You don't say." Rosenthal drops the tablet to his desk with a thud. "Much like your ardor for Miss *Crème Pour le Visage*?"

I don't know what he means, but Leopold leaps. "We will not discuss my past in front of my bride. She is well aware of the man I was before her. I will tolerate no one using my mistakes to make her feel less than what she is — the future Queen of Avalonia!"

Rosenthal lifts his hands for a slow clap. "Quite the speech. You forget that no man is an island, and you, our prince, are a walking beach party. The press is already having a field day. They assume the bride is with child."

"What?" I stand up, too. "There hasn't been time!"

"Oh, but you told the King only an hour ago about how long you've known each other. How he circled back around upon realizing how much he loved you." His voice is a sneer.

Leopold looks like he's about to turn the desk over.

I reach for his arm. "Leo, when I don't produce a baby bump in a few months, those rumors will melt away. Let our happiness be the only thing they can take away from our wedding day."

Leo's nostrils flare as he blows out a gust of air. "The press can do what they want. But inside these walls, I will hear nothing more of it."

I turn to Rosenthal. "Your lack of kindness will be your undoing."

The big man shrugs. "My strength has gotten me where I am."

"That's enough trouble for one day," I tell him. "Leopold is going to show me more of the castle."

"Good day, Sunholia."

I picture Beavis in his Great Cornholio state after drinking caffeine, his T-shirt pulled over his head. Yeah, not a good look.

Leopold pulls my arm through his elbow as we leave Rosenthal and his enormous desk behind. "Let's get out of here. I have so much to show you."

"Where first?"

"You should meet my sisters. You will find them much better company than anyone so far."

We head back through the maze of halls. "Should I be leaving a trail of breadcrumbs or something?"

"You will eventually learn to navigate by the paintings." He gestures to the towering frames filled with images of children playing, some with dogs, others riding donkeys. "The hall of kids."

"So there is a method to the madness."

"Mostly."

We reach a circular room with grand foyers leading outdoors both to the right and to the left. "Our wing," Leopold says. "Mine and my sisters'."

Two guards bow as Leopold takes my hand to lead us through an archway. This hall is wide and bright with white floors and pale gray walls. Colorful portraits at almost life size show a young Leopold with his sisters, all waving from a wooden cart on a hillside. Farther down are other, more dated shots of different children from bygone eras. Near the end of the hall, the images become paintings again.

"This is Lilianne's room, the youngest." He gestures to a tall door with a wreath of pale orange blossoms. "Then Octavia's." Her wreath bears blue hyacinths. As we pass, I let out a sneeze.

"Oh, right. I'll have hyacinths removed from the grounds. They grow abundantly here. We may have an entire hyacinth garden." Leopold's face pulls into concern.

I wave my hand. "That sounds like torture, but really, the occasional bloom won't be a big deal."

Leopold pauses before a door without a wreath, but a plaque bearing a family crest. It has a large A inside a shield. And what looks like two... donkeys?

"Are those—?"

"I don't want to talk about it." Leopold shoves the door open.

Okay. Interesting.

We enter the room. It's three times the size of mine, but of course I'm up in a tower. There's no bed, so it must be more of a living space. It has three sofas, several chairs, a big screen television, a full stereo system, and a small kitchen area in the corner.

"It's like an apartment all your own!"

"It's been modernized. It used to be much more old-fashioned." He leads me to a short hallway. A door to the left opens to a bathroom. To the right is a cavernous closet. We pass on through to his bedroom.

Now we're alone.

The bed is outrageously large, like three normal beds. I picture Leopold with a whole host of girls at one time and have to shake the image away. Large wardrobes fill a wall. There's another flat-screen television and several more chairs. Everything is navy or gold, from the heavy curtains on the windows to the bedspread to the rugs.

It's perfectly neat, but I know that is no reflection of Leopold. He'll have staff picking up after his every move.

"Very masculine," I say. "Is there much bounce to the bed?"

"Let's find out." He lifts me by the waist and tosses me backwards.

I laugh as I land on what feels like air. "Good grief! Did you convince a cloud to be your mattress?"

"There's nothing like them in the States. You all sleep on wood planks."

I turn on my side and watch him as he leans against

one of the carved bedposts. "Some people like to sleep on something firm."

"I have something firm." He plops down beside me and before I can get another word out, his mouth is on mine.

Between the mattress and his kiss, I feel like I'm floating.

> *A leaf*
> *skittering along the bare earth*
> *spinning dizzy*
> *then sent aloft*
> *with a perfect breeze*
> *flitting into the sun*

That's me.

His hands skim my body, taking in my *proportions* outside of the silky shirt. I'm ready to get back to where we were, my head whirling with the prospect of going further.

"Oh, brother! I hear you brought home a bri-ide!" The sing-song voice is followed by the sound of laughter. Not one voice, but two.

Leopold stills his hand and lets out a long sigh. "My sisters. I haven't seen them in months."

I quickly sit up and straighten my shirt. "I'm excited to meet them."

"If only it could wait." He shakes his head.

"Where are you? Are you naked? Based on the news reports, you're usually naked." The voices are in the other room.

With that, Leopold launches to his feet. "Hush now! If

you two stepped one foot outside this castle, you'd see what the papers have to say about you!"

"Touchy, touchy!"

I stand as well, just as two cell phones appear at the end of the hall, followed by arms and then two young women.

"First shots of the happy couple!" one says.

"Upload them!" the other says.

Leopold shakes his head. "Isn't there a geofence around this wing that blocks digital uploads?"

They lower their phones. "We figured out how to get around that ages ago."

Now that their guard is down, Leopold runs forward and grasps them both around the necks. "Noogies all around!"

The sisters shriek and try to work themselves loose. I stand at the end of the bed to watch. My sister and I were never like this. Greta is serious, and playing wild was never her thing.

The cousins, of course, were an entirely different matter. They were always roughhousing and goofy.

Leopold hangs onto both their necks. "Do you solemnly swear to delete any pictures you just took?"

"Oh, Leo, you're such a killjoy," one says.

"We should yeet you into the sun," the other says.

Leopold laughs and lets them go. "Yeet. Nobody in Avalonia says 'yeet.'"

Now that I can see their faces properly, I sort out which is which. The younger of the two has to be Lilianne. She's nineteen. She flops on the bed in her ripped jeans and off-shoulder top. She looks like any teenager, long straight hair falling everywhere.

The older one, Octavia, is twenty-two. She wears pale green leggings under a short pink skirt, which she twists back into place now that the tussle is over. Her hair is rolled into two tight balls, rich black striped with pink and blue. She holds out a hand. "I'm Octavia," she says. "I can't believe anyone can stand this lughead for more than ten minutes, but you seem sane. So I guess he has some good qualities."

I laugh. "He does. I'm so glad to meet you."

Octavia points to the bed. "That's Lili. She's probably already updating her followers that she met you."

"No pictures!" Leopold says, lunging for her phone.

Lili rolls away from him. "I didn't take a picture. It was video!"

Leopold snatches her phone. "You made a TikTok?"

"I have three million followers waiting for my opinion!"

"You haven't been in the room long enough to form an opinion!" Leopold swipes around on her screen. The recording of their voices calling out to us comes from the phone. I peer over his shoulder. There's the end of the hall, the bedpost, then Leopold lunging for them. Then everything's a big blur.

She's already typed a caption. "The royal couple are at the castle! They're all over each other!"

"How did you have time for that?" he asks.

Lili examines her long nails. "I'm fast. You have to be fast these days."

There's nothing there to worry about. The video doesn't even show me anywhere. The suggestiveness in the video is Leopold lunging at the camera with a bed in the background.

"Stop it," Leopold says. "We want to introduce Sunny in our own way." He holds Lili's phone high in the air, swiping through screens. She leaps from the bed to snag it, but he whips it out of her reach. "Promise?"

Lili jumps, trying to get to her phone, but Leopold is way too tall.

"I promise! Jeez! For a guy busted wearing a cocksuit, you sure are suddenly picky about your image."

Octavia snaps pictures of them. "Don't forget that Instagram spread."

"She put stickers over stuff," Leopold says as he continues to hold Lili's phone out of reach.

I stand back, watching. They're all clearly very close.

Lili bends over, wheezing in and out from her efforts. "Did you realize that Insta model put you in her stories, too?"

"What of it?" Leopold takes a quick photo of himself with his tongue hanging out, then holds the phone high while he turns it into Lili's home screen.

"Gross!" Lili says. "And I'm happy to tell you that anyone can remove stickers from a video! There's an app!"

Leopold lowers the phone. Lili instantly snatches it.

"So people can see the raw video?"

"Totally! Weeza's team has been on it, but I'm sure the royal junk is all over private servers."

"Did you see it?" His face is ash.

Lili rams her shoulder into his belly, knocking him backwards. "No! Gross!"

Octavia drops onto a leather chair, the window light

making her hair balls shine. She has tinsel or something woven into them. "Mom and Dad have been beside themselves about you this last year. Why didn't you tell us you found a princess? The cock thing was only a couple of days ago. There were girls hanging all over you." She meets my eyes for only a moment, then stares out the window.

I sit in a chair near the bed, waiting for Leopold to explain himself. We fudged all the details for his parents and certainly to Rosenthal. But these are his sisters. I can already tell by the way they interact that he probably doesn't lie to them.

He sits on the end of the bed, and Lili curls up beside him, her head on his shoulder. Despite their fighting only moments before, it's easy to see what they were like growing up. He's a decade older than her, and she likely idolized him, a lot like the way Greta and I felt about our oldest cousin Jason.

"I screwed up. I enjoyed being the life of the party. But the girls living a life like that are generally only looking for a good time, too."

Octavia moves to the bed to sit on the other side of him. "So how did you meet Sunny?"

I hold my breath, wondering what he will say.

"I was running from the photographers. You know how they get."

The girls nod.

"I ducked into a restaurant, and Sunny was there. She helped me hide, then sent them away, then helped me escape out the back. From the moment I met her, she understood what it was like to be me. She called me out on it, even. She saw all those photos."

Lili's gaze shifts to me. "And you went out with him anyway?"

Time for me to speak. "Not right away. In fact, I think I threw some choice pieces of pottery at him."

"Oh, I want to hear that story," Octavia says.

"She had the guards terrified," Leopold said. "Pace was hiding behind a chair."

"I'm going to tease him about that forever," Lili says.

"Your brother calmed me down." I finger the sparkling overlay of my gold skirt. "He told me that from now on, he pledges me his faithfulness."

"And you believe him?" Octavia asks.

I meet both of their gazes, Octavia, then Lili. "I do."

The girls are nineteen and twenty-two, but they act younger. I think of how jaded my coworker Rachel is at eighteen. Maybe it's the difference between Avalonia and New York. Or maybe they've been sheltered in the palace. But they're adorable.

"We get to be your ladies-in-waiting," Lili says, pretending to hold out a big skirt, and turning in a circle. "I don't normally wear dresses unless Mother makes us, but I will do it for you."

"You're going to get a million more followers for that," I say.

Her eyes go bright. "I will!"

Leopold reaches for her phone again, but she jerks it out of his grasp.

"No live streaming the wedding behind our backs," he warns her.

"Oh! That's a great idea!" She shoves her phone down

her cleavage, which is too slight to hold it. "Dang, I have to find a place it can go!"

Octavia laughs. "You'll be too busy. It's the first royal wedding in ages. It's going to be videoed from every angle already."

Lili presses the phone to her forehead. "Not from *my* angle! I need a strap!"

Leopold walks over and holds out his arm. "Come on, Sunny. We'll be with my sisters again later. We have much to see."

I take his hand, and he lifts me from his chair. Lili snaps a picture. "I won't post it. I promise!" She and Octavia look at it with a sigh.

"See you soon!" I call back at them as Leopold leads me out of the room.

I love them already. It's nice to have people in the palace who are on my side. For the first time, I think — I can live here.

Another limerick forms as we walk back down the long corridor.

There once were two girls in a palace.
A change from the staff who were callous.
They took pictures and laughed
At their brother's huge gaffe.
And made fun of his world-renowned
phallus.

CHAPTER 16

Prince Leopold

Sunny looks lost as we cross through the main hall and out the back doors to the gardens.

I turn her back to face the palace, which encloses the gardens on three sides. "Okay, so the big box in the center, that's where we were at first. It has the throne room, the ballrooms, the big sitting rooms, the dining rooms, and the kitchens."

"But we didn't drive up through these gardens."

"Right. We came in on the other side of that wing." I point to the left. "Beyond it is the airstrip."

She points to the right. "And the children's wing and the offices were all on that side."

"Yes."

"Was my tower on that side?"

"No. You were in the left tower. That side also has the King and Queen's quarters, as well as the Crown Prince's apartments. We will move there next week."

"Why wouldn't the King and Queen want their children close?"

"In the event of a fire or a bomb or an attack on the King, the heirs would be far enough away to survive and escape. There are secret ways to cross through without traversing the halls, as well as paths the staff use. I'll show you them."

"What is the other tower for?"

"Most honored guests. Other royalty. Dignitaries. The guest rooms are spread throughout both wings, and fill much of the main building."

"I can't imagine having to clean all that."

I chuckle. "You never will."

"Never say never! Cinderella certainly never thought she'd be in charge of evil stepsisters."

"All right, all right."

Sunny sneezes, and I spot the hyacinth garden ahead. "Let's cut to the left. Roses are okay?"

She sneezes again. "Roses are fine."

I hold her hand as we wander the path. "I've arranged for a picnic lunch in the hills. I thought it best if we got away from the palace since we have so much getting to know each other to do."

"We do." Two birds flit around each other, crossing our path. "If one of them rests on your shoulder, I'm going to assume I'm in a coma or something, because it seriously won't be reality anymore."

"I'm no Snow White," I tell her, happy to make her smile. "More like Shrek."

"Hardly."

We reach the end of the cultivated gardens. A guard is at the gate.

"Sire." He swings the wrought iron aside. "Your cart is waiting in the first stable."

I nod at him, but Sunny spins around. "Thank you. What is your name?"

The guard's eyes meet mine. "Miss?"

Interesting that he calls her *miss* rather than milady. How do the guards not know that this is my intended? Didn't Grisholm brief the staff? Perhaps there hasn't been time to reach all the shifts. I lift her hand, revealing the betrothal ring.

The guard's eyes grow wide. He bows. "I am so sorry, sire. I didn't realize you had taken a bride. A thousand pardons."

Sunny lets go of me to approach him. "It's okay. I barely know it myself. My name is Sunny." She holds out a hand. "I'm American, so we shake hands."

His eyes flit to me, and I nod.

He takes her hand. "I'm Vellemond, milady."

She shakes it firmly. "Nice to meet you, Vellemond."

We walk along a winding stone path toward the long row of stables.

As we approach, a man in brown overalls waves. Only when he turns do I see it's Sid, our long-time head of live-stock and breeding. He was a father figure to me before my sisters came along, taking me out to the stables to learn the ins and outs of the donkey trade.

He gives only a hint of a bow for propriety before drawing me into an embrace. "Leo, my boy. You have been gone too long from my stables. I hear you have been all over Europe and America!"

"I have. And I brought back a bride."

He releases me to look at Sunny. "I had hoped it was so. An American girl! This is new!" He draws Sunny to him, and she easily accepts his hug. "A girl for Leo! I am so happy! Avalonia has a future queen at last."

He pulls away to look at her. "And so lovely."

"I'm Sunny," she says. "And you are?"

"Sid. At your service. I have the finest donkeys of the royal selection set to pull your cart."

"You have royal select donkeys?"

Sid stands tall, his thumbs locked in the straps of his overalls. "I breed the royal selection myself from the finest stock. No country has finer donkey stock than Avalonia!"

Sunny looks over the long stretch of stables, going as far as the eye can see, rising and falling with the roll of the hills. "Is this your export? Donkeys?"

"It is! We breed a very specific kind, trademarked and all." He steps back and clucks his tongue. "They are known for their stature and their signature laugh."

Wheels squeak, then there they are. Six miniature donkeys hitched to a small cart lined with blankets, a picnic basket positioned in the front.

"They're adorable!" Sunny rushes up to one and pets the puff of white hair on its gray head. The others shuffle and shift, trying to get to her.

"I packed some apples and sweet potatoes to treat them," Sid says. "They are well trained to take you into the hills and will know the way back." He hands her a slender, gnarled sweet potato. "For later, when they've taken you where you want to go."

I try to summon some enthusiasm for the creatures. It

is true I loved them as a child, but once the breech was made, there was no going back.

Sunny holds the sweet potato, fumbling for a pocket, but has none. I take it from her and slide it into the back pocket of my jeans.

Sid seems to remember my reason for losing my fondness for the breed, his face pulled into a frown. "These are good ones."

"Oh, they're absolutely precious." Sunny moves around all of them, petting each of their heads. "Aren't we too heavy for them? Should we walk aside?"

"I breed them strong and reliable," Sid says, pride evident in his voice. "And these are the best."

"I love them." She leans down to kiss one on the nose, and it happens. The first one laughs.

Hee haw haw haw haw.

"Oh, my goodness!" Sunny steps back. "They really do laugh."

Soon all the donkeys are going.

Hee haw haw haw hee hee haw haw haw.

I grit my teeth. The sound sets me on edge.

"They will love you right back." Sid walks among the donkeys, clucking his tongue until they all go quiet and stand at the ready. "I must get back to my duties. Call me if you run into trouble, and I'll send someone out. I heard you wanted to go this alone."

"I do." I give him a quick salute. "You ready, Sunny?"

"Completely!"

The cart is small but well appointed with cushions and blankets. I help Sunny step up onto the back of it, and we settle onto the floor. I pick up the reins and give them a quick flick, and the donkeys move together to set out across the short-shorn fields of grass and clover.

"There aren't any pens?" Sunny asks. She shields her eyes to look across the landscape.

"There are holding pens behind each stable, but mostly the donkeys are allowed to roam. The herders gather them at night. They have trained dogs to help."

"What a life! Oh, I see them!" She points to a small herd of donkeys as we crest a hill and sits up straight. "And this is Avalonia's only point of trade?"

"It used to be. For generations, donkeys were bred for the specific qualities we are known for."

"And what are those?" Her face is animated and happy as she scans the hills for more herds.

"Size and, uh, sound."

She turns to me. "You mean that laugh they did?"

"It's unique only to our breed."

She smacks my knee. "Get out of town! You all created miniature donkeys with a specific laugh?" She pulls on the reins. "How do I stop them? I want to hear them again!"

I glance back. We're well away from the stables, a long expanse of hills. "Let's head to the place I have in mind. There will be tons of them there."

"Okay! The weather is so perfect. Warm but not hot." She lifts her face to the sun, and it's a joy to watch her. I can't imagine any of the other women I tangled with in the last few months being so happy to merely soak up the sun, driven by donkeys, in the middle of nowhere.

I flip open the basket. "Water? Wine?"

She grins. "Water is good." The breeze lifts her hair. "I

could live right out here. Do you not come out here every single day?"

I pass her a bottle. "I did when I was young. I was seven before Octavia was born, so my playmates were the stable boys."

"You must have loved that childhood."

"I did. Until I didn't."

"What happened?"

"It is nothing. Just an unfortunate comment that struck the heart of a young boy."

Her hand covers mine. "Clearly it still gets to you."

I take a long swig of my water. Is this what proper couples do? Share their embarrassments? Perhaps so.

"I don't like to recount it."

"That's okay, then. Maybe when we know each other better." She withdraws her hand and stares out to the hills.

I've disappointed her.

"I was eight. Octavia was a baby."

She turns back to me, eyes bright.

"I wanted to hang out with some of the older stable boys, but they didn't like having the Prince around. That meant guards. And they couldn't smoke or cuss."

She smiles. "Such a killjoy."

"Exactly. But I stubbornly would show up in their hangouts, anyway." I roll the water bottle between my hands. "Once night I snuck up on them, and they were saying they would have to change their favorite spot because I kept coming. This would have been bad enough, but then one of them told the others that my laugh sounded like the donkeys, and they all started mimicking my laugh. It was great sport for them."

"Oh, that's awful."

"Not only that, suddenly I remembered all the times they had made that sound. I always thought they were imitating the donkeys, but it turns out they were mimicking me. They'd never been my friends at all."

"Oh, no."

"So I quit the stables, other than sometimes working with Sid. But things became different anyway. I started my education as future King. I moved on."

Sunny tucks her water bottle back in the basket and takes one of my hands in hers. "For what it's worth, your laugh sounds nothing like a donkey."

"I don't laugh."

She frowns. "Of course you do. I've heard it. Right?"

"No. I don't really laugh. I haven't since then. Chuckle, sure. Smirk, always. But I haven't truly laughed since I was eight years old."

"Oh, Leopold. That's awful. Laughter is so important to happiness!"

"I'm plenty happy."

"Are you sure?" She shifts closer. "Are you really sure?"

Of course I'm not sure. I've been running from my responsibilities since I was old enough to go out on my own.

"I'm happy now."

She gives me a sidelong glance. "I won't believe it until I hear you laugh."

"I wouldn't pin your hopes on that." I gesture to the meadow ahead. "And we've arrived at our destination."

She sucks in a breath. It's an impressive sight. The

valley leads to a meadow edged by a pond surrounded by trees. The slopes are filled with a riot of wildflowers.

"There will be hyacinths, I'm afraid." I pull a handkerchief from my pocket to pass to her.

She accepts it. "A small price to pay." She can't stop looking. "Oh, Leo, it's paradise."

And on that point, I can agree with her.

CHAPTER 17

Sunny

The view takes my breath away. Pink and blue flowers, long swaying grass, the pond, and a vast blue sky. The donkeys munch on the grass beneath a canopy of trees. I suck in a great gulp of air. I never thought of air having a taste, but it does here. And it's fresh and sweet.

I'm in love with a country.

But the man?

I watch Leopold close the picnic basket and lift it out of the cart. How could anyone not fall in love with him? He's gorgeous and funny, and good grief, a freaking prince!

But he's also clearly stubborn, tricky, and if social media can be trusted, unable to keep his pants on. He's certainly shown his rush-to-get-physical side with me. Practically every time we're alone, we're all over each other.

And we're definitely alone.

"That looks like a suitable spot by the water." Leopold carries the basket a few yards into the privacy of the trees.

Really alone.

I pull out a thick blanket to sit on and follow him. Will things go further here? Now? My belly quivers. I've done it before, certainly. There was that one time with Billy Amos in junior college. He was in my poetry class and I thought for sure we would be the next Robert and Elizabeth Barrett Browning.

But I think I did something wrong. Or he did. Or both of us. Because after that infamous night, he sat elsewhere in the classroom and wouldn't look me in the face.

I wasn't expecting stars and fireworks the first time. But there was never a single moment with Billy that was a tenth as thrilling as a simple kiss with Leopold. Even a look from the Prince can make the sparks fly in my head.

> *His glance scatters the stars*
> *forming new constellations*
> *in the heaven of our nights*

"Oh, that's a good one." Leopold takes the blanket from me. "Do all poets spout lovely lines like that as they come?"

I've said it out loud again. Thank goodness the limericks don't do that.

"I wouldn't know. I don't know any real poets."

He spreads the blanket on the grass. "None?"

"I guess some of my professors were poets. But I don't count them."

We settle on the blanket. "Why not? Were their verses inferior to yours?"

I don't know how to explain it without confessing everything. "They didn't care for my poetry. I dropped out of the program and got a generic associate degree in

English. Then I never applied it to a four-year college like I planned. I went to work with Grammy."

He pauses, a charcuterie board of cheese and grapes covered in plastic wrap in his hands. "You dropped out? What did they say to you?" His tone is hard, like he's going to charge onto campus astride a magnificent steed and avenge my honor.

"I was told to stop writing poetry. That I didn't have the knack for it."

"The knack? Like playing spoons or catching two jacks before the ball bounces?" His ire is up.

"I switched the class to pass/fail so it wouldn't hurt my grades. It was too late to drop it. The rest of the semester was murder. I had to force lines out onto the page. After that, I just quit."

"You let one person stop you from doing something you loved?"

"I guess so."

"One person." He sets down the board of cheese. "Surely if one person can ruin something, one other person can bring it back?"

"I'm not sure art works that way."

"But you've been doing it! This morning on the plane! And now!"

He's right. Plus the crazy limericks in my head. "I guess something's jogged it out of me."

His face breaks into a smile. "Of course it did! You're home. Avalonia will inspire all the great poems. You will nurture the poets here and inspire them to write beautiful lines just like yours."

Could he be right?

I help him unload the rest of the basket. There's two baguettes and a warm ceramic pan that reveals a quiche when opened. I realize how hungry I am.

Leopold passes me a plate. "Wine now or still water?"

Wine in the middle of the day. It seems like a perfect place for it. "Wine, I think."

"Excellent." He twists the corkscrew into the bottle.

Soon, we both lie on our sides, facing each other like a yin and yang, the food between us, sipping wine and making the cheese and bread disappear.

> *The artist paints in layers*
> *fresh green and bountiful blue.*
> *His details fill the canvas.*
> *Flowers*
> *picnic*
> *blanket*
> *me*
> *and you.*

"I can't imagine anyone thinks you're not good at this." Leopold takes a sip and I realize I've spoken aloud again. I press the back of my hand to my lips. Did this happen before, back when I wrote verses freely, before my confidence was snatched away?

I don't think so.

"My professor did." I take a longer sip of wine, closing my eyes, listening to birdsong, feeling the breeze on my face. I don't want to think of the old things, but doubt creeps in. How can I lead an entire country's focus on poetry if I'm terrible at it?

Leopold lies back, his hands behind his head. "I've never been good at anything in particular, although I guess I tended donkeys well enough as a kid."

"What did you want to do?" I stack our empty dishes and settle them back in the basket.

"I'm not sure I ever wanted to do anything. My life has been defined by what I had to do. Study Avalonian law. World history. Diplomacy. I did rather like learning how to negotiate with terrorists."

I sit cross-legged, the wine glass dangling from my fingers. "Does that come up often?"

He chuckles. "Never. But there were times in Amsterdam I had to convince a shady character or two to move along. It came in handy."

"Tell me how."

He shifts to sit facing me, our knees almost touching. "First, you have to establish a rapport. Some sort of common ground, even if it's only happening in the moment."

"So he points a gun at you and you ask about his family?"

Another chuckle. "No, you make a quick observation. Like maybe, 'Did the temperature drop?' It's natural to respond to something like that automatically. It makes them think about something else for a split second, breaks whatever spiral they're in."

"Oh. That's good."

"Once they are engaged, you repeat anything they say like you're agreeing with them. So if they say, 'It's been cold,' you can say, 'It sure has been cold.' Now it feels like you're coming to their side of things."

"That makes sense, too."

"It's called mirroring. For most things, you can keep mirroring your way right out of the situation. But if you need them to do something, you keep going, usually by labeling what is motivating them to act a certain way. Like, 'You're down on your luck.' Or, 'I'd be pissed about that, too.'"

"Fascinating."

"I think it's fascinating as well. I'm mirroring you right now." His grin is mischievous, and I realize he's sitting like I am, feet crossed, one elbow on his knee, the other hand on the blanket.

"So, what are you trying to negotiate out of me?" I ask, but by the look in his eye, I already know.

He leans forward, and his lips are gentle on mine, as if he wants to test my reaction before moving on.

But those sparks that he's stirred up repeatedly today return with their strongest intensity yet. I wrap my arms around his neck.

He drags me close to him, our legs uncrossing as we fall together across the blanket. We're deliciously alone, the breeze stirring my hair as Leopold shifts me beneath him.

"It's been hours since I kissed you." His breath feathers across my cheeks. "It feels like years."

His gaze holds mine, the green of his eyes repeated in the leaves and grass around us. The donkeys shift nearby, occasionally braying softly. Something splashes in the pond.

If someone photographed this moment, or painted or drew it, the scene could easily find its place in a story book.

"You are the only girl I've brought here," he says. "I would come here when I was upset. It's a peaceful place."

"It is."

His mouth claims mine again, tender after all the words we've shared. I taste the wine, and a hint of cheese. Delicious, intoxicating.

His kisses trail down my cheek, across my hair, and down to my shoulder. He pulls at the sleeve of my shirt to reveal more skin and leaves a warm trail down my neck to my collarbone.

I'm aloft, floating in the summer air. I grip his arm, certain that if I let go, I'll drift away like a bright balloon.

He pulls the shirt out of the waistband of my skirt. My skin cools only for a moment before his mouth is there, finding fresh territory, sliding along the bottom of my ribs and making its way up.

I open my eyes, the branches that shelter us shifting in the wind. This place feels magical, otherworldly. In this space, I can almost see myself as a princess.

Leopold's hand slips beneath me, and a sudden shift of tension tells me he's released my bra. He lifts the shirt up and away, taking the bra with it. It catches a moment on the length of my hair, then hits the edge of the blanket with a whisper.

Being so exposed in the outdoors is an unfamiliar experience for me. Before I can feel self-conscious, Leopold's mouth closes over a breast, and I forget where I am. My back arches up to him. The sparks scatter and swirl, then concentrate in all the places he touches me.

When he moves from one to the other, the cool air tightens the wet nipple so hard I suck in a breath. Every cell in my body feels riotously alive, like most of me was sleeping until the Prince shook every nerve ending awake.

My chest heaves as I take in each breath. His hands move down, reaching for the clasp of the skirt, which has shifted its way to my side.

Then more skin is kissed by the summer breeze. The fabric slips down and down until I'm left in panties and one simple gold slipper, the other falling off somewhere along the way.

Leopold's mouth leaves a fiery trail as he makes his way down my body. I cross my arm over my eyes, unable to look at anything, flooded with a dizzying roar of need and fear. What had made Billy want to go away after we were finally together all the way? Was there something about me that repelled him? Would it happen again?

I almost push Leopold aside, too afraid he will find me lacking. The rejection will be more than I can bear. I'm half a world away from home. I have no friends here, only two funny sisters who would take his side in an instant. Even Aisha's kindness would cool if the Prince set me aside.

But then his mouth fits over the outside of my panties, and all the heat in my body rushes there. My arms fly wide, clutching the blanket. He breathes against those tender parts, and an intense desperation fills me.

I need him to do the rest. It's already a million times better than Billy's fumbling attempts. I want to scream at him to tear off my panties, to do whatever he wants. I'm utterly, helplessly his.

My voice is a strangled gasp. "Leo, please, yes..."

But he knows. He absolutely knows. He yanks down

the panties and his tongue is inside me, then his fingers. He works me and my hips rise to meet him. He clasps my body and lifts me higher.

I'm dizzy, lost, unable to think. He's eager, attentive, and skilled. I open my eyes, shocked at the way my body thrums, like I'm a flute being played, or a violin, the bow creating music as it moves across my strings.

Every poetic thought I've ever had tries to escape me at once. Trilling songbirds. The splash of a waterfall over rocks. Clouds separating in the sky. The glimmer of raindrops.

My muscles draw together, tightening. I can hear my voice saying words. "Leopold. God. Oh. Leopold." Everything is focused, swirling, centering on where he works me.

There's the moment of quiet, like the forest going still, all its creatures tuned in just before the predator is revealed.

Then I'm over some precipice, falling off the face of the earth. A shock wave goes through me and my voice matches the wind, becomes the leaves rustling, the light bleeding through in sun rays. The tension fans out, replaced by a release, a high, a buzz turned into a pulsing of purest joy.

My hand flies to my belly, feeling the rhythmic squeeze that matches the noises I make. The vibration lingers, holding me in place, and my vision fills with the universe, love, understanding. Things make sense, puzzles unravel. I feel high, like I've ingested a drug.

My lungs exhale, and I begin to come down, drifting like a feather, until I slip into a luxurious relaxation.

My muscles still, Leopold following their lead, as if he and my body are the same musical phrase, in unison with the melody he started.

I hear birds again. The donkeys munch the grass nearby. Then funny little footsteps? Shuffling? I tilt my head.

A loose donkey sniffs at my hair. He's tinier than the rest, a mere baby. "Hi," I say to him. He snuffles about on the blanket, and I realize there are others. Some ease toward the water. Others take great interest in the picnic basket.

Leopold places a kiss on my belly, then hovers over me. "Where there are loose donkeys, there's often a herder. Let's get you dressed."

"But…" I know there is more for us to do, but Leopold stands, scanning the space. I quickly snatch up my skirt and hurry to slide it on.

"I don't see anyone close yet." Leopold bends to pick up my bra and shirt, then yelps. "Hey!"

I turn to see what's the matter. Three donkeys have found the slender sweet potato lodged in his back pocket. They nip at his jeans.

"Did you just bite my butt?" Leopold removes the potato and breaks it into pieces. "I shouldn't reward you for that."

I pick up the rest of my clothes, trying to hold back my laughter. The abruptness of how we ended things is left behind as more donkeys realize we are feeding them treats. I pull my shirt over my head and find my other slipper.

Leopold extends a hand to lift me up. "I suppose we can find the rest of the treats Sid packed for them."

We spend another half hour distributing the apples and sweet potatoes, petting the donkeys' fuzzy heads. Even though the intimate moment has passed, something between us has permanently altered. We smile more easily, and our gazes linger.

This is no fool's paradise, and there is no trouble here.

CHAPTER 18

Prince Leopold

Of course, those damn donkeys bit my butt.

It's been a lovely interlude with Sunny. We walk most of the way back to the palace, the donkey cart trailing behind. She picks flowers and admires the countryside, looking deliciously disheveled.

The loose herd we fed follows along, and she laughs when one of them runs up to us to check if there is a spare apple to beg for. Sunny treats them as pets, giving them all names.

She's a delight, and the taste of her is close in memory, as are the sounds of her cries. She turned herself over to me in a way I have never experienced. Most women want to look a certain way or project a certain image. Some bounce around, one eye watching to see if you're admiring them appropriately. Others try to act like porn stars, all show and very little feeling.

Sunny seemed aloft, as if she'd allowed me to take her on an uncertain journey. Jealousy stabs me that she's ever been with anyone else, that some man out there might know the freedom of her inhibition.

But she turns to see why I've fallen behind, and I catch up to her. She moves her flowers to her outside hand, and I reach for her. Three days with her, particularly with this constant level of togetherness, is more than I have ever spent with anyone. Usually I'm making a quick exit, feeling even more empty than I had before the encounter.

But here, I am at peace. Watching her with a herd of love-struck mammals, I begin to believe in fate again. How did I find her? Or perhaps, of all the women who have fallen my way, how did I know she was the one to return to?

Several guards stand outside the stable, including Rubin. Duty calls. A suit fitting, perhaps, or another inane decision regarding the wedding. I don't want my afternoon to end, and my steps slow.

"Are they waiting for us?" Sunny asks. "Are we in trouble?"

"I'm sure they have a message from someone. Rosenthal perhaps. Or Aisha. Or a chef or a florist or perhaps Mother and Father. No telling."

"I guess there is a slightly important occasion just around the corner." Her open, joyful expression when she looks at me swells my chest.

"I guess we wouldn't be a bride and groom if there wasn't stress over details."

Sid scurries out of the stable as we crest the hill. "I'll take the cart!" he says, shooing the loose donkeys back onto the grasslands. "Where are the herders? Marco should have been with these."

I pat the rump of a brown and white one to send him off with the others. "They were besotted with the Princess. I told him we'd push them back out."

"Uribon!" Sid calls. "Come, boy! Get this flock back with the others!"

"Oh, I'm so sorry," Sunny says. "I shouldn't have encouraged them to follow."

"You can't help if they're drawn to you," Sid says. "Now run along. The guards have been waiting nigh an hour."

Sunny holds her flowers as the guards approach. "I guess it's time we faced the music for escaping."

Rubin steps forward. "Sire, milady, your presence is needed for fittings. The tailor and seamstress await."

I suppose it's necessary. We head through the gardens, my fingers locked with Sunny's. "We'll be separated now. Do you have your phone?"

Sunny glances down at her skirt. "No pockets. It's up in the tower."

"You can always ask one of the guards to fetch me or send me a message. Don't feel as though you have to go through anything alone."

She nods, but I can sense the happy calm she felt while we were in the meadow starting to dissipate into anxiety. I don't blame her. She knows no one. Has no friends here. Rosenthal and Grisholm were straight-up harsh with her.

I turn to Rubin. "Who is her maid?"

"I don't know. I'm sure the head matron has assigned someone by now, though."

"Send Matron Mariam to my fitting. I want to meet the maid and instruct her myself."

"Will do."

We enter the rear of the palace. Rubin peels off to fulfill my request. The guards halt.

"I have orders to take milady to the tower for her fitting," one says.

"My phone is there," Sunny says. "I can text you."

I squeeze her hand. "I'll come find you as soon as I'm done."

"Okay." Her voice wavers.

I lean in for a lingering kiss. Blast it all. I'd rather stay with her. The last time we were parted was disastrous, the guards shoving her into a car. I can't have another mistake. Especially not now that I know who she is to me. Who she can be.

The guards lead her away. She glances behind, petals from her flowers dropping in her wake, as if the happiness of our afternoon is falling away like blooms in winter.

I don't see Sunny again until dinner. Twice I try to enter the tower, and both times the guards have to manhandle me to keep me from going up the stairs.

Grisholm intervenes. "Sire, she is being prepared for your wedding. Bide your time. You are behaving like a rutting goat."

This is not an insult. Rutting is an important time, when donkeys are bred and Avalonia's traditions are upheld. And, given the importance of providing an heir at some point, a rutting prince is an asset to his family.

But I don't like not knowing what is happening with my bride. While she held up beautifully with my parents and Rosenthal, I don't know how much that strength is costing her.

I want to be there to catch her if she's falling. She showed her emotional side in the meadow. I would like very much to wring a poetry professor's judgmental neck.

My sisters grew headstrong to manage themselves as they moved from children to young women. More than once I dried their tears when the weight of our family's expectations was too heavy for their years.

"Do not fret about Sunny," Rubin says as he leads me from my quarters to the dining room at mealtime. "Remember how she had Pace cowering behind furniture upon their first meeting."

This is true, and I should not forget it. The Sunny in the meadow is only one facet of her personality. She will bring out the others when needed. Including the one that throws pottery and threatens to banish cultural directors.

When I arrive in the dining hall, my sisters are already seated. I consider the arrangement. The table is long enough for twenty people, easy. The large chair at one end is wide for my father, even though he is not a large man. The opposite end will hold my mother. Ordinarily, my two sisters sit on one side, and I on the other.

I'd assumed my bride would sit on my side, since that would balance the equation. But my sisters sit opposite each other on the end nearest my father, leaving my position next to Lili, and the additional plate next to Octavia.

I will not be able to hold Sunny's hand during the meal, but given the positions, she would have been too far away at any rate. At least I can watch her, meet her eyes.

"Leo!" Octavia jumps up for another embrace. "I want

to hug you and hug you and hug you now that I can see you all the time."

Lili shakes her head. "You're going to be sick of him by this time tomorrow."

"Oh, shush, Lili," Octavia says, her voice muffled against my shoulder. "You missed him, too."

"Not on your life."

I know better than to challenge the assumption. Lili has grown even more jaded in my absence. Being a teenager in a palace is no picnic in a meadow. Perhaps we shall do another tomorrow with my sisters.

Although finishing what Sunny and I started today is high on my list. I'm being kept from the tower.

"Where's Sunny?" Octavia asks, releasing me at last.

"She had a dress fitting."

"Oh, we did, too!" Octavia turns in her pale yellow dress. "I'm wearing sunshine in her honor tonight. Do you like it?"

"It's beautiful." I turn to Lili, who has put on a dress, probably under great threat by our parents. It is black. "Day and night, yes? I like it."

"Funny." Lili picks up a roll from a silver bowl and splits it open. "Why is everybody late?"

"We have a guest," Octavia says. "You know Mother and Father won't be summoned until everyone else is seated."

Right. They did always prefer to make an entrance. God help them if they have to wait too long, though.

Grisholm enters the dining room. "Announcing Lady Sunholia, betrothed of Prince Leopold."

"It's just us, you old geezer," Lili says, and Sunny, who is still outside the doorway, snorts out a laugh.

This gets Octavia going, and by the time Grisholm has stepped aside to let her in, both of them are giggling.

Not me. I only chuckle these days. Especially now that Sunny can compare my laugh to our donkeys.

But Octavia sobers as Sunny sweeps into the room. "Oohhh, look at her."

I already am. Sunny's hair is arranged into shiny chestnut curls dotted with pearls. Her new dress is also gold, but the palest champagne, only showing the yellow in the shadows of the folds. It's off-the-shoulder, cutting across her collarbone in a straight line, then falling straight to the floor with a pearlescent sheen.

Her transformation from a deli worker to a royal is astounding. She seems pleased with the look, which surprises me, given that she insisted on her colorful outfit only yesterday for the announcement.

"You are stunning," I tell her, walking forward to press a kiss to her forehead. "Are you comfortable in this? Is it you?"

She glances back at the door, possibly looking to make sure my parents aren't coming. "It has a secret." She lifts her hem.

Beneath the sedate dress are rainbow tights and black sparkle tennis shoes.

Lili looks at the shoes, her eyes lighting up. "Can I have a pair of those?"

"Of course! I made them myself. When the seamstress was done with the fittings, I asked one of her assistants for some spray adhesive and a bit of glitter. Bring a pair to the tower and we'll do yours."

Lili jumps up as if to go fetch them, but the guards enter, taking their position on either side of the door.

Sunny drops her hem and steps aside. I take her arm.

The head butler, Teristan, steps inside. "The King and Queen of Avalonia!" He walks to the corner, and they enter, Father holding Mother's arm formally, his lifted in the air, hers resting on top. I guess they're trying to set an example for us.

I doubt the lesson is going to land.

But Sunny watches their every move, giving a curtsy as they pass. They part to sit at each end of the table.

They don't acknowledge her, which is a tradition as well, one that I hate. They are the supreme, and the rest of us are less than. It's what often sent my sisters into my rooms, crying.

The whole idea of hierarchy, of a class system, is ridiculous. I've done enough traveling to see that. In some places, like America, it's enough to make people hate you.

My body floods with hot concern that Sunny will feel rebuffed, unaccepted, like she is no one.

But she watches with sharp attention as she waits for the King and Queen to sit, following everyone else's lead. She seems to understand her place at the table, bowing her head until all the royal family has been seated, then finding her spot.

She understands.

I don't want her to understand. I want her to rise up. To protest. To call bullshit on this entire way of thinking.

But she accepts it. Acquiesces. She does this for me, and I know it was our time in the meadow that did it. She wants to belong.

We all sit and are served. Her behavior is impeccable. I want to throw fruit, to splatter sauce on the walls. She speaks only when spoken to and keeps her remarks short and to the point. The donkeys. The scenery. The tower. Her dress.

I've brought her here. I chose her.

And now I only wish to set her free.

CHAPTER 19

Sunny

Dinner is easy. Once I understand where I fit, it's like slipping on an old glove.

Being the lowest is something I'm used to. At Grammy's deli, I served. Occasionally, I had the opportunity to be helpful. Someone could ask, "What do you recommend?" Or, "Is there a specialty here?"

And I gave my opinion or asked questions to refine my suggestion.

But ultimately, I did what I was told. I listened to the order. I executed the command. And I did it properly.

This dinner is no different.

I'm mostly silent, hesitating on each course to make sure I'm the last to pick up a piece of silverware and to use the same one as everyone else.

The Queen asks me if I like the soup, and I reply it is delicious.

Lili asks if she can come to the tower tonight, which makes the King's fork halt halfway to his mouth, but I merely say I would be delighted to get to know her better.

It's strained, mostly quiet, with small bits of stilted conversation. The sisters seemed to be dying to talk to Leopold in his room, but they are mostly subdued, as if they don't want to ask their questions in front of their parents.

At last, we're excused. My assigned guard, a huge, tattooed man named Emilio, arrives to take me back to the tower. Leopold tries to follow, but Rubin and Pace turn him toward his own wing. "Text me!" he calls.

I realize I really will be separated from him.

But only a few minutes after I'm led back to the room where I'm more or less a prisoner until the wedding, Lili barges in. She's changed into jeans and a red T-shirt. She says, "Beat it!" to her guard, and the young woman stands outside the chamber door with Emilio.

Lili launches herself onto my bed, dropping a pair of black Vans on the floor. "Octavia is coming soon. She had to talk to her bestie."

I sort through the drawers for my own clothes. They were unpacked while Leopold and I were in the hills. "So you and your sister can come to the tower, but not Leopold?"

"Yeah, he can't knock you up before the wedding."

My face flares hot. "That's an odd tradition nowadays."

"That's what I told Octavia! Like, you could have been knocked up ages ago!"

"Well, I'm not. Knocked up, that is."

Lili holds up a hand. "I don't need details. But on the female front, I hope you brought your own tampons. You can't pick your own girl stuff here, and the ones they get in are utter crap."

"Thanks for the tip."

"Also, the staff will keep count and go through your trash to look for wrappers to make sure you're not pregnant. Ask me how I know."

"You saw them looking?"

"Totally. Uggh. What a horrible job! So I took mine from Octavia's stash one month and hid all the wrappers. Mother sent Aisha to talk to me! As if I even see any boys. I bet they examined my sheets for blood."

Yikes. "I guess they thought it could have been one of the guards."

"The guards are not banging material. There isn't one under thirty. Father's orders." She rolls over on her belly. "Octavia's not bringing any shoes to bling. She's too afraid of Mother."

It only now occurs to me that sparkling a pair of Lili's shoes might upset her parents. My stomach quakes for a moment, but I set it aside. With Lili, I might make an actual friend.

"I'm trying to get used to gowns. I don't normally wear stuff like this."

"You will. I hate, and I mean *hate* dresses. But sometimes it's not worth the fight."

"I'm sorry you'll be forced into one for the wedding."

"It's all right. Say, why the big delay in telling anyone? Everybody's scrambling like mad to get it done in time."

I wish Leopold was here to help me field these questions. I'm not sure how much he wants to say.

"It was a last-minute thing. I didn't realize it would set off such a fast timeline. I'd have preferred a long engagement."

"I want to hear about how you terrified the guards." Her feet swing back and forth as she props up on her elbows on the bed.

I locate a pair of black jeans and a Grateful Dead T-shirt that belonged to my cousin Max before I stole it. "Let me change, and I'll tell you all about it."

In the bathroom, I swiftly replace the dress with my own clothes and pause by the sink. This day has been a lot. A night on a plane. A first kiss with Leopold, and then so much more. Laughing donkeys. Fittings. Rosenthal, the King and Queen!

I'm exhausted.

But I will sleep eventually. I hear voices in the room and return to find Octavia has joined us. She flings herself against the pillows. "I tried to sneak Leopold in, but he got caught again. They are seriously not going to let him up here!"

"I guess I won't be able to sneak out either."

"No way," Lili says. "Obviously, the guards have orders that supersede ours."

I almost sit on one of the plush chairs, but decide to join the girls on the bed. Octavia is still in her yellow dress although her hair is back up in the two balls. "How is your friend?" I ask her.

"Super great. I'm trying to get her family an invitation to the wedding, but Rosenthal is being all weird about the whole thing. Aisha's working on it. She's one of the good ones."

"I figured that out."

Octavia smacks Lili's feet, which keep getting too close

to her face. "You've probably already figured out that Rosenthal and Grisholm are literally the worst."

"Yep."

"Most of the women are okay. Our maids are good. My guard is good. Lili's guard is horrible."

Lili nods. "She won't let me do anything. That's why I kicked her out. I'm hoping she'll get reassigned."

"I have a male guard," I say. "But yours are women?"

"You have the big guns," Octavia says. "You're the future Queen. We're the spares." She leans back against the ornate headboard.

"That's terrible! You're important!"

"Not like you are. Your babies are the future of Avalonia." Octavia knocks Lili's legs aside again. "Watch it!"

Lili shifts to sitting cross-legged so she can face the two of us at the pillows. "This bed is smaller than ours."

"Really? It's the biggest bed I've ever seen!" But it's certainly smaller than Leopold's enormous one.

Octavia punches a pillow and sticks it behind her back. "They don't want any hanky panky on this one."

"We should do your shoes," I tell Lili. "The ones you brought, I assume?"

"Yeah." She dives over the side of the bed, then comes back up with them in her hand. "Yours were so cool."

"The glitter is in the other room."

We cross through to the sitting chamber. I'm surprised to see a woman sitting there, tying ribbons on a basket full of small balls of white gauze.

Lili runs up. "What are these?"

"Bags of birdseed for the townspeople to toss once the bells toll." The woman demonstrates, placing a small pile on the square of gauze, twisting it up, and tying it off. "Everyone is helping since it's such short notice."

"I'm sorry about that," I say. "I can do some."

The woman shakes her head fervently. "That would get me fired in a hurry." She sets the basket aside to stand and curtsy. "I'm Amelliana, and I'll be here for whatever you need while you're staying in the tower."

"She needs Leopold," Octavia says. "Can you sneak him in?"

Amelliana smiles. "I would if I could. But we all have strict orders to keep the Prince out of the tower."

Lili turns to me. "Told you."

"Don't mind us," I say. "We're going to sparkle up a pair of Lili's shoes." I open a drawer in the desk by the window where I stashed the supplies I got earlier.

"I'll tidy up when you're done," Amelliana says. "Don't fret about it. Glitter has a mind of its own should it want to escape." She returns to her birdseed balls.

We spend a pleasant hour doctoring the shoes, making a much bigger mess than I intended. The shoes are not quite dry when the guard knocks and enters, saying the sisters must return to their own wing.

I'm sad to see them go. But then I remember Leopold asked me to text him and rush back to the bedroom for my phone. It sits by my bedside, already placed on the charger.

I have four texts from him.

Tried to get in. No dice.

Second attempt also thwarted. Not giving up yet!

I guess you're busy with my sisters?

Venturing outside to check the exterior wall to the tower.

He's what?

I quickly text him. *Don't you dare climb that wall!*

When he doesn't respond, I run to my window to push it open.

A few people walk the square below. Couples stroll along the sidewalk. A family leaves one of the restaurants. A lone violinist plays beneath a lamppost, his case open for tips.

Some things are the same here as everywhere.

There is no figure on the wall, so I let out a sigh.

I text again.

Your sisters are gone. Where are you?

It's a few minutes before he responds.

I've penetrated the tower. I'm one level below you, where the old maid chamber is. It's storage now.

Do you think I can come down a level to you?

Unlikely. You have a guard outside your door.

I also have Amelliana in my sitting room.

You can order her to go when you get ready for bed.

I sneak down the hall past the bathroom to peer in. Amelliana continues to make birdseed balls.

My phone buzzes.

You opened your window. Look down.

I hurry back to my bedroom. When I look down, Leopold's grinning face is a level below, hanging out his window.

"Leopold!"

"Shhh." He turns to look at the ground, then holds out his phone.

Mine buzzes. He's sent a message. *Talk this way so we don't alert the guards or get noticed by townspeople.*

I lean out the window. It's not terribly far to the

window below, but the stone wall is way too dangerous. There are no footholds, no trellis, and we're at least six stories in the air.

Don't you dare try climbing up that! You're not Spiderman!

No response.

I tap my foot.

Leopold?

Still nothing.

I peer down. A knotted bedsheet sails by my face.

"Leopold!" I hiss. "What are you doing?"

He looks up and holds out his cell phone.

Catch the end of the rope!

Rope? It's not a rope! It's a glorified strip of cloth!

No way! You can't use that!

I will! Catch it!

I peer out. Leopold has dragged the length of bedsheet back. He holds it out with one hand and gives a thumbs-up with the other.

Oh my God! He's going to die! I'll be a widow before I'm even a wife!

I shake my head no, but the end of the bedsheet sails at me, anyway.

I chuck my phone onto the rug and catch the big knot of sheet.

I ought to throw it back down, but I drag it inside and pick up my phone.

Now what?

Tie it to the bedpost.

Is he serious? Is he staking his *life* on my knot-tying ability?

No way! I don't know the right knots!

Knot it ten times.

He's absolutely insane.

> *A prince tied some knots in a sheet*
> *And scaled a stone wall just to meet*
> *His princess in bed*
> *By his dick he was led*
> *Now his head is cracked down on the*
> *street!*

No, no, no. I don't want to think like that!

I hold the end of the bedsheet, ready to toss it back to him. I lean out the window. He's waiting. "It will work," he mouths.

God. He's determined. I pull the sheet into the room and wrap it around the wide foot of the bed. I tie and wrap and tie and wrap again and again and again. My phone buzzes several times, but I finish the job before I look.

I've done this before. So have my sisters. It will be fine!

Not my kind of fine.

It's an adventure! Don't forget to dismiss your maid.

Right. Amelliana.

My heart pounds as I slow my breath. I walk to the sitting room.

"It was a long all-night flight and a longer day," I tell her. "I'm going to bed."

She stands. "I'll turn down your bedsheets."

"No!" I clear my throat. "I mean, that's not necessary. I already did it."

"Oh. Did you find everything you needed in the bathroom?"

"Yes. Totally. Thank you so much."

I stand and wait, trying not to look suspicious. She sets the basket on the chair. "The old-fashioned phone by your bed links directly to me. Pick it up and it will call me."

"Really? Okay. Thank you!" I wave.

"There is a tradition you should know about. I think it's important."

Goodness, will she not leave? "What's that?"

Amelliana heads to a small chest at the end of the sofa. It looks ancient, the varnish on the old wood almost orange in places, the leather straps serving as hinges wrinkled and worn.

She opens the top, revealing a set of white linens. She sorts through them, then pulls out a very long, extremely old-fashioned nightgown, white cotton with lace edges and pearl buttons up the front all the way to the chin.

"Every bride since Queen Valentina in 1875 has worn this very nightgown, and before that, one like it. It's a tradition during the stay in the tower. I hope you will continue it."

I take the gown. It has been freshly laundered and pressed and smells faintly of flowers. "It's lovely."

"Would you try it on?"

"Now?"

"I don't wish to be presumptuous, but it would be a great honor to assist our next queen on her first night in the palace."

"Oh. All right."

We head to the bathroom, and I look with concern at the tied-up sheet at the base of the bed. I hope she doesn't go in there.

Amelliana waits at the door, holding the gown. Am I supposed to get naked with her there?

This is weird.

I kick off my shoes and slide out of the jeans and shirt. I hesitate.

"I'll be all ready with the gown!" she says merrily. She holds it up to block her view of me.

Okay. My bra hits the floor and Amelliana swiftly drops the nightgown over my head.

It floats down my body. I turn, and Amelliana fastens the buttons so quickly I can barely keep up as I watch in the mirror. She removes the pins from my hair so it can fall in waves across my shoulders.

"A quick brush?"

Leopold is waiting, but I nod.

She takes care as she smoothes out the lengths. "I can see it." She turns me to the mirror.

"What do you see?"

"My future queen."

I stare at my reflection. I've tumbled back into some other age. The old nightgown, the hair, and the gilt wallpaper behind me all suggest I've gone back in time.

Is she right?

I have no idea.

"It's lovely. Thank you."

"It's good to see Prince Leopold settling down. I'm very happy for you." She walks back to the sitting room. "Don't forget, there will be a guard."

Maybe she is on to me. "I feel very safe," I tell her. "Snug as a bug in a rug."

Her head tilts at that, and I can see that it's not an expression here.

"Good night, milady." Then finally, she's gone.

I rush back to the bedroom and peer out the window. Leopold is looking up. His eyebrows lift at my new outfit.

"Ready?" he mouths.

I nod.

He pulls the slack out of the line and disappears.

I look out on the town. There's very little activity. No one wanders the square. Even the violinist has packed up.

Leopold appears again. He sticks a leg out the window, and I almost yelp in fear. This is crazy!

My heart hammers as both legs appear, and he rolls over to bend over the sill. He reaches out for the bedsheet rope and uses it as leverage to stand on the edge of the window.

I feel faint with worry.

He twists the bedsheet around one foot, then he's standing on it. The line goes taut, and I panic, grabbing hold of it as if I'm the only thing standing between him and certain doom.

He grips one of the knots, and he's out the window. With a speed and grace I didn't expect, he rises up the rope so fast that I have to back away to give him room.

His head and shoulders appear in the window, then he's tumbling through and landing on the rug.

"Made it." His face is bright with the achievement.

"You are so crazy." I'm breathless with relief that he's made it in. I think of nothing but him and his determination to get to me — ME — when I step up and press my palms to his cheeks. "But maybe I already knew that."

He wraps his fingers around my hands, then sends them outstretched so he can take me in. The gown is intended to be modest, covering me from neck to toe. But it's thin, and in the light, it has a translucent quality. "What is this?"

"An almost two-hundred-year-old bridal gown."

"Wooooow. It shouldn't be sexy, but it totally is. Totally." His eyes alight on every part of me, then his gaze meets mine. It's not bright in the room, the only lamps on either side of the bed, but I can see a hint of the gray-green.

He reaches out to finger the loose folds of the cotton, then runs a thumb up the line of pearl buttons to my throat. He grazes my chin, and that small touch is enough to make me jolt with awareness of him.

He leans down to kiss me, and I swear the stone floor moves beneath my bare feet as his warm lips capture mine. I know why he's here. It's not for more chit chat. We could have done that on our phones.

We're going to finish what we started in the meadow.

My heart hammers painfully. The fear rushes right back. What if he feels like Billy afterward, like he's done with me?

But his lips keep moving, his hands releasing mine to run down my body in the cotton gown. He pulls me against him, and I can feel the effect the nightgown has on him. Thank you, Amelliana.

His fingers are everywhere, down my back, along my waist, over my hips. The stars gather again, where he touches me. The heat rises so fast, I'm lightheaded.

His tongue touches mine, and I taste a hint of the chocolate ganache from dinner. He drags me even closer, crushing me against him. His fingers dig into my hair, and I nearly lose my footing.

That lost feeling claims my breath. He gathers the nightgown in his fists, lifting it. The hem flirts with my knees, then my calves.

Then he can reach beneath it, and his hands are on my skin, taking in all those places without a barrier. Sparks fly through me everywhere he goes, tracing the edge of my panties, slipping along my belly, then cupping both breasts.

I suck in, the intensity of my need almost painful. My nipples are tight as he grazes each tip. All the energy of the stars trail behind each movement he makes, each part of me he brands as his.

He breaks the kiss, leaning in to press his mouth to my ear. Then the ground is swept away as he lifts me into his arms, cradled against his chest.

He steps over the bedsheet rope to the bed to lay me down upon it, tenderly, like I'm something fragile and precious. He grins down at the millions of buttons, then unfastens them one by one.

Is this how all the other brides felt in this tower? Did their future husbands work so hard to get to them, or did they have to wait until the wedding night?

Air hits each inch of newly exposed skin. Leopold is attentive, watching me as the nightgown opens. I'm not sure which sets me more on fire, when his hands went beneath the gown to find me, or this painfully slow reveal.

He reaches the waist and peels the cotton fabric aside, revealing one breast, then the other. He takes his time, making slow circles with his hand before bending down to take a nipple in his mouth.

There's too many stars now, my body filled with light. I want so much of him, all of it. I'm ready to risk it all. I reach out for his hair, running my hands through the chaotic strands. The urgency between us kicks up, and soon he's pulling the gown up and over my head.

It catches on my wrists, and his chuckle is low and sexy as he locates more pearl buttons on the sleeves.

"But I like this," he says, my arms caught over my head, locked in the gown, my body displayed on the bed in nothing but the tiny satin panties that had matched the pale champagne dress.

Even so, he releases the buttons, letting the gown slip to the floor. His mouth is suddenly everywhere, my neck, shoulders, breasts, belly.

He lifts my knee and kisses all the way up my thighs. "I want to hear those sweet sounds again," he says, grasping the edge of the panties and tugging them down.

His eyes are on mine as he slips fingers inside me. My hips rise and a groan escapes, bringing a smile. He likes doing this to me.

When I finally say, "Leopold, yes," he kisses my belly, then slides his tongue lower, just inside.

I gasp, my body clenching, so ready to find that beautiful space again.

And it comes, so swiftly, so easily, muscles tightening, my hands clenching the sheets.

The quiet space arrives, perfect and still. I hover among the stars.

Then it explodes. I say names. Bits of poetry, mine and

others. Tears squeeze from my eyes. There is nothing like this. Nothing.

I hear the thud of his shoes hitting the floor even as he gently brings me down. He pulls away for only a moment, his shirt flying. His pants fall to the floor.

I learn something few know. The Prince of Avalonia wears silk boxers. I want to do something, so I reach for him, grabbing the waistband. I take them down myself, looking at all of him. His shoulders and chest, those tan abs. His thighs, muscles bulging as he leans over me.

Then the most private part of him, long, hard, and straining toward me as if I am the answer to all of his questions.

I look up at him. "I'm not on birth control. Are we going for an heir already?"

He shakes his head. "I came prepared." He ducks for his pants, dislodging a long line of condoms in their square wrappers. He rips the last one off the end, unrolling it over his length.

I kneel next to him to watch, my hair flowing over his shoulder and down his chest.

His eyes meet mine, then swift as a jaguar, he grabs hold of my waist and moves me to his lap. My knees barely hit the mattress before he's inside me, spreading me open.

I gasp, clutching his shoulders. This is nothing like my first and only other time, where I wasn't even sure what was happening. Leopold fills me so far, so high, that I swear he's reached the center of my body.

He holds me firmly, lifting me up, then bringing me down again. There's a small, sharp pain, but it's eclipsed by everything else. Leopold's mouth on my breast. His hand squeezing me, moving me over him. The heat rises between us as we move together.

I lose sense of what is up or down. There is nothing but the feel of him inside me, and a tight, feverish need building more deeply than the times before.

It's an itch and I must scratch it. I drive down on him, rocking against his body in a frenzy I've never felt before.

"Yes, my love," he whispers.

We both tumble back on the bed, and I'm over him, feeling wild and powerful, like nothing that has ever come before even touched who I was before now.

CHAPTER 20

Prince Leopold

She's wild and uninhibited and beautiful and mine.

It takes all my will not to unleash in her as she sits astride my body on this bridal bed. Her hair tumbles and rolls like the sea itself as she moves. I could watch her forever, her eyes closed, her breasts swaying, hands gripping my shoulders.

I want to imprint this vision of her on my memory. No woman has been so free with me, so completely mine.

She grinds down, and I hold her hips, focusing on her so that I can keep going, never let this moment end.

But her time is arriving again. I feel it in the clench of her muscles, the rising of her voice. One day and I already know her. She has let me see, let me do everything.

"Leo!" she cries, her eyes flying open. She halts her movements, but her body clenches around me. "Oh my God!"

Her hot gaze on me is my undoing. I hang on to her, driving her body down. It takes very little. I've been held on this precipice for so long.

The release is glorious, a purge into pure bliss. The sight of her, the feel of her skin, the sound of her calling my name. It's like nothing I've felt. And being here, in the palace, after fighting to get to her, heightens it all.

We are living an epic love story, the pages written as we go. And I long for each line to keep coming. I want to see what each day brings.

I'm not running away. I'm running toward this place. To her.

She collapses on my chest, a wetness on her face transferring to my skin. I wrap my arms around her. "Are you all right?"

She nods. "I'm perfect. It's emotional." She trembles.

"Sunny? What is it?"

She lies very still.

"Can I help?"

She slips off my body to lie beside me. I lift a blanket from the end of the bed to cover us. "Tell me."

"It's so awful. I can't."

"All right then. Just be here." I pull her head to my shoulder and kiss her hair.

She cries a while longer, and I keep a firm grip on her. It's been a lot, I'm sure. My guards practically kidnapped her only two days ago. And since then she's been questioned by the press, flown to a new home, denigrated by staff members. My anger burns. I swear to God I will fire every last one of them if they still live when I take over. There is no excuse for their behavior. None.

I will take it up with Father, although he and Mother were not much better themselves. What is wrong with this family? This life? Why would anyone be horrid when they could be kind?

Something here must be set right.

Sunny sniffles. "I told you about my poetry professor."

"Right."

"There was another thing about that class."

"Oh?"

"I was seeing a guy in it."

I wait this one out.

"And he was… my first. And after… after that one time, my only time, he wouldn't speak to me again. He wouldn't even look at me. He never even bothered to break up."

"Oh, Sunny. What an utter shit."

"And the professor had already told me I couldn't write. And now this… this man made me feel like I couldn't love properly. I wasn't worthy of… anything. So I went home. I got my apron, and I worked for Grammy. I didn't want to ever leave again."

I cup her head and press it to my chest. My poor girl. "That boy was utter shit and don't think of him another minute."

She sniffs.

I pull away so I can look at her. "You're amazing and perfect. And honestly, I'm not sure how long I can hold out before I must have you again."

Her smile is small, but then a giggle escapes. "You sure?"

The sight of her, so vulnerable, her bare shoulder gleaming in the low light, her warm body pressed against me, makes all the blood rush to my groin.

Shit, the condom. I reach for the Kleenex box and swiftly remove it before it can become a problem.

"I think I'm already there." I pull her closer so that she can feel me against her belly.

"We can do it again? Now?" Her eyes brighten.

"Absolutely." I roll over her, pressing her into the bed. "I want to know all the things you like. I want to enter you in every position imaginable."

She draws in a sharp breath. "Yes, please."

I reach down to slide a finger inside her. "You're not sore?"

"I felt a pinch last time, but it's gone."

My eyebrows draw together. "A pinch?" I slide the blanket away from us.

And there it is, on my belly. A smear of blood.

She sees it and sits up. "It's not my period. I'm not due."

My eyes meet hers as I snag another tissue. "And this asshole who broke your heart? You sure he accomplished the deed?"

"Yes. I mean, he was there. He put it in." She bites her lip. "It didn't feel anything like what we just did."

I have to laugh. "Sunny, I don't think he got anything done at all. And the reason he couldn't look you in the eye again had nothing to do with you. It was his lack of, let's say, water pressure."

Her mouth drops open. "So he didn't actually, you know, get in there?" She points to her thighs.

"Not properly." I push her down on the bed. "How about I show you again how it's supposed to go?"

She wraps her legs around me. "I would very much like

a proper demonstration. I might have missed some of the finer points."

A gentleman never disappoints a lady.

CHAPTER 21

Sunny

Day Four

Leopold slides back down the bedsheet rope before dawn, and I untie the rope so he can stash it.

I don't have the patience to button all the pearls again, so I throw the gown over my head. For a while, I'm too jazzed to sleep. My phone lights up.

Safe in my quarters. Goodnight, my love.

My heart turns over. Maybe the Prince is this demonstrative with every lover. But I'll take it. We will be the one that never ends. I tap out my reply.

Goodnight, my love.

It seems I've slept only a moment when the door creaks open. "Milady?"

It's Amelliana.

I roll to the side of the bed closest to the door. "Yes?"

"I'm so sorry to bother, but we have breakfast and then

another fitting. The seamstress team has worked through the night."

Oh, good Lord. "Do we have to do the entire beauty routine before I go down? Gown and all?"

Amelliana opens the curtains, looking curiously at the window lock. I wonder if I left it in a different state than usual.

The light is fierce as she pushes the heavy drapes wide. I'm sure I'm a fright, my hair a snarl and I never properly removed the makeup from yesterday.

She turns and catches sight of my unbuttoned gown. Then her eyes drop to the pristine white quilt. Right there, smack in the middle, is a smear of red.

Oh, God.

"My period!" I say. "I got it! So sorry."

Her eyes shift again to the open gown. Then back to the window.

Yeah, she's figured it out.

She bites back a smile as she whisks away the soiled quilt. "That is all well and expected. There are supplies in the cabinet."

I slide out from under the sheets. I can't come up with any reason for the unbuttoned gown. I was hot? I stammer an excuse, but Amelliana holds up a hand.

"Your prince is not the first ardent groom to climb the tower to get to his bride. In fact, staff rumor is that the King himself may have scaled the wall. Extra sturdy bedsheets, sure not to tear and bring harm to the future sovereign on the eve of his wedding, have long had a home in the storeroom beneath your chambers."

Oh, gosh. I stare at the quilt in her arms. Is she going to give a report to the Queen?

"No worries, milady. Your secret is safe with me. But tonight perhaps allow me to lure the guard into the sitting room so that the Prince need not risk life and limb each night until your wedding day."

Oh, I like her. "Thank you."

She opens a small closet and removes a mesh laundry bag. "I'll clean this myself so no one else needs to see it, regardless of its origin or significance."

"Thank you."

She stuffs the quilt into the bag and sets it by the door. "So, are you ready to begin your morning? Aisha will be styling you today to train me so that my everyday work is to her liking. You will only see her on special occasions otherwise. We will prepare your things while you shower. Should I ring for some coffee?"

A shower sounds heavenly. "Yes, please, on the coffee. I'll be quick." I hurry to the bathroom, but pause outside the door. "I'll let Leopold know about the guard."

She opens the wardrobe that holds my official clothing and winks. "Good."

I head into the gold-tiled room with its claw-footed tub and sparkling walk-in shower. I can't wait for the night again. Knowing I will spend it with Leo will help me get through what is sure to be a grueling day.

Breakfast is thankfully less formal than dinner. Octavia and Lili don't even show.

Aisha dressed me in a calf-length gray linen skirt and a fitted yellow top. The slim lines force me to stand up very straight lest I dissolve into pudge in the middle. The shoes are impossibly high, and the glossy waxed floor tests my already questionable balance.

Amelliana expressed her concern, but Aisha waved her away. So here I am.

The King and Queen are elegant in classic business wear, but Leo wears jeans and a plain white T-shirt that hugs his chest like a layer of skin. My belly warms at the sight of him.

Leo jumps to his feet when I enter. I take careful steps, grateful for a rug. He kisses my cheek and whispers, "Those shoes are seriously hot. I want to see you in them later, and nothing else."

A rush of heat runs the length of my body. He leans in to kiss my hair, and I squeeze his hand.

"Do sit," the Queen says. "We have quite an agenda together today, you and I."

Do we? I manage a small smile. "That's wonderful."

There will be no relaxing today.

My plate is across the table from Leo, but we smile at each other over a line of unlit candles.

"I'll leave you to it." The King grabs a piece of toast and his coffee and takes off.

The Queen shakes her head at him. "He never eats a proper morning meal."

A server, or I guess a butler if I have my *Downton Abbey* cast right, extends a silver platter for my perusal. "Toast, soft-boiled eggs, or fruit?"

"Yes to everything," I say, feeling starved. I barely ate

dinner and last night burned some calories.

After a heaping amount has been added to my plate, the Queen says, "You have an appetite."

Should I eat less? Am I going to be weight controlled? Food shamed? My gaze darts to Leo.

"The kitchen staff is going to love you," Leo says. "Nobody seems to actually enjoy food around here."

I stab the egg and slice it into pieces with a rebellious clink. "I'm from a food family. I'm going to make up for you all."

"I saw that," the Queen says. "Delicatessens. Known for their flavorful pickles."

I assume they've read an entire dossier on me. I swallow my bite. "Yes. And dill dough."

The Queen's eyes go wide, and Leo almost chokes on his orange juice. I let her shock hang a moment, then add, "It's bread dough with dill pickles mixed in. Did you think I meant something else?"

Her long fingers festooned with rings grip her china cup. "It might be best to avoid mention of the more colorful dishes by your establishment around the press."

My blood boils. "Fat chance," I say, and Leo nearly sprays OJ a second time. "I'm extremely proud of my legacy. I can't control the ugliness of others."

She tilts her head. "I concede the point." She pushes back from the table. "Leopold, when Sunholia has completed her meal, please show her to my office. We have much to go over."

I wait until she's gone to say, "Please tell me you will never say Sunholia."

"I would never." He picks up his plate and walks

around to my side of the table. A butler instantly moves a chair next to me.

I have a sudden realization. "It's going to be in the wedding vows, isn't it? The priest or preacher or whatever is going to call me Sunholia?"

His beautiful lips pull into a frown. "I'll try to stop it. But even if he does, I won't say it."

"What's wrong with my name? My mother is going to have a fit!"

"Mother's name was Mary," he says. "It was changed to Pulmaria to match our naming conventions. You won't find too many American-sounding names here. The guard James is one of the few."

I butter my toast. "I see. I should try to fit in. Even England's King George was originally Albert." I'm about to take a bite when I add, "Have you ever seen *Beavis and Butthead?*"

His mouth falls open. "What's that?"

"A TV show. I'll find a clip." I search YouTube for a moment and find a Cornholio video.

He watches it while I eat. When he sets the phone down, I say, "See? I'm going to be a joke in my country."

"You made this connection between your new name and this show yourself?"

"It's the first thing I thought of!"

His face is serious. "Perhaps we should come up with our own version of your name. We can present it to Mother, and perhaps that will placate her."

"Okay. I've noticed lots of names ending in -anne and -avia and -aria."

"Yes. Sunianne. Sunavia. Sunaria. Any of those?"

"Maybe. What else? Aisha isn't like that."

"She's not royalty."

"Oh, right."

"There is a Sanskrit word. Hold on." He pulls out his phone. "Yes, Sunandia. It means 'having a sweet character.'"

"Sunandia. I can live with that. Though I don't think I'm much of a sweet character."

He glances at the butler in the far corner and leans in. "I thought things tasted very sweet on the hillside."

My face blossoms, and the stars gather again. "Did you?"

"So think of that anytime someone calls you Sunandia."

"I will be in a perpetual state of blushing."

His thumb slides along my cheek. "It's a good look."

He lifts my chin, so I face him, and his lips press softly to mine. It takes willpower to keep it light. I want to fall again, to feel the world drop away.

"Ahem. The Queen awaits milady in her office."

We turn. It's Grisholm, of course.

Leopold jumps up to pull out my chair. "I'll walk her."

Grisholm grimaces, his trademark expression. I'm still thrilled from the kiss and the much improved royal name. I'm taller in the shoes, so it's easy to press a quick kiss to Grisholm's cheek as we pass. "Thank you for fetching me."

His eyebrows lift, like he can't quite decide what to make of my display of affection.

Leopold leads us away, but it's far too fast for the shoes. "Leo! I'm dying here!" I shuffle to walk more quickly, but the narrow skirt keeps me from taking a step any longer than a foot.

"That outfit looks like torture," he says. "Here." He picks me up and throws me over his shoulder.

"Leo!" I laugh, holding on to his belt loops as we jog through the main concourse of the castle.

We head into a hallway, and his hands rove up my legs. "Oh, I like this a lot." He keeps going along the outside of the skirt until he squeezes my butt. "Maybe I'll make off with you to my man cave." He grunts like a caveman.

The guard outside a gilded door averts his eyes as we approach.

"This is Mother's office." Leo sets me down, holding me carefully until I find my footing in the heels. After this meeting, I'm kicking them off. And if they try to put me in heels for the wedding, I swear I'll wear the black sparkle tennis shoes instead. How about starting a trend with *that?*

Leo kisses my hair. "Good luck."

"Will I see you again after?"

"I will do everything in my power." He winks. "And I am the Prince."

Don't I know it.

When he's gone, I turn to the guard. "What's your name?"

The man frowns. "Shall I announce you to the Queen?"

"Only if you tell me your name first."

"Mandolian."

"Oh, that's nice. We changed mine to Sunandia. I'm about to tell the Queen."

His expression suggests he isn't sure that will go over. "Should I announce you as that?"

"Oh no. Just do Sunny. I need to tell her myself."

He raps on the door three times, pauses, then turns the lever.

"Your majesty, I present Lady Sunny."

I don't get to see her reaction to my given name, and by the time I'm through the threshold and up from my curtsy, her face is a mask of controlled pleasantness.

She sits on a delicate Queen Anne chair covered in ivory silk. She gestures to a chair opposite a marble table with a silver tea set.

"Thank you," she says to the guard, who returns to his post and closes the door.

The Queen watches me quietly for a moment. I sit tall and formally, my ankles crossed, knees together, hands in my lap. I watched *The Crown*. I know the pose. And it's excruciating.

My back is already cramping when she finally says, "So I understand my son took your virginity last night in the tower."

I almost leap to my feet, but force my butt to stay in the chair. "I don't think that's any of your business!"

"When a royal wedding is at hand, everything's my business. Do you know how many paternity claims we've had to squash in the last year while my son gallivanted across two continents?"

She doesn't wait for me to guess. "Seventy-two."

"That's a lot."

"Women who were photographed with him. Many who knew where he was staying. So many pregnant opportunists. Not a single one of them had shared his bed. We have a list of those. Probably incomplete."

I don't know why she's telling me this. "I guess that will stop now that he's getting married."

She stares me down. Her eyes are hard, dark, and glittery on a beautiful, perfectly made-up face. Her pale hair, threaded with gray, is swept into an elegant chignon. "One would hope. I was surprised to learn you were not one of his wild conquests."

I almost say, "I barely know him," but remember my bold cover story yesterday. "I think perhaps he liked that I initially turned him down."

"Good for you." She relaxes in the chair, and I too, let out a breath and stop sitting so stiffly. "I apologize for shocking you. And don't blame your maid for blowing the secret. Matron Mariam misses nothing and spotted her washing the blood out. The sheets in the storeroom were wrinkled from the knots. It wasn't hard to fill in the gaps. We need to keep assurance of his paternity if you fall pregnant."

I have no intention of giving her the whole story. The point is still valid. It's not possible that I'm pregnant by anyone else. And now that I know Billy got almost nowhere, she's not that far off.

But I'd prefer we change the subject. "Leopold and I spoke of my new name this morning."

That gets her attention. "Oh, did you?"

"He was not aware of a cartoon in America that renders the name Sunholia an ugly joke."

"And yet you told me yourself this morning that you could not control the ugliness of others."

She's a sharp one. "It's one thing to be the originator of

the joke. In this case, it has been foisted upon me. We did, however, come up with a solution."

"Proceed."

"Sunandia is an old Sanskrit word that means 'sweet character.' We feel it would solve the problem."

The Queen runs a hand along the arm of the chair. "That is acceptable. I will inform the staff."

"Thank you."

Her gaze rests on my face, and I try not to squirm. "I watched your press conference."

Oh. That. When I refused to dress like a stereotypical princess. Rather than comment, I play her game, meeting her gaze.

"You've worn Aisha's styling since you've been here." Her voice is cool. "Why did you refuse in front of cameras?"

"I think it was my turf versus your turf."

She stands. "Well, you are definitely on our turf now. And on that note, I will take you on a walk."

I follow her to a side wall of the room to stand before a large tapestry.

She lifts the bottom corner. "Some clichés are true."

There's a hidden door.

Instead of a book that moves, or a long key, however, she punches an electronic keypad. She points to a battered metal lever higher up. "There is a manual override if the power is cut. It's hard to move, though, so I had this installed."

The door clicks open and she pushes it wide. Lights affixed to a stone wall pop on. "Also flashlights for the same reason." She points to a bucket hanging on a nail.

"Nothing fancy once you're in here. It's maintained by my personal guard. The regular staff isn't informed of this interior path."

"So nobody would find me here," I say.

She doesn't respond to that.

I follow her down, terrified of the rough stone and my precarious heels. I'm tempted to slip them off.

She floats down like an apparition, a grace long practiced. I will never take stairs like that.

We curve down and down, occasionally passing a landing with a door. I want to ask where we're going. I picture a dungeon. Is this some sort of test?

"How far does this go?" I ask.

"Out of the city, as I understand. It's intended for an escape. I rarely go beyond the palace with it. Mainly we use it when we want to move about the castle's wings without anyone's knowledge."

I tug my phone out of my cleavage, the only spot I could stash it.

No signal. Of course. We have to be deep underground.

We come to the end of the stairs. Two guards wait below. Oh no. This really is it. Will they lock me up and tell Leopold some sob story? Or escort me out of town to be smuggled back to America?

We pass the two guards and reach a fork in the path. We go left and encounter two more guards by a steel door.

They bow. "I would like inside," she says.

One turns to another electronic pad. I guess they've upgraded their prison. I swear I hear the drip of water. The air smells dank and moldy. For all I know, they've got a dragon down here.

The pad buzzes, and the guard drags the heavy door open.

"Come now," the Queen says.

I hesitate a moment, but the guard moves close to me to force me inside.

We enter the space, and lights pop on gradually, illuminating each wall.

My jaw drops.

It's not a prison. It's a vault.

The walls are lined with thick glass, each one filled with black velvet shelves lined with jewels.

"You will need everyday jewelry, which will move to a small safe in your chambers the day after the wedding. You will also need your wedding jewelry. We'll take a few choices to your gown fitting to see if they complement the neckline."

She opens a glass door filled with tiaras. "And you will, of course, need to select your crown. It will be hidden beneath your veil until the end of the ceremony, then Leopold will reveal it before your first kiss."

I can't even take in all the jeweled headpieces filling the space. There are big ones, dainty ones, some all diamonds, others with rubies, emeralds, and all manner of gems.

"I think for your features, something like this would be a fit." She extracts an elaborate looping tiara with large diamonds swinging in three central sections. "What do you think?"

"It's beautiful. They all are."

"Let's try it." She places it on my head. "Hmm. Maybe. You look."

The front wall of the vault is a long mirror. I turn to it.

Good lord. The white sparkle of diamonds on my dark hair is mesmerizing. I am absolutely a princess.

I look the part.

I press my hand to my chest. "Wow."

"Let's try this one." She chooses another, this one with points rather than loops.

We exchange them, and I turn back to the mirror to place it on my hair.

"That's better," she says. "You need crisp lines, I think. There is another."

The third one is larger, heavier, and more regal. As soon as I put it on, I know it isn't right. "Too big," I say.

"Agreed." We turn back to the display. "Any others?"

I spot a regal one with pearls surrounded by dainty diamonds. "What about that one?"

"Ah, yes, it's similar to Princess Diana's crown." She takes it down, and we trade again.

It settles into my hair like it was made for me. It feels like nothing, comfortable and easy. "I love it."

The Queen comes behind me. "It's a good choice. Understated but complex."

"Yes." I can't stop looking at myself and touching the crown.

The Queen returns with a necklace. "I think this one will fit the décolletage of your wedding gown. Plus it has pearls like the crown." She fastens the jewels around my neck.

It's unbelievably beautiful, a network of diamond leaves and pearls, and heavy on my chest. I could buy a block of New York with this tiara and necklace.

"There are several earrings that could pair with it. You want to look?"

I turn to see. There are many large pieces laden with jewels. They look like they might drag my ears to my elbows. I spot a dainty waterfall of tiny diamonds and pearls. "These."

"Yes. You don't want to overdo it." She hands them to me, then turns to the back wall. "And your wedding ring." The case includes diamonds of every shape and cut. Some are encircled with smaller diamonds or other gems.

I fasten the earrings. They're not too heavy. "Can I come back here with Leopold to choose?"

"You're sentimental," she says. "Of course."

We go through the more casual jewelry, gold chains, diamond stud earrings, and tennis bracelets. We fill a small box with our choices and the Queen passes it to the guard. "Take this to the lockbox in the Crown Prince's chamber, please."

He nods, holding the box as we start up the stairs. I press my hands to the necklace and earrings, then touch the crown. I'm going up a lot fancier than I came down.

"Have you traveled much?" she asks.

"Not really."

"We will assign you an attaché to help you understand the customs of other royalty. Leopold's former one will do nicely. He probably needs a refresher as you travel."

"We're traveling?"

"Yes, for eight weeks, commencing after his birthday celebration. He becomes the Crown Prince upon marriage, so he will meet them as a more powerful presence than before. You will have to adjust to their customs. Some of them have less progressive ideas about women."

"You mean they don't lock them in towers?"

"Touché. It is only a tradition, last completed by me. Would you like to stay in the main palace? Change the way we do things?"

"No." I hesitate. "The gown was lovely. I didn't like Leopold scaling the side of the palace, though."

She laughs, and for the first time, I think maybe we will be all right. "You are correct there. I did not like it when Francisco did it either. Funny how they plant the bedsheets. And the grooms always come up with the same solution. Do you think they tell their sons the story?"

"They might. I thought I would have a heart attack when he asked me to tie the bedsheet."

"I had my maid do it. I was too afraid."

"You let your maid in on it? I had to trick her into leaving!"

She laughs again. "I will have the order to keep Leopold from the tower rescinded. He shouldn't have to keep climbing."

"That's a relief. We don't need a scraped-up groom."

We share another laugh, and my concern feels completely erased. This will be fine.

My life here is going to be perfect.

CHAPTER 22

Prince Leopold

I spend the morning with the tailor. I wonder if there is something I can do to make the wedding suit more personal, a secret that can connect it to Sunny.

Then I have it.

"Can we make the inner vest pale gold instead of white?"

The portly man with his gray speckled beard looks up at me in astonishment. "Sire?"

"For my bride. Sunny. I noticed the seamstresses were dressing her in gold, and even my sisters were in on it. Wouldn't it be clever? All the magazines would talk about it."

The tailor glances over at Rosenthal, who is supervising the fitting. They pass some sort of silent message I don't quite follow.

My annoyance is pricked. "Is there something wrong with gold? It scarcely matters. There's no law about the color of the groom's vest."

"I shall look at my fabrics," the tailor says. "I'm sure

there is something suitable."

His assistants remove the suit with its new set of pins. The vest has only been cut but not sewn, so hopefully I haven't asked for too much. Surely.

As they pack their things, I turn to leave, but Rosenthal catches my arm. "Prince Leopold, you are needed in your chambers. There are some items there to review."

"Like what? I'm trying to catch Sunny before lunch." She texted me to say they had picked out jewelry and were on their way to the fitting. I assumed we would finish at roughly the same time.

"They will be a good hour yet. The dress is far more elaborate than your suit."

I frown. "All right. But what have you put in there?"

"Some trinkets for you to consider."

Trinkets. What is he talking about?

Rubin and Pace follow us to my wing. Both of my sisters' doors are open, their rooms empty.

"They are doing their fittings alongside the American," Rosenthal says.

"You mean my bride, your future queen?" My anger rises by the moment.

"Let us come." Rosenthal pauses outside of my antechamber and waits for Rubin to open the door. What is this man's game?

But I don't have long to find out.

The windows are open, flooding the space with light. And perched artfully throughout the room, as if it's a magazine photo shoot, are three women.

I halt. "What is this?"

"The brides you refused to meet," Rosenthal says.

"Unless you want to create a negative incident with some of our country's finest merchants and traders, you will give them your attention and civility."

It's almost impossible to put on a mask of politeness in the face of this ambush. But I pause in the center of the room as they stand and curtsy.

"Sire," each one says, head bowed.

This is what I was talking about. If they have any decent thoughts in their heads, they've been trained to keep them to themselves and act in a way they think will please me.

"What are your names?" I ask. I'm already thinking of ways to get out of this lasting more than five minutes.

The first one, dressed in a pale pink dress, says, "Carindalia."

"Hello, Carindalia."

The second one curtsies again, a single black curl trailing down the front of her green sundress. "Ivalaria."

Classic Avalonian names. Probably given by eager parents hoping this day would come.

The third one is going for broke, wearing a white dress with beads along the low neckline. She curtsies extremely low, allowing the dress to fall and reveal creamy breasts unhindered by a bra.

I avert my gaze. Yeah, she thinks she knows what will work on me. Perhaps a week ago, she'd have been right.

Her eyes lift, checking to see if I'm watching. I keep my head turned, although I can see her movement in the periphery.

"I'm Helenista. At your pleasure." Her voice purrs on the last word. Yeah, she's got my number. My old one.

I imagine Sunny is in the corner watching and strive to conduct myself in a manner that would not cause her the least concern.

"It is a delight to meet some of the women of Avalonia. Thank you for coming here today." I turn to Rosenthal, whose eyes are fixed on the girl in white. She got his attention, apparently.

"You will spend time with each of them," Rosenthal says. "Carindalia, Prince Leopold, let's adjourn to the other room."

He's really going to make me take each one into my bedchamber?

"This seems terribly inappropriate," I hiss at him as we pass through the short hallway.

"You cornered the market on inappropriate this last year," he hisses back. "This comes at your father's order!"

We can say no more. Carindalia steps into the room. She curtsies again.

"That's not necessary," I tell her. Rosenthal disappears into the short hall between the rooms, closing the door behind him.

Great. I'm alone with this woman.

I gesture to a chair by the window. "Please, have a seat."

Carindalia does as I request, perching on the edge, ankles crossed, once again posing as if I'm about to take her photograph.

I take a chair a good distance away. "So, what are your interests?"

She sits taller. "I would like to honor Avalonia with a life of service."

"In what way?"

"However I might best support my country's goals and aspirations."

"It sounds like you're applying to college," I say, then catch myself. I shouldn't be unkind. "What do *you* like to do?"

She doesn't meet my gaze. "Walk alongside the herds in the hills. Read about history. And volunteer for charities."

This sounds scripted. "What's your favorite song?"

"'Montero.'"

"That's a good one." Then I remember that this song was playing in Amsterdam when I was videoed at a club dancing on stage with the DJ. I'd shouted, "I love this song!" and made everyone cheer. It had gone semi-viral.

Right, she did research.

I try to come up with a question they couldn't have predicted, but feel exhausted just thinking about it.

So I play along. "What does your father do?"

"He is the lead manufacturer of the Jessup dolls. He designed a new and more effective assembly line."

The Jessup dolls are female donkey toys. There are stuffed plush versions, plastic versions with snap-on bridles and saddles, and entire sets with stables, riders, and grooming tools.

"Sounds like he is quite an asset to Avalonia, as are you." I stand. "Thank you for spending time with me."

She stands and curtsies again, then remembers she's not supposed to and mumbles. "Sorry."

"It's okay! Thank you."

I run my hand through my hair in frustration. I have to sit through three of these? Does my father think I'm going to be swayed by this?

Ivalaria arrives next. I motion her to the same chair. This is going to be a long morning.

CHAPTER 23

Sunny

The second fitting is a dream. The train is miles long, gauzy and sparkling. For a while, Octavia and Lili are with me, taught where to stand and how to straighten the train, which will be their job when I exit the car to go into the abbey. At that point, no ordinary staff is allowed near me, lest they wind up in the video or images. Rosenthal is adamant about that.

"Watch Pippa Middleton. Epitome of grace," he says. "She straightens Kate's train and keeps the air of aristocracy."

The three of us burst out laughing, making Rosenthal turn beet-red. "You must respect the ceremony!"

Practice bouquets are tried out, but two have hyacinths. When Amelliana learns I am allergic, she gives the florist an earful about keeping them out of the arrangements. I wonder why Rosenthal didn't bother to tell them. Seems like critical information.

Of course I know why. He'd like to see me sneeze my

head off at my own wedding. I might take allergy meds as a precaution in case I'm sabotaged.

The girls are sent away and more specific alterations are made to the bodice, neckline, and front length. I win the argument about sensible heels.

I feel good when at last the dress is unpinned and I'm back in my own clothes. I don't bother putting the heels on again and loop them on my fingers to walk with Emilio back to the tower.

He strolls ahead of me, and I dally, wondering if I can escape him and get to Leo. We pass the kitchen, and a woman in a white apron pops out, hurrying to rush a silver platter somewhere.

I see my chance. I duck to the left and push through the kitchen doors. There's a small room with hooks filled with bright white aprons and the round hats the kitchen staff wears.

I hide my shoes behind a shelf and tie on an apron. Thankfully, a guard took the jewels away. My pale yellow shirt blends into the white and the linen skirt is hidden.

I snatch a hat and shove it on right as a butler in a black suit passes through with another platter. He doesn't even spare me a glance.

Right. Nobody notices people in lower stations.

I'm barefoot, but it's not like the ruse will hold up for long.

I pass through the second door into the clatter and warmth of the palace kitchen.

Oh, this is my happy place, the closest I can get to feeling like I'm home at the deli. Long chopping blocks fill the center of the space, and two lines of stoves gleam silver. Several cooks rush around, pouring soup into tureens and stirring sauce. One slices a large ham.

They are all busy so close to the midday meal, and I keep my head down, passing among them. In a far corner, a half-dozen women work swiftly, sifting flour and mixing batter at a table near a wall of ovens.

"The tasting is tomorrow," one says. "We need all four recipes so that they might choose their wedding cake flavor."

A cake tasting! The pantry door stands open, and I rush to it, stepping into the shadow. From here, I can see the women baking, but no one will notice me unless they walk this way. I want to get a first glimpse of the cake. Once I'm caught, I will laugh and thank them and return the apron.

But their work is fascinating. They are so intent and concerned. All for my wedding!

A woman enters the space with a large round cake frosted white. "Let's look at the colors," she says. "I have bright white, blue-white, gold-white."

Another woman cranes her neck. "We should write something on the top, get a gander of how the colors work together."

"I wish he'd pick his bride," the first woman says. "Once I have the letters, I will know what script works best for the monogram on the tiny cakes for the square."

I step back, my hand pressed to my chest. What do they mean, pick his bride? I've been picked! I've been in the wedding dress! I've chosen jewels!

Maybe the staff hasn't been told?

I'm about to walk out there and make myself known when the next sentence freezes me in my tracks.

"Did you see that American walking with him in the gardens yesterday? Surely she is only a diversion."

"I hear she's in the bride tower," another says. "But the other three are in his bedchamber."

The women laugh. My throat constricts. What are they talking about? What other three?

It can't matter. Leopold wasn't in his own bedroom last night. He was with me. This is idle talk. Probably it makes their long days more interesting.

"He's with 'em now," another says, her gaze flicking to the main kitchen before she continues. "My husband is a guard on their wing. He says they all get time alone with him today."

Time alone? Today?

"Good. I hope he chooses a proper Avalonian girl."

I sink farther back into the pantry. I need to find Leopold. See this for myself. I want to know how far the staff gossip strays from reality.

I glance down. There's a pair of white Crocs tucked below the bottom shelf.

I nudge them out and slip a foot inside. They are a little big, but they stay on.

I tuck my hair more securely in the hat. I'm going to Leo's wing.

To help me blend in, I snatch up a big metal bowl from the bottom shelf and dump a bag of apples inside. I don't know if staffers wander the palace with giant bowls of apples, but I will not worry about it. I'll get as far as I can.

I lean out of the pantry. No one is looking this direction.

I lift my bowl of apples to chin level and walk confidently toward the door.

I'm almost there when a hand grabs my shoulder. "Hey!"

Oh, no.

My bowl is taken away and a platter with a covered dish given to me instead. "Take this to Lord Rosenthal. He's entertaining in Prince Leopold's chambers. Do not serve it yourself. Give it to the junior butler I've sent ahead with a drink cart."

I nod, careful not to look the man in the eye.

I scurry to the door.

This is perfect. I'll figure this out for myself. By the time anyone figures out who I am, I'll have the information I need to know.

If Rosenthal is involved, it's bound to be no good.

CHAPTER 24

Prince Leopold

Finally, we're on the last one.

This has been painful. I was so right to choose my own bride. I'm sure these women are lovely in any other circumstance. But they're so afraid I will reject them that they say nothing of consequence or interest. Every word out of their mouths has been studied and practiced.

I wait for Rosenthal to send in the final girl. I can't imagine this has ever been a good system. No wonder Father raised hell to change the law.

Helenista saunters in like a belly dancer, leading with her hips. She pauses and surveys the room. "It's your bedchamber."

"It has a bed."

"And a view." She walks over to the window.

At least this one has a mind of her own.

"Is that the hyacinth garden?" She turns, and I see why she chose this spot. The light behind her reveals her silhouette. She rotates carefully, ensuring that the outline of her breasts is easily seen.

She did the right research. I recall a picture very much like this on that Instagram model's feed. She stood at a window in a see-through dress, me watching her from the bed, a shocked-face sticker over my junk.

But I'm not interested in reliving my greatest hits of social media mistakes. "It is. The flowers are lovely. There's a chair for you."

She turns to me, pressing her hands to her belly, pulling the white dress tight against her skin. She's seducing the prince who partied too hard, who might once have tossed her on the bed the moment she showed she was willing.

I'm not that man now.

I shift in my chair, wishing I could escape. Sunny should be done with her fitting. If I could get her here, we could make proper use of this bed. My fingers twitch just thinking of getting her naked again.

Sex with her is transcendent. I care. She cares. This connection matters so much more than I ever knew.

Helenista senses she's lost my attention. She sidles over to the footboard. "Is it true what they say about the palace mattresses?"

I don't want to encourage her, so I don't answer, crossing an ankle over my thigh and straightening the leg of my jeans.

"I'll find out for myself." There's a squeak, and she's flung herself back on my bed. I'm startled enough to turn. Her skirt puffs in the air, revealing her utter lack of underwear.

I hold back my sigh of annoyance. What does she think

will happen here? I'll be unable to control myself and ravish her? Then, considering herself soiled, her father will insist on our marriage?

Wrong century for that.

I stand. "I believe it's time I resumed my duties."

Helenista leaps to her feet. "But we haven't even talked."

"It's been the same amount of time as the others." I don't know if that's true, but it feels like a year since she entered the room.

She rushes to me. "Please, sire, don't cast me away. I understand you. I have an appetite as well. It's strong, but I will save it for you. I like to learn new things. Do new things. Wild things. I would like to do them with you."

Well, that's an angle. I don't play along. "You mean like hang gliding? I've also considered taking up parasailing."

She doesn't miss a beat. "I'll do any of that with you. And you can do anything you want with this." She shrugs and lets the straps of her dress fall, the bodice sagging to her waist.

Oh, boy. I step back from her.

"Helenista, I can't have anything to do with this." I give her a quick nod and don't even bother with the door to the corridor between my chambers. Instead, I open the main door to the hallway, startling a member of the kitchen staff holding a large tray.

"Sorry," I say, circling her and barreling down the corridor. I know I just left a bare-breasted woman in my room, but I've had enough. I'm speaking to Father about this. We shouldn't encourage these girls. It's not right.

I've made my choice.

No one follows me. Rubin must be in the chamber with Rosenthal. For the moment, I'm without a guard.

I yank out my phone. This is perfect. I'll find my actual bride. If I'm spending the day with anyone, it should be her.

CHAPTER 25

Sunny

I'm frozen, staring into Leopold's room. The woman seems pleased with herself, lifting her dress back into position and smoothing it over a set of boobs that I would kill for.

And Leopold was just there with her. Looking at that. Maybe more. What had gone on?

She spots me. "You may go," she says. "Stop staring."

I back away. I don't know what to do with the tray. My courage faltered when I arrived at Leopold's door. He'd know me. Rosenthal would. I paced a few minutes, unsure how to proceed.

Then out Leopold came, not giving a common kitchen worker a second glance.

Was his appetite too large for one woman? I don't doubt that he liked what happened between us. He didn't slink away. He was attentive this morning at breakfast.

But he's spent years going from bed to bed. Would this continue after all?

I leave the platter on the floor outside Leopold's door

and hurry to Octavia's open room. I duck inside and yank off the hat and untie the apron. There's a laundry bag by her door like the one Amelliana used, filled with bedsheets. I stuff the kitchen clothes inside it and smooth back my hair.

I'll have to wear the Crocs for now, and my heels are in the kitchen. Those things don't matter, though, if everything has changed. It's not too late to cut loose, to escape.

The moment I exit the hall and enter the grand foyer, Emilio and two other guards rush toward me. "Milady!" Emilio says. "I lost you."

"You did!" I say, trying to fake a light tone. "I got turned around. I've been wandering in circles."

His shoulders relax. "It is time to take your lunch."

I press the back of my hand to my forehead. "Please have the kitchen send up a tray to the tower. I'm exhausted from the excursion with the Queen and the fittings."

I don't take no for an answer, heading straight for the far corner which leads to the tower.

Emilio waves off the other guards and follows at a fast clip. "Your maid can send for your lunch."

I hurry up the stairs. I want to be alone. To think.

When I make it to my chamber, I ask Amelliana to fetch my shoes from the kitchen and return the Crocs, giving no explanation for either thing.

I fall across the bed. What do I do?

Tears don't come. I'm in shock. If what I heard in the kitchen is true, the woman I saw is a potential bride.

Was Leopold trying them out?

I shudder.

Surely not.

He pledged me his faithfulness! That's what brought me here!

I need someone on my side. Someone to talk to outside these walls.

It's noon here, which means it's six a.m. in New York.

Grammy will be up. Even if the deli is closed, she will keep her hours. I know her.

I put through the call, running my fingers along the stitching in the quilt as it rings.

"Sunny? Are you all right?"

Just the sound of her voice makes tears spring to my eyes. I want to say, "Yes." And, "It's beautiful here."

But the words won't come out. Instead, those first tears become a flood.

"Baby girl. Talk to me. What's he done to you?"

I say all the things I planned to keep secret. "I slept with him."

"Oh, Sunny."

"He's been so great."

"All right. That doesn't sound so bad."

"I think I'm falling in love with him."

"That doesn't sound bad either."

"There are other brides."

Her explosive, "What!" makes me pull my phone from my ear. The background noise grows as things slam about.

"Grammy, what are you doing?"

"I'm packing. I'm going to get there and give him a piece of my mind!"

"No, no. I can handle this."

"Nope. I'm coming. That family has messed with the wrong Packwood!"

"I don't know that he's done anything." And I realize this is true. The girl was there, but Leo was running out. Maybe he was as blindsided as me.

The slamming noises stop. "All right, child. Tell me everything from the beginning."

I explain about meeting the King and Queen, and Rosenthal, and that Leopold has been perfect. Then about the jewels, and the kitchen gossip, and finally, the woman.

"Sunny, who is getting fitted for a wedding gown?"

"Me."

"And who is having meals with the royal family?"

"Me."

"And who got to hang out with the Princesses?"

"Me."

"We always knew there were brides waiting for him. There's no telling what the King and Queen promised those families. It sounds like one of them went too far, and your prince got the hell out of there."

I sniffle. "You're right."

"Sunny, the basis of any good relationship is communication. If you want to know about these women, just ask him."

"I'm never alone with him."

"It sounds like you were plenty alone last night."

She has me there. "You're right."

"Give him a chance. Okay, love? Have some faith."

I mumble an okay.

"We all got the call that the royal plane is leaving La Guardia early tomorrow morning."

I sit up. "Nobody told me."

"All the cousins are coming, plus your parents. Sherman, too. And Greta."

"Caden is going to be the ring bearer."

"Oh, lovely. I'll let your sister know."

I should have been talking to everyone. I was here all day yesterday.

"I'll call Mom later, when it's not so early."

"You do that. She's beside herself about what to wear."

"She can reuse what she wore to Greta's. It was lovely. Maybe add a hat."

"I'll let her know."

"Thank you, Grammy."

"You take care, love. Have the time of your life. Remember, weddings are stressful even in normal circumstances."

"I remember." My sister Greta's had been difficult. "See you tomorrow."

"See you tomorrow."

I let the phone fall to my bed. So I've overreacted. I should talk to Leopold.

But even with Grammy's advice barely five minutes old, I already have doubts.

My relationship with Leopold is so tender, so new. We've only just found each other. How will he respond to my insecurity? Will he feel an affront that I doubted him, mere hours after we slept together?

I vow to try. We will talk. We will work through this.

And worst-case scenario, if I sense he is lying, I bail.

Words start to flow, so I find my glitter notebook in my old purse and write them down.

Clouds gather
Tears spill from the sky
Petals fall from their stems
Their bright colors
Disappear into the dark earth
A bird flits through the raindrops
Searching for shelter
But the grasslands have no home
For the creatures who dare to fly
Into the tempest

So it's not happiness and wonder that bring out the words in me. It's fear and sadness, too. Had I felt anything at all in a long time? I'd been numb to the world, so the world gave me no poetry.

There's plenty of it now.

A perfect storm is worth a thousand words.

CHAPTER 26

Prince Leopold

I'm unable to get to Sunny all day. She takes lunch in her tower. Even though her guard lets me through, it's her maid who stops me and says she needs some time to herself.

I walk the gardens, disliking the juxtaposition of our separation after the arrival of the brides. I want to do something for her. Something big. Something no one could do for her unless they knew her, understood what makes her soar.

Then it comes to me. The perfect wedding gift. It will take time. And memory. And work. I want to do much of it myself.

I ask Grisholm to make inquiries among the staff. If Sunny can't be with me this afternoon, then I will spend the day in service for her.

I'm relieved when Sunny arrives at dinner. She wears a midnight-blue gown with a back cut so low I have to force myself not to slip my hand down inside it.

I lean close to her ear when she arrives. "You are more stunning than a twilight sky."

She smiles at me, accepting a brief kiss before standing behind her chair to wait for my parents.

But she's subdued. The dinner is quiet, Mother asking a few questions about my suit fitting. Then she says, "Sunny asked for you to be with her when she selects her ring."

Father's head snaps up and meets her gaze in a challenge. She lifts an eyebrow. This tells me plenty. Father is insisting on the other brides. Mother is displeased with his interference.

Sunny will be happy to learn of her support. Her gaze flicks between the two of them, and I wonder what she thinks of their intense expressions.

But they are the epitome of control. Father says, "That sounds like an excursion for tomorrow."

Mother lifts her wine glass. "I agree. The bakers report that there will be a tasting for the wedding cake." Her gaze rests on me for a moment. "I trust you will be there without distraction."

"Of course," I say. "We both will."

Sunny nods. "Of course."

"I hope you have sushi at the feast," Lili says. "We never get sushi." She turns to Sunny. "Do you like sushi?"

Sunny chats with Lili about the superiority of Tekka-maki over Unagi.

I pay attention to my parents, how they observe the

interaction. Mother has relaxed considerably since yesterday. Father maintains a state of disgruntled concern.

My day was fruitful. I am pleased. I notice a smear of paint on my knuckle and smile. Sunny will be so surprised on our wedding night.

At long last, the meal ends, and the family disperses. I wonder how quickly I can get Sunny naked. "Should we go to my chamber tonight?" I ask her.

Her expression changes completely, but her voice is steady when she says, "The tower is better."

She's probably right. My sisters might attempt to commandeer our time. I pull her close to whisper, "I have longed for you all day."

Her smile is small. "All day?"

"All damn day."

Another expression flits across her face. Uncertainty, perhaps? "Did everything go well with Mother? Was the fitting difficult?"

"Oh, no. Your mother was lovely. I chose my crown and the jewels for the wedding." She bites her lip. So something *did* happen.

We arrive at the stairs, and this time the guard merely bows as we pass. They've been called off when it comes to me, that's for sure.

She's quiet as we ascend past the storage room where I tied a rope to get to her. Are we already past those lofty feelings of last night? She seemed fine this morning.

Her maid greets us as we arrive at her rooms. "I'll be nearby if you need me." She curtsies and quickly exits.

Sunny sits on the bed, immediately removing the

sparkling black heels. "I have to find out who can get me normal shoes."

"Aisha can do that." I sit next to her and take her hand. "Although maybe keep a pair of those around for that fantasy of mine."

"Oh, right," she says, leaning down to pick one up again.

I stop her. "No, no. It's fine. Plenty of time for fun. I'm worried about you. Can you talk to me?"

Her gaze meets mine. I sense torture there, and I long to sweep it away. At last she says, "I sneaked into the kitchen earlier."

This is a surprise. "Have you missed preparing food? We can arrange a time for you to chop pickles to your heart's content."

"No. I was seeing if I could escape the guard."

"Did you?"

I finally get a smile out of her. "I did. He totally panicked."

"It's great sport, isn't it?"

She nods. "The bakers were working on the cakes for the tasting tomorrow." She pauses. "They didn't seem to know you had chosen a bride."

Ah. Perhaps this is the concern. "I'll speak to Rosenthal about it. No, he's useless. I'll have Mother speak to Matron Mariam. She's head of the staff. She can make sure everyone is informed."

"It seemed… well, it seemed like there was still some question as to who you would pick from a selection."

"There is no selection to be made. It is done. I'm glad I'm allowed in your tower."

I lean in to kiss her. She seems reticent at first, but I pull her to me, moving her to my lap.

Soon, her breathing has sped up, and when I pull away, I hold her face with both hands, gazing into her amber eyes.

There is trouble there, but that is to be expected with so much happening, and so many new things to learn and do. I wait, looking at her, wanting her to come to me. I will not push any further than I have.

The moment is infinitely long. Is there something more wrong? Have I upset her? I'm about to ask when she crashes into me, lips eager. I kiss her with all the depth of my concern, of my need for her. And I'm drowning in it. I want every part of her in my hands, in my mouth. I want to hear her cry out.

Her long hair falls from its coil as I roll her back onto the bed. The dress is slit up the thigh and I trail my tongue on all the places it exposes.

My hands slide up the fabric, following the curve of her hips, her waist, her breasts.

I remember how the dress plunges and roll her to me, slipping my hand down her back, then dipping inside the gown. I find bare skin, no panties, and my dick goes into overdrive.

"The cut was too low," she whispers. "They showed. No bra, either."

Dear God, she was naked the whole dinner beneath the dress.

"I want to take you on that table one day," I tell her. "Let the silver candlesticks hit the floor."

She laughs. "I'm game."

She's returned to me. The seriousness that discolored the evening has lifted.

I peel the dress off her shoulders. Her skin is lustrous in the low light of the wall lamps.

I can't get enough of her. Soon the gown is puddled at her waist, and she is mine to explore. I watch her face as I touch her, my fingers light, trailing along her neck, the line of her collarbone, and down the swell of a breast.

The taut nipple begs for my mouth, but I watch her face. She opens her eyes and I drink in her gaze. Her eyes are dreamy beneath the long, curling lashes. I think of her words, the ones that were my focus today. She has talent, street smarts, and the wealth of life lived. I am in awe of her.

She reaches out to touch my cheek, and the emotions flow, not just the heat of our need. I can't resist leaning in to kiss her, our breath mingling.

Then my thumb crosses her nipple and her body arches up to me. The connection shifts, catching fire, and I want to consume her. The kiss is fiery, deep, and her arms clutch me as if I'm the only thing that keeps her from falling into an abyss.

But I will follow her there, do anything. I've missed this part of the equation all along. This fervor, not only for her body, but all of her. It was so easy with my past conquests to leave the next morning, or even the next hour. There was no pull, no fitting together of any part of ourselves other than what could easily be done with a stranger.

Sunny is no stranger. Not anymore.

I slip the dress the rest of the way down her body. I want to worship every inch of her, and I start my pilgrimage, first at her mouth, then her jaw, her ear, her neck. I miss nothing, let no territory go uncharted.

When my lips close over her breast, I slide my hand down her belly and fit my fingers inside her. She enters that space I already understand, anticipation, a quickening. She moves not only beneath me, but toward me.

My mouth continues its journey down her body, even as I knock away my shoes and unfasten my clothes. This is one thing my promiscuity has given me — a proficiency at getting undressed one-handed. I remember the condom and ready myself. When the moment comes, I will not delay.

My tongue joins my fingers. The smell of her, the taste — it's all so familiar already. She's open for me, vulnerable, mine. I want to hear her respond to me, to let her inhibitions fall away.

She writhes on the bed, saying my name, calling for God, for the ghosts in these towers to remember their own sweet surrender.

But I don't let her over the edge. I move up her body, our skin in full contact. One of her arms is flung over her face, her cheeks and breasts rosy from her arousal. I sear the vision into my memory. I will never tire of it.

My fingers work the little bud that has her so overwrought, so near to her own release. I keep her there, fitting myself over her. I want us to fall off the edge of the world together.

I slip inside her, and her eyes fly open. "God!" she cries.

She can barely catch her breath, body moving rhythmically with mine. I slide carefully in and out, still touching her as well, easing us up to the precipice, controlling both her moment and mine.

Her hand clutches my arm. "Leo!" She's in agony, and I love every minute of it. "Please!"

I continue my gentle movements, holding back the moment, until I sense she can no longer take the delay. I hesitate, waiting for her to open her eyes.

Then I slam into her, drawing an astonished gasp. I shift my touch, remembering exactly what pushed her over the edge. My body pounds against her again and again. Her eyes squeeze closed and her hips tremble with the intensity of the contractions.

The moment she squeezes down on me, I lose control. Both of our bodies vibrating with the height of the orgasm at the same time is heady and disorienting, like we've lost our grip on the world.

Sunny's eyes open, looking at mine. I hold on to her, neither of us moving, letting our bodies do the work. The rhythm stretches out, elongates, and settles. I drop my head to the bed next to hers, our skin fully connected, breathing the same air.

This is what they mean by becoming one, I realize, the wedding vows suddenly making sense like never before. We are the same being in this moment. Nothing separates us.

My cheek goes damp and I turn to kiss the tear that has slipped from her eye to the valley between our faces. I think she must feel as I do, and the cosmic whirl that surrounds us continues to rarify the air. I kiss her forehead, threading my fingers in her hair.

I want us to feel this connected for always.

CHAPTER 27

Sunny

Day Five

With no real duties until the tasting at lunch, Leo and I request breakfast in bed.

Amelliana sets it on the bedside table with a smile. I'm curled with Leo under a mountain of blankets.

When she's gone, he snatches up a small silver bowl of lingonberry preserves. He dips a finger into them and snatches the covers away. He draws a line from my ribs straight down past my belly button and proceeds to lick it off.

"You're delicious," he murmurs, then his mouth is farther down, his hands lifting my hips so he can taste me freely.

I never tire of this, the bed swept from under me, that airy sensation taking over. I'm getting addicted to it. I'd rather never leave this bed, letting our meals be brought and going in and out of this undulating pleasure until we die of it.

My cries fill the room, startling a pair of birds who landed on the windowsill. Leo chuckles as I gasp for breath, finally sinking back down on the mattress.

"I think we need more preserves," he says.

I touch my finger to the tip of his nose. "I think you're hungry."

He plants a kiss on my belly button. "Starved. And I'm going to keep eating this." He bounces more kisses down until he's there again.

"Leo!"

He chuckles and rolls to his side to reach for a piece of toast. "Fine. We'll gather strength for the next round."

I'm not sure what possesses me to ask this, but I say, "Were you this way with those other women?"

His hand freezes. "What do you mean? What women?"

I instantly realize he isn't thinking of the years before me, but of yesterday. My belly quivers. "Never mind."

He sits up, holding the toast stiffly like it's turned to stone. "You seemed upset yesterday."

This is the moment I can bring it up. Communicate, like Grammy said. Ask about the brides. Tell him what I saw.

I can't handle this conversation naked, so I locate a sheet and untangle it so I can cover myself.

"I was. A little." A lot, actually.

Leo returns the toast to the tray. "Can we talk about it?"

It's hard to swallow around the thickness in my throat. "Okay." I pull the sheet over me and tuck it under my arms.

He waits, propped against the pillows. I wish he'd make

it easier. Why can't he just tell me about the brides? About the half-naked woman in his room?

But he watches me, waiting.

"You once told me there were choices if you failed to bring a bride home. It seems that even though you did bring me, they were here anyway."

His jaw clenches, and his gaze fixes on the far wall. I wait him out.

He finally asks, "Did someone speak to you about them?"

That's not an answer. He's fishing for what I already know. Anger flashes through me. I want to scream, just admit they were here!

I'm afraid if I start talking I will fly apart. Our easy happiness has flown out the window. Now it's hard. The kind of hard I don't want. I already regret saying as much as I have.

"Sunny—"

He's only said my name when there's a knock at the door. A voice booms. Grisholm, of course. "Sire, you are needed with the King immediately."

"No," Leo calls. "He can wait."

The latch jiggles, then the door flies open. I'm hugely grateful that I've already covered myself when Grisholm and two guards enter the bedroom.

"What the hell!" Leo leaps from the bed. "I'll have all three of your heads for barging in here like this."

Grisholm is unfazed, his lips tight. I swear his hair has gotten grayer since I met him. "You'd defy your King for those soiled sheets?"

Leo leaps forward, his fist striking Grisholm's face.

He hit him!

No one moves. Grisholm stands straighter, working his jaw back and forth. "Sire, you can come with us dressed, or you can give the entire staff a show as we traverse the palace."

Leo stands close to the man, his fists tight. "Your days here are numbered."

Grisholm doesn't budge. "Not while your father is King."

I'm impressed by Grisholm's unflappability. And by Leo's anger.

Nothing here is what it seems.

Leo snatches up his jeans and shoves them on, then drags a shirt over his head.

"I'll be back," he says. "I will answer all your questions."

Grisholm leads him out of the room as I clutch the sheet. Amelliana rushes in, gathering the clothes. "I'm so sorry, milady. Things are tense with the wedding so close."

She's right. Grammy said the same thing. Everyone is on edge.

Most of all, me.

I lie back on the pillow as Amelliana rushes around, picking up and straightening the room with nervous energy.

"I'll get your shower ready and choose an outfit for lunch," she says. "You have a wedding cake to test."

I work to slow my breathing. I'm the one tasting cake. I'm the one with the dress. I'm the one who spent all night with the Prince.

I need to calm down.

CHAPTER 28

Prince Leopold

I know something is wrong.

It started when I was forced into my bedchambers. Grisholm supervised my shower and dressing.

Father waits for me when I get out. He hasn't shown up in our wing since my sisters were children.

He crosses his legs in the armchair near the window. In certain light, I see the resemblance between us, mainly in the eyes and jaw. This was once his room, and as he looks around, I wonder if he is recalling his time here.

"I heard the report from Rosenthal," he says.

"Report on what?" I remain standing by the door. I'm not certain I will stay much longer. I am eager to get back to Sunny. Our time apart yesterday was a disaster and I do not wish to see a repeat of it.

"The brides. It seems the third one felt the meeting went well. When she was seen in a state of undress, Rosenthal brought her to Mathis."

That's not good. Mathis is the head of religion and ethical practices.

"She told Mathis that you engaged in relations, and she hoped she was not with child, as she is not on birth control. With the wedding so close, this was naturally a concern."

"What the hell?"

Father holds up a hand. "I wasn't born yesterday. You're not the first future sovereign to deal with such a matter. Did you sleep with her?"

"No. We didn't even get within five feet of each other."

"I accept your word on the matter and will convey this to Mathis. However, her father is an ambassador, so I would prefer you show her the respect her station deserves."

"She's a hot mess. I don't want to be alone in a room with her."

He frowns. "I agree. But please meet with her once more, so that she can feel she was fairly considered. That's all I ask."

"Sunny will be devastated if she learns of it. She already noticed that the staff has not been given the name of my bride."

"That's because officially, I have not declared it."

"I performed the ritual. We had a press conference."

"You also disappeared for a year, and your swimsuit video at the pool got far more visibility than your announcement. I find a ritual no one saw, and a press conference that garnered little notice, inconsequential given the magnitude of your choice."

"But you would have me give a second chance to a conniving nymph who would lie to the head of religion? What sort of queen is that?"

He taps his thigh in agitation, a habit the two of us share. "Your point has already been made. You will have your American as a bride. By all accounts, it's a love match. I didn't think you had it in you, but I'm glad you proved me wrong."

"And yet you force me to go through this charade."

He stands. "You will find when you wear the crown that this charade is the least of the pointless actions you must take to keep peace with those who make Avalonia a safe and harmonious place."

I blow out a gust of air. "All right."

"We will keep Sunny entertained until you can get to her. All will be well." He grips my shoulder for a moment as if he might say more, but then he's gone.

Rosenthal enters right on his heels. "Helenista will be here shortly. I think you're crazy not to take advantage of that one before you're locked down, but then, if you take after your grandmother, your rutting days are far from over."

It takes a lot of self-control not to punch a second person on this frustrating morning. I walk to the window. "Do I have time to see Sunny before that girl arrives?"

"Sunny is being prepared for the day. You'll see her soon enough."

I should text her. I look around for my phone, then realize I left it in the tower. "Send someone for my phone in her room."

He rolls his eyes. "Don't you have a butler?"

"Grisholm has been serving that role but he's an attaché, not a bellboy."

"Fine." He heads down the interior hall.

I sit at the window, looking out on the hyacinth garden. It feels as though the entire castle is thwarting my relationship with Sunny.

Even the damn flowers.

CHAPTER 29

Sunny

Grammy texts to say everyone is on the plane and on their way. They will arrive late afternoon. I spend the morning approving their rooms and talking to the head chef about a meal that will work for everyone.

Emilio escorts me to the dining room, where the table is filled with cakes for us to try. The head baker, a woman I recognize from my kitchen stint yesterday, stands at one end of the table, her hands behind her back.

Rosenthal arrives, peering over the cakes.

"Will the Queen come?" I ask him.

"No, it's all on you," he says. "It's not important. All the choices will be excellent."

The chef beams and nods to a young woman who begins cutting slices from each one.

"We should wait on Prince Leopold," I say, but Rosenthal shakes his head.

"He's not coming either."

"What?" I tug my phone out of my cleavage. Today's

outfit doesn't have pockets either. I quickly send a message. *You're not tasting the cakes?*

Rosenthal picks up the first plate and takes a bite. "Delicious." He eats it eagerly and moves on to the next.

I frown. I refuse to eat a single one without Leo.

But my phone is silent.

I wait five minutes, watching Rosenthal make his way down the line, rubbing his fat belly in a striped jacket.

Still nothing.

Leo?

And I wait.

Rosenthal makes it to the end of the line. "Please send a piece of each of these to my office later," he tells the chef. "Excellent, all of them." He shoots me a dark look, then leaves.

What the hell?

I plaster on a smile for the chef and her assistant. "I need to use the ladies' room. I'll be right back."

As soon as I'm out of the dining hall, I take off in a run across the grand foyer.

Emilio spots me. "Milady!" He catches up easily, but jogs behind me. "Where are you going?"

"I'm on my period and going to wipe up the *blood* in Octavia's bathroom! It will be messy! Full of menstrual leakage!"

That gets him. He stops. "I'll wait at the end of the wing."

Some tricks always work.

I enter the children's hall. Octavia's door is open. She sees me and jumps from her bed. "Sunny! Hey! Come in here!"

I hold up a hand. "Later."

She rushes into the hall. "I need to show you something!" Her face is panicked.

"In a minute." I will not be slowed down.

Octavia calls out to her sister. "Lili! Help!"

Lili comes out of her room. "I'm not doing a damn thing."

Octavia doesn't give up. She races to catch up with me and grabs my arm. "Come sit with us. Didn't you taste the cakes?"

I keep moving, dragging Octavia with me.

"Come on, Sunny, don't do it. Don't go in there." Octavia's voice is plaintive.

My heart falls so fast I feel lightheaded. They're protecting him. Whatever's happening, they know about it. They're keeping me away.

I was foolish to think anyone in this family was on my side.

Rubin stands outside Leo's door.

"Let me in," I say.

"My apologies, milady. I can't."

I shake Octavia off me and dig in my heels to push the big man aside. "You have to."

He doesn't budge. It's like trying to move a wall.

"My apologies, milady."

I run down to the other door, the one to his sitting room.

Pace blocks this one. "I can't let you in either."

He's not as big as Rubin, but equally impossible for me to move.

Maybe I can run outside and climb in through the

windows. Tears form. Something is wrong. Really, really wrong.

Octavia takes my arm again. "He'll be done in a minute. Why don't we go eat some cake? I'd like to try some."

I want to scream at her, or cry, or hit something.

Instead, I sit on the floor. I'll stay here until he comes out.

Octavia kneels next to me. "It will be okay."

Lili walks up, standing behind her. "Sunny, you can't take this personally. It's a big decision, and he needs time."

So I'm right. He's in there with the brides again.

I want to say he told me he'd already made his choice. That we've been so good together that he can't possibly be considering those other women.

But my voice won't work. I plant myself on the cold tile and wait.

A female guard arrives. "Octavia, Lilianne, come with me."

"I don't want to," Octavia says. "Sunny needs us."

"Just go," I say, my voice a croak. "This is between me and Leo."

Octavia slowly rises. "Come see us. Okay? It's going to work out."

Is it? I don't know that. I don't want to be in this position. I didn't come here for a fight, especially if the odds are stacked against me.

The girls leave with the guard. Rubin and Pace avoid looking my way as I sit on the floor. I don't cry. I don't scream. I just sit.

Maybe I'm wrong. Maybe it's some other thing.

But the sisters know.

And so do I.

There's a burst of laughter from behind the door. Female. Rubin shifts uncomfortably.

A young woman in a white apron hurries up the hall. I probably looked like her yesterday, hat and white Crocs. She stops before Rubin. "I need to give this to the butler."

Rubin glances at me, then opens the door.

In the slice of the room I see before it closes again, I spot the same woman I saw yesterday. She's turning in a circle, then smiling over her shoulder, kicking up the back of her dress to flash whoever she's looking at.

In Leo's bedroom.

She looks annoyed at the woman, then realizes she has food, and bounces toward her. Without a bra. Again.

That's enough. I can't be here anymore. I can't do this.

I stand up. There is no love here. Not really. Some good sex. A few good times.

Leo cured me of the lingering disaster of Billy. I'm grateful for that.

But I shouldn't have been left naked in a bed, my questions unanswered.

I shouldn't have had to taste cake with no one but a staff member who hates me.

I shouldn't have to endure the sympathy of two princesses who see the handwriting on the wall for their brother.

And I sure as hell shouldn't have to be watching this woman, who was nearly naked with him yesterday, laughing in his bedroom again today.

It's over.

It's really over.

My first urge is to cry, but I stuff it down.

No. I refuse to hate what happened here. It was good. I need to remember what was wonderful.

I want to memorize everything.

> *Stone walls, stalwart, protective.*
> *Gilt frames and paintings.*
> *Princes and princesses long gone.*
> *Halls that smell of roses and fresh grass.*
> *Lights crisscross on the high ceiling*
> *forming their own coat of arms.*
> *The ting of my stilettos on the floor.*
> *I walk away from splendor*
> *into silence.*

I reach Emilio at the end of the hall, and he follows me through the foyer to the offices on the other side. I pass Rosenthal's door, reading the gold plaques until I find the one I'm looking for.

Grisholm Pachin.

There is no guard to announce me, so I rap on the door.

"Enter."

I push it open and stand only a few feet inside. His office is not so large as Rosenthal's, nor as elegant as the Queen's. He has a blocky desk, a tall chair, and shelves on either side.

"Lady Sunny." He stands. "Did you choose a cake?"

"When does the plane arrive?"

"In a few hours. Is there a preparation you need?"

"Why would you bring my family here if I was not secure as the Prince's choice?"

He has the wherewithal to hesitate, as if unsure of his words.

I keep going. "I know about the other brides. I know they were here yesterday, and I know they are here now."

He clasps his hands behind his back. His gray suit is somber in this light, as though it's a funeral. "I see. There is only one who was called back. She, uh, seemed to make some headway with the Prince."

*Head*way. Right. I get it.

My last shred of doubt dissolves. So the half-naked woman was exactly what I thought.

The playboy prince.

King of Cock.

He had slept with someone the day we met. So why would he have stopped?

No doubt, this bride is as besotted as me. He's that good. She seemed absolutely elated to be in his room, and perfectly happy to flirt and flash her panties.

If she was even wearing any. That's apparently his kink.

My anger hardens into a cold, hard stone in my gut. "There's no need for him to decide between us." I step up to his desk and lay the betrothal ring on the desk. "She can have him."

Grisholm's frown deepens. "I see."

"Now may I be driven to the airstrip? I would like to wait out my time there instead of here."

"What shall we do when the Prince asks for you?"

"Tell him I have invoked the escape clause."

I think this will make him finally smile, but he maintains his signature stern expression. "As you wish."

"Don't quote *The Princess Bride* right now or I will cut you." I whirl around. "I expect the car in fifteen minutes. I need to grab my things." I won't leave my old wardrobe behind. I can't afford to replace it.

I take off running for the tower, Emilio on my heels. I burst into the room. Amelliana works on the birdseed packets in the corner.

"Help me pack!" I turn to Emilio. "You, too!"

"Oh, milady!" Amelliana pulls clothes from my drawers while Emilio fetches the bags. "What happened?"

"It didn't work out. He has another choice of a bride."

"But he was sleeping here! You two were so..." She falters.

"Well, he's in his own room with her right now, and apparently he was yesterday, too."

Amelliana's tears drip on my clothes as we both frantically shove everything inside my suitcases. "What about your gowns?"

"Leave them."

"All of them? They were made for you!"

"I work in a deli. I have no use for them."

The last bag doesn't want to latch, but Emilio leans on it and we get it fastened. The three of us carry them down.

The grand foyer echoes with our steps as we exit the back of the palace. Grisholm stands by the black car that brought me here. It's like my life is on rewind.

"The driver and the car will stay with you until the plane lands," he says.

"Can it fly right back?"

"I'm not sure. This wasn't expected." Grisholm's face is grim.

I'll figure it out. I just want away from here.

Emilio opens the door. "Milady."

I shake my head. "I'm only a miss."

He frowns. "Miss."

I crawl inside while the driver stashes my bags in the trunk.

I don't look back at the small group as we drive away. I already know Amelliana is wiping her eyes with her sleeve. Grisholm is standing like a gargoyle. And Emilio is broad and tall, somewhat in shock.

I don't need to see.

We arrive at the airfield all too quickly. It's quiet and empty. The driver rolls down the glass partition. "We can wait here until they arrive."

"Thank you."

When he rolls the window up again, I stare out at the fields. Fences separate the airstrip from the rolling hills, but I spot a herd of donkeys in the distance, wandering the long grass bending in the wind.

I lower my window. The faint sound of their signature laugh rides the breeze.

I have hours to wait. So I open my purse and tug out my sparkle rainbow notebook. I open to a blank page and begin to write, first slowly, then faster and faster, the verses coming so quickly I can barely stay ahead.

I have so much to say.

CHAPTER 30

Prince Leopold

I know something's wrong by how everyone treats me after Helenista finally leaves.

She was flirty and tried sitting on my lap, but I kept a contingent of staff around us at all times.

But now that she's finally gone, Rubin won't meet my eye, nor Pace.

Rosenthal seems pleased with himself.

When I finally get my phone back, I realize the cake tasting has long since passed. I text Sunny furiously, assuring her I'll get the cakes.

I glare at all the staff who'd made me miss. "Damn it, what is wrong with you all?" I take off for the dining room.

Rubin follows, calling out, "Sire, I think it's done."

I wave him off, crossing the palace at a rapid clip.

When I arrive, the table is empty, not a crumb in sight.

I won't be thwarted. Even though my parents expressly discourage the family mingling with the staff, I burst into the kitchen.

"Where the hell is the cake?"

A young cook drops a bowl of oranges, which roll across the floor.

"Sorry," I say, kneeling to pick them up. "I was supposed to be tasting the wedding cake with my *bride*." I realize they still don't know who that is. "Sunny. The beautiful one with long dark hair."

They all watch me. Finally, Matron Mariam shoos them away. She's formidable in her all-black dress and stern demeanor. I was terrified of her as a child. Lili and O still are.

"Sire, let us deal with the oranges." She waves the young cook back to finish the job.

I stand. "What happened at the tasting?"

"I'll take you to the chef."

I follow her through the kitchen to the ovens.

A stout woman comes forward at Matron Mariam's urging.

"Did Sunny try the cakes?" I ask.

"No, sire. She wanted to wait for you."

"But they weren't in the dining room."

"I had to clear them for lunch. I can send a platter of them to your chambers."

Right. I missed the entire meal with Father's insistence on my spending time with Helenista. At least that's over. If she reports to her father that I shafted her, I can't control that. I've done enough.

"Can you send it to the tower? We'll try them up there." That will be better. I can eat them off Sunny's bare belly.

The very idea makes me feel better.

The chef bows. "I will send them up straightaway."

"Thank you."

"Now, out of the kitchen," Matron Mariam says. "You know how the Queen would scold you if she knew you came in."

I feel ten years old as she escorts me out.

But at least it's all resolved. Surely nothing else can go wrong before the wedding. It's only two days away. Sunny might have acted a little off last night, but we got past it. If she's upset that I missed the tasting, I will do whatever it takes to make her feel better.

I feel sure that if we can spend the remaining time together, even this short courtship will be enough.

I cross the main foyer. Rubin falls in behind me. "I'm heading to the tower," I tell him. "In fact, have some clothes and toiletries moved there for me. I'm not leaving Sunny's side for any reason until the morning of the wedding."

"Sire."

"Just do it!"

Rubin waves a member of the staff toward him to convey the message.

I take the steps two at a time. I'm on the first landing when I encounter Grisholm. This can't be good.

"What are you doing here?"

"I left instructions for your bride."

"Is she mad?"

"She seems quite happy, sire." Despite saying this, his expression is grim. But then, it always is.

"She wasn't upset that I missed the cake tasting?"

He stares me down. "I'm sure it can be rescheduled."

What's with the look? "The chef is bringing some up."

Grisholm points behind me. "Looks like it's here."

A kitchen server pauses a few steps below, holding a silver platter.

"I'll take that," Grisholm says.

"No, I will," I say. "You all have done enough." I accept the tray.

Grisholm lingers on the stairs, but I leave him behind. What is wrong with everybody?

When I approach Sunny's door, her maid is waiting. Her face is blotchy, and it looks like she's been crying.

"Is everything all right?" I ask her.

She takes the tray. "Is this your lunch with your new bride?"

"No, it's the wedding cake. We were supposed to taste it."

She heaves a gulping sob. What in the world? "Why are you so upset? Please leave it on the table inside. Good Lord."

I open the door to Sunny's bedroom. It's empty for the moment, the windows thrown wide like she prefers.

The maid sets the platter on the side table. "Should I get you drinks?"

"Some champagne, I think," I tell her. "And strawberries. And cream." We should go all out with the food fun. "I apologize in advance if we leave the sheets messy."

The maid looks horrified, then cries again. She must be going through something.

"I'm sorry if we're a burden to you in your grief," I say. "Shall I ask the matron to find a replacement for today so you might have time to yourself?"

Her tone turns sharp. "A replacement, you say?" For a moment, I think she's about to get angry at me. But then she shakes her head. "I'll be fine. I'll fetch the items you requested." She curtsies and leaves.

I let out a breath. The last few hours have been absolutely maddening.

The curtains billow in the breeze. I walk there to wait on Sunny. It's a bright day. Perhaps we can take another excursion. I haven't had an opportunity to show her the town.

Unlike other royalty, my family walks the streets of Avalonia on the regular. We eat in the restaurants. I could take her to the toy shop to collect something for her little nephew, who will serve as ring bearer. She will like that. Her family should arrive by dinner.

Things will settle down. This troubling bit with the other brides is behind us. Soon, the staff will recognize her as the Princess.

All will be well.

The bathroom door opens. Finally.

I turn to the room. "I brought the cake —"

My words catch in my throat.

The woman in a glittering blue gown isn't Sunny at all. She steps into the room. "We get to taste the cake?"

I can't speak for long seconds. She walks across the room to look at the platter. "They all look delicious."

She turns to me. "You seem surprised. I don't see why. Your father was quite taken with me. That cultural director, too."

The last ten minutes blast through my memory. The

empty table. A concerned Rubin. A subdued Grisholm. The weeping maid saying "new bride."

This woman is not the one I chose.

Standing in the bridal tower, lifting a fork to take a bite of cake, is the very woman I just set aside.

Helenista.

CHAPTER 31

Sunny

I've seen millions of videos of military families being reunited. Mothers in camo sneaking in behind their children in the lunchroom at school. Fathers showing up at a sporting event. Brothers popping out of boxes. Families at the airport with balloons and signs, jumping and crying at the sight of the one they've been waiting for.

But none of those moments comes close to the feeling that overwhelms me when I see the plane land.

Crew members from the metal building adjacent to the landing strip push out a rolling ladder. The door opens, and more crew affix the steps to the side of the plane.

Then they're coming down. Mom. Dad. Greta. My sister's husband Jude leads little Caden down. Uncle Sherman is next, his big shoulders barely fitting through the door. He turns to help Grammy with the stairs.

Mom rushes forward to envelop me in a hug. Soon we're a big ball of Packwoods and Pickles, including my three cousins.

I want to put on a bright face and welcome them, but

the moment Grammy sees me, she asks, "What did he do to you?"

And I'm crying, sobbing, barely able to stand. Grammy wraps her arms around me, rocking me back and forth, her hand smoothing my hair.

"Where is that asshole?" Max says. He's a brute of a cousin, a bodybuilder. He looks ready to smash the castle.

I shake my head. "It's done."

"What happened?" Mom asks.

"There were other choices." I can't even say it without picturing that woman in Leo's bedroom, covering up those perfect boobs.

I bend over, clutching my stomach. I'm going to throw up.

"Let's get you back in the car," Grammy says. "Sit down."

The driver opens the door, and I perch on the seat, leaning out. There is no red carpet here, only the warm asphalt. They've all come for my wedding, and it's not going to happen.

At least not with me.

Grammy bends down next to me. "So something happened with the other choices?"

I nod. I can't talk about what I saw.

Dad seems confused. "So, did he choose somebody else?"

Mom smacks his shoulder. "Shut up, Martin."

It's too much, sitting here, surrounded by all this family. I'm such a failure. This is so much worse than keeping my head down at the deli, nobody noticing me. I'm the central figure in an unprecedented nightmare.

Greta shades her eyes. I expect my sister to say, "I told you so," but she surprises me. "Is that the castle up there? I'm going to give this asshole a piece of my mind." She takes off across the asphalt.

"Jude, go stop her," I say. "There's a million guards. She won't get in."

He passes Caden to Uncle Sherman and takes off after his wife.

Grammy holds my hand, squeezing it tight. "Do you want us to help you sort this out?"

I shake my head. "He's seen this other girl at least twice. It's too much. I'm not interested in competing for a stranger."

Inside, I want to shout *he's not a stranger!* But I stuff it down. If he could keep up this competition, then he really is. He's good at making you feel you know him. Like you're the center of his world.

And maybe you are at that moment. Just not in the ones where he's with someone else.

A breeze kicks up, sending the scent of the hyacinth my way. I sneeze. Everything's out to get me, urging me to go.

Suitcases appear all around us, the crew hurrying to drop them and head away. A woman in a gray uniform appears with a small bag. "We have to go pick up more wedding guests. Is this one of yours?"

Grammy accepts it. "Thank you."

"Of course." She looks at the car. "I don't think all of you are going to fit in that."

The driver stands uncertainly by the bags. "I think she was hoping for everyone to go back to the States."

The woman shakes her head. "That's not possible. We

have to go straight to Milan." She glances back at the plane. "They're refueling and taking off again."

Sherman looks around. "We're in the middle of nowhere. What do we do?"

"I can take the first group into town to get rooms at the inn," the driver says. "Then return for the others."

Sherman nods. "That works."

Jude makes it back with Greta. Her face is bright red. She's furious. "What's the plan?"

"We'll stay in Avalonia until we figure out what to do next," Grammy says. "Have you texted the Prince? Is he trying to reach you?"

I realize I haven't thought about my phone since the mad dash to pack my suitcases. I dig through my purse. It isn't there.

I race to my suitcases, pawing through my clothes and books.

Nothing.

"I left my phone in the palace."

"We'll get you another one," Dad says. "Forget about it." He leads me to the back seat of the car, and I slide in.

Grammy sits next to me, then Mom squeezes beside us. Dad sits in front.

The woman who broke the news leads the rest of the family to the gray building to wait.

The car is quiet. I will myself to pull it together. I'll go home and forget this ever happened. I realize I'm wearing one of the princess outfits, a yellow skirt with a shiny pearlescent shirt. I guess I'm taking this one. Maybe I'll send it back. Or leave it in the inn.

I don't know anything.

We take a road that circles the palace. Dad lets out a low whistle. "That's quite the digs."

"Martin." Mom's tone is hard.

I don't want to look at it. The gardens. The towers. The hills stretch far and wide beyond the gates. A herd of donkeys wanders in the grass, a man following them in a cart.

How could such a perfect place be so harsh?

There was a lot at stake. I should have known — and Leo should have known — that you can't simply bring a Brooklyn deli worker to the palace and make her a princess. Maybe Octavia and Lili will be able to choose more leisurely, since their husbands won't be King. But Leo was picking the future Queen.

And I'm not it.

We turn toward the township, arriving in front of the palace at the square I'd only seen from above. People roam about, looking curiously at the black car with the Avalonian flags. A few curtsy and bow, assuming royalty is inside.

Hardly.

I stare out the windows at the shops. A toy store. A bakery. Flowers. Hardware. Coffee. I blink back tears. Things I will never explore.

We pass a truck with a tall extension. Workers add white bunting to the streetlights. They've already done several blocks, and farther down I spot a banner emblazoned with the words, "The Royal Wedding." Naturally, there are no names. They were hedging their bets to the very end.

Signs point to where spectators can gather. We must be

approaching the abbey. Then, I see it. The church is enormous, the same stone as the palace. The facade is draped in white, several crew members affixing more decorations around the door.

I tear my gaze away. I will never see the inside of that abbey.

"This is the inn," the driver says. "Shall I make inquiries?"

"I'll go with you," Dad says. "We'll be right back."

The two of them set off.

Grammy threads her thin fingers through mine. "You're going to be okay, my love."

"I know."

"I wish I understood what was happening," Mom says. "Maybe you could start at the beginning?"

So I start the story, from the afternoon Leopold crawled through the deli. I get as far as the plane ride and the kiss when the driver and Dad return.

"What happened?" Mom asks.

"No luck," Dad says. "With the wedding, there isn't a single hotel or inn in Avalonia that isn't booked to the gills."

"Now what?" I ask. "Can we get to an airport?" The urge to leave is strong.

"We'll have to get flights," Mom says. "Surely we can drive out to Belgium or Luxembourg and find a hotel while we figure out the best course."

"Take us back to the others," Dad tells the driver. "We can Uber over the border. We're done with Avalancha or Avoidalonia or whatever it is."

I snort a half laugh, half sob. It's such a Dad thing to say.

It's two hours before three cars full of Packwoods and Pickles make it to Belgium and are situated in hotel rooms.

I lie on the bed in the room I'm sharing with Grammy. We have most of a hall dedicated to our family, and Sherman pops in to say we're all having dinner in the restaurant downstairs.

I don't want to go, but Grammy pulls out my favorite rainbow dress and red boots. "We need to talk this over as a family."

My feet drag as we head to the restaurant. Sherman has secured a private space for us. The waitstaff take our orders, and when they leave, he pulls the accordion door so we're separated from the rest of the patrons.

He stands at the head of the table as if he's about to give a speech, and I sink down in my chair. Grammy pats my hand. Mom sits on the other side of me, and Dad next to her. Greta and her family are close to Sherman's position.

Across the table are my three cousins with their ladies. Max spots me looking and gives me a wink, smacking one meaty hand into the other to remind me he's ready to rough somebody up.

"I think we should decide as a family our next course of action," Sherman says. "The delicate flower of our clan has been wronged."

Oh, God. Delicate flower?

I want to shove the limerick away, but I've been writing poetry all day, so it jumps into my head as easily as a toddler spills milk.

There once was a delicate bloom
Who thought that she'd found a groom
But he banged several brides
Wrecked the flower's sad pride
Till her Grammy whacked him with her
broom

Okay, that was funny. I almost crack a smile at myself.

Sherman slams his cup on the table. "What are we going to do about it?"

"Storm the damn castle!" Max says, eliciting a whoop from the group.

Jason catches my eye. He pours a glass of wine so full that it sloshes when he pushes it across the table.

Why not? I sip the top so more won't spill. It's good.

Dad shakes his head. He's often impatient with Uncle Sherman and the cousins. "I see the hotheaded side of the family is jumping to wild conclusions."

Uncle Sherman crosses his arms over his chest. "What's wild about them? You saw the press conference. That prick prince said they were getting married. Then he goes off and looks at other brides? That's screwed up."

"They haven't even known each other a week," Dad says. "Why were they getting married, anyway?" He turns to me. "What sort of scheme did you get mixed up in?"

Grammy stands so fast her chair screeches on the floor. "Do not assume Sunny did anything wrong. I met this boy. I saw them together. Don't you talk that way about my granddaughter!"

"She's my daughter!"

"Then be her dad!"

Sherman holds out his hands. "Okay. Whoa. Whoa. Mom. Martin. Let's discuss it."

Mom raps her knife on the table, hushing everyone. "There is nothing to discuss. Sunny has decided to leave without marrying the jerk Prince, so we're going home. Sherman, you and the boys figure out a way to New York. Ladies, we're going to have a spa day tomorrow while they figure it out. No sense wasting a vacation."

Mom has never been much of an authoritarian in this group full of extroverts and hotheads, but everyone sits down.

The food is served, and the men look up flights while the women go over spa options.

I drink wine as fast as I can, and when this awful, awful day finally ends, I'm happy to fall into an exhausted, drunken sleep.

CHAPTER 32

Prince Leopold

I shouldn't have even been shocked to see Helenista in that tower.

I spare no haste in getting the hell out of there, but no one will tell me anything useful. Grisholm only says Sunny came to him to invoke the escape clause, so he sent her to the airstrip.

Emilio only says she was crying, and he helped her pack.

I can't find the horrified, crying maid.

I text and text Sunny but hear nothing back. She might be in the air, already on her way to New York. I apologize for the cake. I promise to not leave her side again.

I tell her I love her. And that I should have said it before now.

Nothing.

Since no one has answers, I refuse to talk to anybody and escape the castle for the stables.

I find the old loft hammock I would sleep in as a kid, and I lay awake to the sounds of the donkeys shifting and braying below. The occasional laughing *hee hee hee haw* no longer conjures the upset of my youth, but makes me think of Sunny. Feeding the herd apples and sweet potatoes. Walking through the grass.

I can't get her out of my head. Leaning out the window as I climbed the tower. Dragging the sheets to her chin. Naked in my arms.

This agony is wholly unfamiliar. I can't even recall the names or faces of anyone else. But Sunny is crystalized in my memory. Her leaving has ripped something from me, something essential to my ability to move forward.

Damn it all. I fell in love.

I can fly to New York, perhaps. It won't be easy. With the wedding the day after tomorrow, the plane isn't even here. And I'm sure the pilot has orders to prevent me from leaving. But if I could find a way to Belgium or Germany, then I could fly on a commercial airline or hire another private plane.

Except my money has been confiscated. That happened the day I proposed and turned myself in. But my sisters could help. Hell, I have things I could sell. I understand about pawn shops. Wouldn't that be a lark? Grandfather's things alongside gold chains and fake diamonds in a case.

I ought to do it.

But Sunny left. It might be a waste. She might not talk to me.

We're as far apart as two people can be.

Sid lumbers up the ladder shortly after dawn. "I thought I heard someone up here. You want to talk about it?" He sits on a stool, elbows braced on his knees.

"No."

"Looks like you slept here."

"Maybe."

"When the next King sleeps in a hammock with donkeys, something's up."

I sigh. "Sunny left me. I told her if she wanted out, she only had to say so."

Sid opens a jack knife and pulls a block of wood from his pocket. He begins to whittle, cutting away the edges. "You know what led to it? You two seemed tight the other day."

"I missed our cake tasting."

"That sounds upsetting, but not enough to run."

"That's what I thought. Oh, I punched Grisholm. You think she was afraid I would be violent?"

"Could be. No sense of trouble before that?"

"She was out of sorts the night before. Said the staff didn't seem to know she was the chosen bride."

"Was she?"

"She was to me."

"But not to anyone else?"

"Father had me meet with others. Ones he'd chosen."

"Did she know about that?"

"She shouldn't have."

"But if the rumors that she wasn't the chosen one got to her, who knows what else did?"

I lie back on the hammock, staring at the shadows in the rough-hewn roof. "I don't know. She won't respond to my texts or calls."

"So how did you end up here?"

"I stormed out."

Sid shakes his head. "You always did run away from things."

I sit up. "What do you mean?"

"When your parents were too harsh, you ran here. When the stable boys upset you, you ran to the hills. Then you ran off to avoid settling down. At some point, son, you have to stand and face what's coming."

I almost jump out of the hammock and walk out after that speech.

But that proves it, right?

I run. I avoid.

I sit with the discomfort. I suppose I don't ask the right questions. I listen only long enough to figure out a way to move on. Sunny tried to talk to me that night. I convinced her to do other things instead.

My life flashes before my eyes. Me, leaving one bed after another. Moving between cities, hotels, friends. Never getting to know anyone long enough to be annoyed by them.

Never having anyone expect anything from me but a good time.

Now I've done it.

The one person I wanted to stay with. To have for the long haul.

Gone.

Sid's knife scrapes along the wood. He's good, waiting me out.

I can't stay here.

I have to find her.

I drop my feet to the floor. "Thank you for the talk," I say. "You really busted my balls."

"Anytime." He closes his knife and sets the wood on the floor. It's the ass-end of a donkey, the front not yet carved. Nice, Sid. Poetic.

I climb down the ladder and head to the gardens. Someone knows where Sunny went. The pilot. A driver. Guards.

They will speak to me. And they will speak *now*.

CHAPTER 33

Sunny

Day Six

When I wake the next morning, I feel like my head is going to fall off. I groan in the dim room. Grammy has the curtains pulled and sits in the corner with a lamp, knitting.

"What time is it?" I can't open my eyes more than a crack or a thousand shards of pain shoot into my head.

"Coming up on noon."

"Oh!" I sit up. "Do we have plane tickets? Are we leaving?"

"We do, and not yet. They're for tomorrow afternoon. It's the best we could do with as many of us as there are."

I lie back on the bed. "So it's spa day or whatever?"

"The others have already gone. I told them we'd join if you were up for it."

"I'm not. I've had nothing but spa days since I met Leo."

She pauses in her knitting. "Your hair is looking rather lustrous."

I hold out my hands. "And my nails are perfect. And my face moisturized. Amelliana had a whole daily routine to do before breakfast."

"A princess has to look the part, I guess." Grammy clicks her needles.

"What are you making?"

"A baby blanket."

"For who?" Both Jason and Max got married in the last couple of years. "Is someone expecting?"

She tucks the pastel rectangle into her bag. "No. I'm just getting a head start. With everyone paired off, there could be a baby boom any time."

Not here. I'm glad we were careful with the condoms. There should be no lasting consequences from my time with the Prince.

Other than my shattered heart.

It's over. Done. I can't dwell on it anymore.

"Let's eat something decadent," I tell Grammy.

"Belgium is known for their waffles."

"Sounds perfect. Let me take something for my head."

But when I get in the bathroom, my reflection scares me. My hair is only partially coiffed, the other half a snarl. I have makeup smudges everywhere. I need to get castle life off of me.

When I step into the shower, I realize I'm washing away everything. The hair products Amelliana so lovingly used. The body lotion. The perfume.

I'll be scrubbed free of everything from the life I've been leading.

I kneel on the floor of the shower, unable to hold myself up. I can't even think about Leo. The anger is gone, and a desperate loneliness washes over me. How am I going to recover from this? When a prince has scaled a tower to get to you, how can you start swiping Tinder photos?

No. None of that. I'll be a spinster poet. The woman who was loved by a prince and never recovered. I can conjure verses, speak to the brokenhearted.

Yes. I have a mission. I have a plan.

When I get out of the shower, I twist my long hair into a tight knot. I'll be a modern-day Emily Dickinson. I'm quite sure my intense longing will sustain my poetry for decades to come.

I choose a black tunic top over silky red pants. No more pastels. Only drama and angst. I should get a cameo pin.

Grammy looks up when I come out. "Well, that's certainly a look for a countryside vacation."

I want to tell her it's not a vacation. It's the funeral of a princess.

Oh, that's good. *Funeral of a Princess.* I can use that for the title of my first collection. I already have the opening poem in my head.

Death of a Princess

Slash the beaded gown.
Scatter the glitter.
Smash the wedding cake.
The sugar is bitter.

Break apart the jewels.

Toss them to the poor.
Let the pearls roll
into the cracks of the floor.

Tear down the white bunting.
Silence the bells.
The princess is dead.
She discarded her shell.

Hey, I'm rhyming. That's weird. It's like my limericks and my free verse had a love child.

Grammy's baby blanket foretold this.

I'm about to scribble another poem about the blanket and the prophecy when there's a loud bang on the door.

My stupid, stupid heart leaps. It's Leo. He's found me. He's going to scoop me into his arms and take me back to the tower. We'll tie ourselves in strands of pearls and feast on each other—

It's room service.

Grammy ordered waffles for the room while I showered.

The devastation is harsh, but I lean into it.

I scribble another idea.

Tragic Waffles

Syrup makes its final fall
leaving its glass prison

"Sunny. You should eat. We're going to meet up with

the others and tour some of the old churches this afternoon." Grammy sets the tray on the table and lifts the lid.

I want to stay in the dark, making woe out of waffles.

But they smell so good.

There will be time for poetry.

And time to mourn.

For now, I'll be glad my Grammy is here. I will eat for her sake.

Tomorrow I will go home.

The first day of the *real* rest of my life.

CHAPTER 34

Prince Leopold

When I leave the stables, the whole palace is in overdrive preparing for tomorrow's wedding. Rosenthal is giddy. Helenista is the perfect canvas, he says. He will have her face on plates. He's already got an operation in Brussels churning them out to be sold from carts. He's trying to find a T-shirt vendor.

It's gross.

When I cross the foyer, a banner is already flying.

Prince Leopold and the Lady Helenista.

So much for Father finding her inappropriate. He probably applauds her initiative, her cunning in finding a way in.

I refuse to go to the tower and deal with that woman. I stop a passing maid and ask her to fetch Amelliana and send her to the billiards room. It's one of the least-used rooms in the palace, and it's unlikely anyone will look for me there.

Amelliana is clearly nervous as she curtsies her way

into the room. I'm sitting in the far corner, where a person passing the door will not spot me.

"Sire?"

"What the hell happened with Sunny?"

"She packed her bags, sire."

"Why would she do that?"

"She said you had another choice of a bride. And the other one has been spending her days with you, even as your nights…" She trails off.

I get it now. Sunny thinks I was double dipping.

"Why didn't she talk to me about it?"

"I don't know, sire. But maybe… it was hard for her. Maybe… she thought that this is how things are, and it isn't for her."

My heart falls. "I see. You were kind to her. Thank you for that."

"I loved her, sire."

"That makes two of us."

Her eyes soften. "So, the other bride?"

"Not going to happen."

She stares at the floor.

"Did you see who drove Sunny?" I ask.

"The older gentleman. I believe his name is Carmichael."

"Can you find out where he is? And tell no one of my whereabouts. I don't wish to be disturbed. Particularly by that other woman. Or my parents."

"I understand, sire." She curtsies again and leaves.

The driver search is no good. Matron Mariam sent him to Luxembourg to pick up items for the wedding. So I don't know where they went, or if they're still in Europe.

I avoid the new bride, my parents, and the guards for most of the day, but midafternoon, Lili and Octavia find me drinking behind the billiard bar.

They sit on the floor on either side of me.

"The whole castle's looking for you," Lili says. "Wedding guests are arriving and you're supposed to greet them."

"They can shove it." I swallow another inch of brandy.

"It's our fault," Octavia says.

"Hush up," Lili hisses.

I set my glass on the tile. "Why do you think that?"

Lili glares at Octavia, but Octavia talks anyway. "When you had that woman in your room yesterday, Sunny knew. She showed up in the hall."

The liquor curdles in my belly. "What?"

"We tried to get her to come with us, but she insisted on staying. She knew something was going down. She sat on the floor in the hall to wait."

This is what Amelliana was talking about. "What did she see?"

"Rubin wouldn't let her in, but obviously she saw something." Octavia sniffs.

I groan.

"You blew it," Lili says. "She shouldn't have even been in there!"

"Our father insisted!"

Lili's face moves close to mine. "You should have said no!"

"You can talk. You don't even have any friends outside this castle."

"Neither do you!"

We shouldn't have yelled. Within minutes, two guards arrive.

"And now you're busted," Lili says.

"Out, please," Octavia says to the guard. "Stand in the foyer, not in the billiards room. This is private."

The man eyes her a moment, but eventually does as he's told.

"You think our parents are going to show up here?" Lili asks.

"I'm sure." I drain my glass.

We sit in silence for a moment.

"I liked Sunny," Octavia says. "We should have told you she was in the hall. Maybe you could have done something."

"It's not your fault," I say. "Sometimes our circumstances get in the way of what we want."

"You want Sunny, right?" Lili asks.

"I did." I pour another glass. "I do."

Rubin appears at the end of the bar and looks down at us. "You all right?"

"Do we freaking look all right?" Lili snaps. "No guards!"

I wave her off. "Hold on a sec. What's the situation out there?"

"We've been looking for you, and all guards have strict orders to keep you inside the castle walls until the wedding."

"They're going to make you do it," Lili says. "I knew it."

"We're allowed to use force," Rubin says. "I'm not saying I will. But we're all stuck because of the King's orders."

Of course they're making me do this. Nobody cares

about my chosen bride. The staff never even knew her name. I'm trapped.

We move to Lili's room, the guards left in the hall to keep us in, but also Helenista out.

I keep texting Sunny, trying to find something to say that will make her write back. Even if she did fly home, she'd be there by now.

I don't think she's blocked me. When I place a call, it's her normal voicemail. I've left a half-dozen pleas.

"We'll think of a way," Octavia says. "We're pretty sharp. If there's anything we can do to get you out of here, we'll find it."

But we can only hide out there so long.

You'd think a prince would never be a prisoner in his own palace.

You'd be wrong.

Guards take me to my final suit fitting.

Guards walk me to dinner with my parents and the new bride.

But when the guards try to force me in the tower with her?

Hell, no.

I have Amelliana to thank for my tower escape. I'm all set to tie bedsheets to go out the window when she gets the Queen up there to suggest that it's bad luck to see the bride on the wedding day, and therefore I should spend the night in my own quarters to avoid any face-to-face in the morning.

Mother walks beside me on the way down. I feel ten years old again, like she's come to fetch me from the stables.

"I know dinner was difficult," she says. "I'm sorry Sunny didn't work out." She seems genuine about it.

"Sunny saw me with the other brides. No one can blame her."

Mother is pensive as we walk through the palace, not to the children's wing, but below ground.

"We don't have a dungeon," I remind her. "Are you going to make me sleep in the vault?"

"I need there to be no windows," she says. "I promised your father."

We wind up in the butler's quarters. I currently have no butler, since I was gone traveling for so long. So I'm put up in his empty room.

It's well appointed, as expected for a such a position. But no windows. And terrible cell reception.

Mother stands by the door, lingering before having the guards lock me in. "My wish is that tomorrow is everything you hoped it would be."

Right. I had hoped it would never happen, and now it's the worst-case scenario.

"That's impossible," I say.

"I know." She slips out. The door is shut and barricaded.

The damsel in distress?

That's me.

CHAPTER 35

Sunny

Day Seven

Our plane to New York doesn't depart until afternoon, so we leave our bags with the hotel to walk around Brussels on the morning of what was supposed to be my wedding day.

And it's still a wedding day. We're close enough to Avalonia that everyone's talking about it. Quite a few of the hotel guests are wearing tiaras, carrying folding chairs and coolers to drive out and make a day of it.

Out on the streets, vendors hock royal wedding souvenirs. I can't stop myself from looking.

There are cookie plates with Leopold's face next to that other woman. His picture is old, from when his hair was short.

Grammy drags me away. "Don't look at that stuff."

"How did they get her on there so fast?"

The man hears me. "We got the pictures in yesterday

morning. Shut down everything to get them done. Just ten euros, miss."

I reach for my bag. "I'll take one."

"Sunny!" Grammy tries to lead me away. "No!"

I only have dollars. "Will twenty US do?"

"Certainly, miss." He accepts the bill. "Shall I wrap it up for you?"

"That's not necessary." I accept the plate.

Uncle Sherman catches up with me. "Are you torturing yourself?"

"Oh, no. You watch." I head to the nearest trash can, which is a concrete rectangle surrounding a metal can.

I look at the plate. Leopold. That woman. I lift it and smash it against the edge of the bin.

It shatters into a dozen fragments. Most of it falls into the bin, but a couple of pieces hit the ground. I reach down to pick them up. One of them has the woman's eye.

I grab a rock and smash the shard of plate on the concrete edge of the bin, feeling pleased as her face disintegrates, then sweep it all into the trash.

"I got a dozen," Max says with a grin. He brings the stack over. "Let's do this right."

We spend several giddy minutes smashing the plates. When we're done, I feel better. "How long until the flight?"

Uncle Sherman checks his watch. "We can fetch our bags and head to the airport. No sense being out here when all the talk is about the wedding."

We pass a bookstore. Outside of it is a cart with several featured books and local newspapers. There's a copy of the latest issue of *The Universe of Poetry*. Even though I have a subscription, so one is waiting for me at my apartment, I decide to pick it up to read on the way home. Maybe I'll end up in those pages eventually. That's one good thing to come of this whole disaster.

The poems.

The young woman at the till sees me looking at it. "Did you see their website this morning? They featured the Prince! He did a crazy gift for his bride. They're going to do a special edition on it."

"Sunny, that's enough wedding talk," Grammy says. "Let's get to the airport."

But I turn to the woman. "Why would the Prince's gift be featured in *The Universe of Poetry*?"

"Because of what he did." She pulls out her phone. "All the poetry world is talking about it."

My heart hammers. "Show me."

She angles the screen toward me. At first, I can't believe it. I pinch the image, looking closely, then zoom out again.

"Sunny, what is it?" Grammy asks.

I can't speak. My eyes have blurred. Then great gulping sobs.

Grammy takes the phone.

"What's it say?" Mom asks.

Grammy reads, and I clutch the side of the cart. "Avalonian prince creates a space fit for a poet bride."

Everyone's trying to see. It's Leopold, sitting in a chair in a palace room, one I've never seen. His arms are covered in paint, and he's smiling.

Behind him, the walls are stenciled with poems, verses only he could have known. I barely know them, and they are mine.

His glance scatters the stars, forming new constellations in the heaven of our nights.

The artist paints in layers, fresh green and bountiful blue. His details fill the canvas. Flowers. Picnic. Blanket. Me. And you.

The perfect letters fill the space, pale blue over gray. My words. All of them I said to him. He'd remembered them, painted them, planned to surround us with them in our new world, the Crown Prince's wing, where we would live as husband and wife, the royal pairing he'd traveled for years to find.

And now I know.

I know he didn't want those other women.

He'd had no choice but to entertain them.

They'd done everything they could to change his mind.

But instead he'd painted poetry — my poetry — on the walls of our future home. Because he chose me.

I know what I have to do.

"We have to get to Avalonia," I say. "Now. Right now. What time is it?"

Uncle Sherman frowns. "Coming up on noon."

"The ceremony is at one." I feel hot and panicked, like I've been jolted with electricity and every cell is blazing.

Everyone stares at me, unmoving.

"Snap out of it!" I yell. "We have to stop the wedding!"

CHAPTER 36

Prince Leopold

I sleep very little in the butler's quarters. I dream of monsters in towers, and Sunny wandering lost among the donkey herds.

Grisholm arrives early with a younger man in formal butler attire. "This is Jacoby. We'd hoped to have him start before the wedding day, but as you know, things were rushed. He will travel with you and the Princess on your honeymoon and tour."

"Fine. I guess you're done with me." I'm not feeling very generous toward Grisholm, but he was at least a known quantity.

"Your father has requested I return to my normal duties now that you are situated." Grisholm steps aside to let the younger man by. "Jacoby is well trained. He will serve you well."

Jacoby bows. He's already dressed in black tie. "I have your suit ready in your new chambers. All your personal effects have been moved to the Crown Prince's wing."

Right. I'm no longer near my sisters.

Ten guards stand at the ready, completely surrounding me as we cross the palace to my new wing. This movement was clearly well planned, as a huge contingent of staff plus many of the wedding guests in the palace stand in the grand foyer to watch me pass.

I wonder what they think of all the guards, if I'm being well protected rather than well contained.

Entering the bedroom I prepared for Sunny hits me like a ghost has passed through my body. Her words surround the bed, dancing along the walls, echoes of a life I thought I was entering.

The fallout of today will be tremendous.

Everyone wants to be born into royalty, or to marry into it.

They have no idea how torturous a path it really is.

The new wing has two floors. Down below are offices, a meeting room, a living room, and private dining. The bedchamber, closets, and sitting rooms are on the second floor.

I head straight to the window. My parents might assume I won't climb down, but as soon as I push the panes open, I see that they prepared. Three guards wait below.

No tying bedsheets to escape.

I spend overlong in the shower, pondering whether I can dissolve into the drain. Jacoby eventually raps on the door. "Sire, we are behind on your preparations."

I shut off the flow. A team is outside. One to do my hair, such as it is. One for the suit. The tailor arrives to oversee any necessary adjustments.

But there is one oversight. The vest is pale gold, as I requested.

I run my hand down the silk fabric. She's not with me. She will not be my bride. But the way I felt when I requested the color remains. In that way, I get to carry a part of her with me today.

I'm brought simple food to carry me through the ceremony to the feast. I eat only the minimum to avoid alarm. It tastes like dust. I have a long day ahead.

The events of the next few hours are going to change everything.

But first, I'm going to the bridal tower.

CHAPTER 37

Sunny

The Volkswagen Beetle definitely looks like a clown car.

There were zero Ubers or Lyfts or any other service to drive us into Avalonia. When an old lady in a 1984 lime-green Bug showed up to drop off a cookie delivery to someone at the hotel, Dad offered to pay her a thousand dollars to take us to the palace.

Mom, Dad, and Grammy are squished in the back. I sit in the front, hanging out the window to get a load of traffic on the long, winding road through the hills.

Uncle Sherman, my sister, and the cousins insisted they'd find their way there. I can't worry about them. I have to get there myself.

As we approach the Avalonia border, the line of cars along the highway comes to a complete stop.

"What's happening?" I press both hands to the dash and lean forward as if I can x-ray vision through the cars in front of us.

"It's the border checkpoint," the driver says. "With the wedding, I'm sure security is higher than normal."

No, no, no!

We're miles and miles from the palace.

"I'm going to walk and check it out." I can't just sit here.

Dad passes me his phone. "You'll need to communicate with us. The passcode is the year you were born."

"Thanks." I take it and walk alongside the cars. They occasionally move forward, but it's not enough for the Beetle to catch up.

I wish I were an athlete. A runner. And that I was wearing something other than a long black tunic that is absorbing the heat. My brooding poet look was not meant for hoofing it.

Still, I speed up. I reach the checkpoint stopping traffic into Avalonia. There are two people working, peering into cars before waving them through. One elderly gentleman seems particularly chatty.

I should hitch a ride with someone who's already passed through. It's only fifteen minutes to the palace from the border.

I wave my arms, trying to get the attention of any of the cars as they leave the checkpoint. But they gun their engines, trying to make up for lost time. They don't even see me.

I have to try someone who is about to go through.

My feet crunch the gravel along the edge of the road as I look for a good candidate. I pass a middle-aged couple who avoid eye contact.

Then there's a family with a bevy of kids who stare out the window at me. No room in that inn.

I spot a group of girls in an ancient Volvo and approach.

The one in the passenger seat rolls down her window. "You trying to get to the wedding?"

"Desperately!" I say. "Can I hitch a ride?"

She turns to the girl driving. "What do you think?"

The driver leans over. "Where are you from?"

"America. New York."

"She looks familiar," the girl in the rear seat says.

They all stare at me. I stare back.

The girl driving slams her hands on the steering wheel. "You're that girl from the press conference! Aren't you the bride?"

"It's complicated, and I ran away. But I have to get there before the wedding starts!"

"Oh my God!" The girls scream. "Get in!"

We're only two cars away from the checkpoint.

"Are they looking for you?" one asks.

"I don't know."

They squeal, and one of them shoves a wedding T-shirt at me. Then a wide-brimmed straw hat sails at me.

I switch out the shirts. Thankfully, that other bride's face isn't on this one, only the words THE ROYAL WEDDING with hyacinths. Damn Rosenthal. I shove on the hat right as we approach the checkpoint.

"Where are you from?" the man asks.

"Brussels!" the girl chirps, showing him her license. He bends down and peers in. "Any fireworks or illegal substances?"

The first girl holds up a shiny royal wedding mug. "Just herbal tea!"

He waves us through.

Whew. So they aren't looking for me. Of course not. Hardly anyone in the castle even knew I existed.

We sail along at full speed for several miles, and my hope soars. This will work! I will get to the palace and find a guard who knows me. Emilio, if I'm lucky. He'll understand.

It's the best plan I have.

I text Mom to let her know I'm only a few miles from town.

And then, traffic slows.

Then comes to a stop.

The line snakes on and on. People park by the side of the road and hike in.

We're at least five miles from town. I can see the palace, but it's far off in the distance.

I'll never make it in time.

"I guess we're walking from here," the driver says. She pulls off into the field like many others.

The car chugs to a stop, and we get out. Despite all the people stopping to park, the line of cars on the road winds for miles.

"I have to run," I tell the girls. "Thank you for getting me this far." I pass the hat back.

"Keep the shirt," one says. "Take a picture in it someday and tag Marcia Bennett."

"Thanks. Will do." I tie my tunic around my waist. "I'm going to run."

"Good luck!" they cry as I take off down the road.

I jog only a short way when I decide that cutting across the field will be a faster route to the rear of the palace. I'll enter like I did from the airstrip. I know the way.

I'm only half a mile into the jog when everything hurts. Lungs. Legs. Head. Still, I push on, sweating and huffing up a hill.

The road is far behind me now. It's just me and the swaying grass.

I crest the hill and look down. There are donkeys everywhere. They see me and approach with their funny *hee hee hee haw.*

I pet their heads. "Where's your herder?" I ask, gasping for breath.

The creak of wheels makes me turn. It's Sid. He's on a gleaming gold wagon festooned with white ribbons and bright peonies. He's dressed in gray finery, a plume in his hat.

He shields his eyes to peer at me. "What are you doing out here?" he shouts.

I run to him. "Can you take me to the palace?"

He hops down to help me up on the cart. "I thought you left. The poor Prince has been beside himself. Slept in the stables to avoid that other woman."

Of course he did. I've been so, so dumb. So incredibly dumb.

"I made a mistake. I didn't think things through."

"We'll fix it. Don't you worry. Move along, now!" he calls to the donkeys, who speed up at his command.

"Why aren't you at the wedding?" I ask him.

"My job isn't until the end. This cart will be led by my finest donkeys to take the bride and groom from the abbey to the palace."

"But you're in the fields."

"I had to search out Angus. I believe he's the one who led your picnic." He gestures to the gray donkey in the front of the line of eight.

"That feels like a lifetime ago."

"You and I agree on that."

"Will we make it before the wedding starts?"

"Definitely. I have to stage the carriage in position as soon as the cars drop off the bride and the Princesses."

I realize something. "Do you have a cell phone? I couldn't text the Prince from my family's phone because I never memorized his number. Do you know it?"

"Not his specifically. Never needed it. But I have Grisholm's and Rosenthal's and Matron Mariam's."

"They're no good. I'd just be tipping them off that I'm coming."

"Probably so."

I grip the padded seat. This cart is fancy, unlike the one we took on the picnic. It has a tall bench in the back. I can already picture Leo and that bride sitting there, waving to the throngs in the square.

No. That won't happen. I'll make it.

And then what?

I haven't thought this through. Do I barge in, stating my opposition to the marriage? Does everyone laugh and the guards haul me away?

It doesn't matter. I have to try. I have to hope that when I get there, it's Leopold who takes charge. That he is the one who refuses to marry the other woman when he sees I'm back.

I have to believe.

Sid hurries the donkeys along. "Prince Leopold will have already left the palace. Your best shot is the abbey. There's a side door by the cemetery."

We arrive at the edge of town on a street blocked off with guards. They move the barricade aside for the cart. No one pays me any mind.

"We're coming up on the square," Sid says. "I'll be stopping shy of the street. I can't go in yet."

I lean over to kiss his cheek. "Thank you."

He stops the cart near the back side of the square. The steeple of the abbey is visible over the rooftops. I'll have to make a run for it. Again.

I jump down from the cart. I know I have to stay within the cleared area as long as possible. If I don't, I'll be part of the masses trying to see the wedding procession from the palace to the abbey, and I'll never get through.

I cross another street filled with long black cars sitting idle, drivers waiting for wedding guests to come out, no doubt. I keep going until I reach an alley and turn in the direction of the abbey.

Every intersection has guards facing the main street. I can't let them see me or they might force me into the crowd.

My phone buzzes. I creep along a brick wall and glance at the text.

Dad and I through the checkpoint. Sherman found a helicopter for the others.

Of course he did. Why didn't he think of that before I ran in the hills?

It doesn't matter now.

The crowd noise grows. I inch to the end of the building. There are more guards at the end of it, and then, gobs of crowd. I've gotten too close to the spectators.

But then I see what Sid was talking about. An iron gate surrounding a small cemetery. The guards are at the front of it near the street, preventing anyone from getting in. I'm in the back.

I open the gate and move swiftly among the statues and tombstones, whispering an apology to anyone whose grave I might be trodding on. I can't use the open path.

I hide behind a raised concrete tomb topped with angels. There's the side door Sid mentioned, but it's guarded. That won't work. I'm too obviously not attending the wedding as a guest.

The street is currently empty, backed by throngs of townspeople waving Avalonian flags, many wearing tiaras. They are kept back by a white barricade guarded by police.

I'm not sure what to try. I'm so close, but there's no way in.

As I wait and watch, the church bells start to toll.

No, no, no! It's almost one o'clock!

A sleek, low black car approaches slowly. Inside, I see my veil. My dress. It's been modified in the front to fit the other woman's far more ample chest.

I'm so mad. So so so so mad. This isn't right. She shouldn't be here!

If she thinks she is going to sleep with my prince, surrounded by my poetry, which he painted on the walls for *me*, she's got another thing coming!

The bride steps out of the car. I dash for the front gate

of the cemetery and hide behind a pillar. This exit leads directly to the street. I could throw a rock and hit the guards lining the steps up to the church.

The crowd cheers as the woman gets out.

I inch the gate open as she moves forward to make room for her train. Everyone's looking at her, so nobody notices the random girl slinking toward the abbey.

Octavia and Lili step out of the car, wearing the dresses they had fitted with me. They bend down to help with the long train the way they were shown to do with *me*!

My anger drives my every move. I make it to the end of the fence while everyone watches the bride, who's looking down as the sisters straighten the dress.

But they're doing a… bad job? Why? I stop to watch.

It's intentional. They flip the bottom over. They leave the sweep of the train uneven.

Rosenthal, resplendent in blue and gray, storms forward. He kneels to organize the train. He's clearly angry. He wanted this image to be perfect, the bride and the sisters only. He told us this repeatedly as they practiced.

But by the time he's done fixing the dress, the sisters are gone.

Where did they go?

I make a rush for the abbey steps. I shouldn't have paused. I should have barreled forward.

Rosenthal glances up, and he sees me.

Then the bride.

The steps are wide and steep, with a guard at every level.

I don't know why I thought this would work.

Everyone gasps as I dash full-tilt up the stairs.

I don't make it past the first guard. He steps in my way and grabs my arms. Then another gets his hands on me. Then another.

Rosenthal rushes the bride up the steps into the safety of the building. I lose my footing on the steps as they close the doors behind them.

I'm too late. I didn't make it.

One of the guards orders, "Let her go, I've got her."

He must be in charge of the others because they obey. I'm led around the corner of the abbey, out of sight of the crowd.

"Dear girl, what are you doing here?"

I finally peer up at him. It's Vellemond, the guard from the garden on my first day at the palace.

There's no point in lying. "Stopping the wedding."

"But you're supposed to be the bride."

"Can you get me in?"

"No, miss. Not even a guard can escort a guest."

"It's supposed to be me in there!"

"Why isn't it?"

It's too much to explain. I slump down on the ground by the wall. The concrete is cold in the shade. I want it to rain, really bring on a storm, but the day is stupidly bright. A perfect Avalonian wedding day.

The bells stop tolling and inside, an organ rumbles with a tune. The ceremony has already begun. I don't know what to do.

Poor Leo. He's had to go through with this thing, even

though he wanted me. I left. I didn't do what Grammy told me to. Talk to him. I'd been too afraid.

The crowd suddenly gasps, then there's a commotion near the street. A second guard peers around the corner to look at us. "Something's going on." He takes off.

Vellemond walks to the edge of the abbey wall. "Don't move," he says to me.

But of course I do. I can work with a commotion. Maybe Leo has refused to marry her. Maybe the sisters created a diversion.

I lean around Vellemond to look.

Rosenthal is out on the steps, shouting at guards. More of them are spilling out from inside the church. Then there's Grisholm. Then a man in religious vestments, holding a Bible.

I don't think the wedding's happening.

The crowd noise grows. A few guards spot Vellemond and come over. "Did anyone run this way?" they ask.

"No," Vellemond says. "Who would run?"

"Prince Leopold." He peers into the cemetery. "Could he be in here?"

"The Prince is gone?" I ask.

The guard looks from Vellemond to me. "Who is this?"

"A friend," Vellemond says. "What are you saying?"

Another guard passes by to enter the cemetery. "He's saying the Prince disappeared from the abbey just before he was supposed to enter the sanctuary. His sisters are also gone."

Vellemond glances at me. "And nobody knows where they are?" he asks the other guard.

"Nobody."

I back away. "I'm going to go now."

No one follows as I run around the cemetery fence and back the way I came.

They might not know where the royal siblings went or how they got there — but I bet I do.

CHAPTER 38

Prince Leopold

Lili's face is briefly lit as she shifts her flashlight through the tunnel. Even though she says, "Leo, our parents are going to kill us," her face is glowing with glee.

"Probably so."

Octavia lifts her skirt so she can move more swiftly. "Isn't it great?"

I'm glad they can be so glib about it. "I fear I've gotten you both in a lot of trouble."

"Worth it!" Octavia sings.

We approach a short flight of stairs, and I shine my light on them so the girls won't trip.

"Good thing we used to run these tunnels as kids," Lili says. "Because they are creepy deluxe."

We arrive at a fork. Right should take us from the abbey to the palace.

Left goes to the hills.

"Ugh, I want to chuck this dress," Lili says. "The shoes are torture."

"I told you to stash some clothes in the tunnel," Octavia says.

"Did you?"

"No."

I smack the backpack I've slung over my shoulder. I planned ahead. "You can borrow a T-shirt or something."

"Are you leaving?" Lili asks.

"Yes. Claude is meeting me on the border as soon as he can manage it, and we'll get a flight out of Luxembourg."

"Take us with you!" Octavia pleads. "We're due an excursion."

"I'll do that if you want," I say. "But you have to commit to couch surfing. Hotels leave a paper trail."

Lili stops. "Is that why you slept with all those women? To crash at their places to avoid the guards finding you?"

I shine my light on my face. "Let's say *sure* on that."

She punches my chest. "You're so gross."

We keep going.

"What about Sunny?" Octavia asks. "Can you stay with her?"

"If she'll have me. I don't know."

Lili huffs as we climb a set of stairs in the dark. "I should do more cardio."

A crack of light ahead tells me we've almost made it to our destination. "I'll go out first," I say. "Mother and Father will have figured out our ploy. There might be guards."

Lili's voice is a sing-song. "But it's too late to make you get married!"

I grimace. I hadn't wanted to embarrass Helenista. I went to the tower this morning to tell her I had no intention of going through with the wedding.

Aisha was there to dress her. She insisted we could not see each other on our wedding day and made Helenista stay in the bathroom.

I sat on the bed, thinking of Sunny, and how to form the words to get through to Helenista that the wedding wasn't going to happen.

Then I found Sunny's phone. It was sitting right there on the charger by the bed. All the notifications were lined up, a few words previewing each of my texts.

Helenista had told no one that she had Sunny's phone, and on top of that, had clearly been reading what she could without unlocking the screen.

She knew I wanted to marry Sunny. That I loved her.

And she had actively worked to make sure Sunny never learned the truth.

I took the phone and walked out without telling her my plan.

I feel no remorse.

I tug on the lever of the ancient stone door. I'm not sure when it might have been opened last. I haven't used the tunnels this far from the palace for a decade at least. Possibly no one has.

Dirt showers from the seams as I push. If anyone is on the other side, they'll know we're coming through. The metal hinges screech in protest.

At last it's open wide enough to pass through. Sunlight pours into the tunnel.

"Anybody there?" Lili asks.

I peer beyond the door. "Not in the ruins."

I shut off my flashlight and put it in the bucket by the door. The girls do the same. I step out. The tunnel leads into the ruins of a stone stable several hundred years old. The stone wall holds a hidden door impossible to open from the outside without serious equipment to pull on the door or detonate it. The passage was intended as an escape out, but never a way in.

I walk through the crumbling stones grown over with grass and vines and peer through an opening to the hillside. We're not far from the meadow where I took Sunny on our first day. It's my destination, a place to find some peace on this unprecedented day.

The girls emerge, dusting off their white dresses.

"All clear," I tell them. "We made it."

"What now?" Octavia asks. Her perfect updo lists to one side, and she pulls the pins, letting the hidden pink and blue stripes show again as it falls.

"We wait in the meadow under the cover of trees."

Lili stomps up beside me in her delicate dress, no longer caring about posture or grace now that we're away from the abbey.

We watch the sky as we traverse the open hillside, as if helicopters might ferret us out.

But the clouds are unaccompanied, and we arrive at the meadow without incident.

"I think we can lower our assessment of our parents' intelligence," Lili says. "They should have figured out what we did and had someone waiting. It took forever to get here."

I agree. But I also know the delay means the wedding is clearly off. Even if they collected me now, at least I've accomplished that.

Octavia plops onto a fallen tree log. "They probably

think we went to the palace. We are spoiled little royals, after all."

Lili sits next to her. "True. If they're searching all those rooms, it will take them a long time to figure out we're actually here."

I unbutton the stifling jacket. "The guards are all scattered due to the wedding, so it might take more time to get them organized."

"Now if we only had a picnic," Lili says. "And a blanket. I could use a nap. They got me up at five a.m. for hair and makeup."

Octavia bends over, resting her head on her crossed arms. "Six for me."

I wish I had food for them, or somewhere to sit. "You could head back," I say. "I'm going to walk to the border the moment I hear Claude has made it there."

Octavia's head pops up. "No way. We gave you all our cash. I say we go, too."

Lili shuffles her feet, digging her stiletto heels into the dirt. "Don't be ridiculous, O. If we all go, the entire country will come after us. They can't let the entire royal family disappear."

She's probably right.

I walk up to the edge of the trees to look out. Herds of donkeys roam the grasses. I spot one herder on a cart. He's off in the distance. We'll make sure to avoid him.

"See something?" Octavia asks.

"Just a donkey cart."

Lili kicks out her legs. "Maybe he has water. Or apples for the donkeys."

"I should have planned better. You probably missed lunch."

"Oh, I'm just whining," Lili says. "We both ate a crap-ton of pasta. I'm mainly having cell phone withdrawal. We totally should have put those in the tunnel."

"No," I say. "They can track us through those. I burned through a dozen of them to stay away from the guards last year."

Her shoulders slump. "Right."

We sit for a while, the wind rustling the grass and the donkeys laughing. Then the squeak of wheels and the bray of donkeys makes me leap to my feet.

I press a finger to my lips to keep my sisters quiet as I slip through the trees to get a visual on the hillside.

A cart is parked on the edge, six donkeys pulling it. I spot a dark head on the other side of it and drop to the ground.

This person walks on the other side. I can see a pair of feet.

In red boots?

And red pants?

I only know one person who would wear red satin on a Saturday afternoon.

I jump up. "Sunny?"

She turns, her hair in a topknot that spills tendrils everywhere. "I knew it!" she cries.

She rushes around the cart, and then she's in my arms. I clutch at her, wondering if she's some strange stress dream, and I'm actually asleep by the log with my sisters.

But then I'm kissing her, and if this isn't real, no one better wake me up. She's delicious and warm, and I can't let go of her, ever. I squeeze her so close to me that she breaks the kiss. "Leo, I'm not made of stuffing!"

I can't wait a minute more to say how I feel. I've been given this second chance. I won't waste it.

"I love you, Sunny Packwood of Brooklyn, New York, queen of the pickle sandwich, stealer of my heart."

She smiles at me. "I know. And I love you, Leopold the Second, Prince of Avalonia, totally King of Cock."

I laugh, and she laughs, and even if this laugh sounds exactly like the braying of the donkeys standing nearby, I don't care. I'll laugh this way until the end of my days, as long as Sunny's arrival means she's come back to me for good.

CHAPTER 39

Sunny

The four of us sit amongst the trees. Lili uses my black tunic for a dress and we split her long white gown down the seam to serve as a blanket to sit on.

"Where is your family?" Octavia asks. "Didn't they all fly in?"

I lean my head on Leopold's shoulder. He hasn't taken his arms from around me since I arrived. "My parents and grandmother are stuck in traffic on the highway to Avalonia. My uncle, sister, and cousins are apparently in a helicopter trying to find where we are." I lift my chin to look up at Leo. "Should I drop a Google pin so they can come, or send them back to Belgium?"

Lili claps her hands. "Oh, please let them land out here. I've never ridden in a helicopter!"

"I guess it's fine if we're caught," Leo says. "There's nothing they can do to make me marry that other woman."

"They didn't succeed the first time," Octavia says. "They won't risk this fallout again. But there's going to be hell to pay."

"I'll pay it in America, then," Leo says. "There's no reason in the twenty-first century for a monarch to marry because of some outdated law."

"You'd think Father would know better," Lili says. "I say we bust this royal family right open."

Octavia elbows her. "I highly doubt we're the first royal kids to think of such things. And yet here we are." She nudges my leg. "Bring on the helicopter."

I send the text to Uncle Sherman with the pin. "Done."

"I hope they have snacks," Lili says, fingering the rough stitching on the hem of the tunic. "I rather like this shirt-dress. I hope you don't mind if I steal it."

"Go right ahead. I have this dazzler of a shirt." I point to THE ROYAL WEDDING. "Could they have made the words any bigger?"

"Leo's going to be on all the gossip sites," Lili says. "Prepare for a return of every meme ever made about your Instagram models and your cock."

"Don't say cock in front of me!" Leo shouts.

"Then don't wave it around the Internet!" she shouts back.

We're all laughing when a buzzing sound makes us all pause to listen.

"The helicopter!" I jump to my feet.

We rush to the edge of the trees. The dark green oval hovers two hills over, then moves this way. The sisters wave at it, and it comes close enough that I can see Max in his headphones looking down.

They fly farther away, the long grass blowing madly with the whir of the blades. They drift over the slope for a moment until they seem to find a spot the pilot feels safe enough to land on.

The side door opens, and Max spills out, then Uncle Sherman, Jason, and Anthony. Then Greta. That seems to be all who fit.

Max reaches me first, sweeping me up in a hug and spinning me around. "You did it! We heard it on the news. Everyone's talking about the runaway groom!"

I let him sweep me in circles, then bang his shoulder to put me down. "He wasn't running away from her as much as toward me."

When my feet are back on the ground, I dizzily focus in on the rest of the Pickles standing menacingly around Leo. Octavia and Lili have backed away.

"Hey! Stop glaring at Leo!" I jump in front of them, waving my arms. "He got away. He's here." I thread my arm though his. "We figured things out."

Uncle Sherman shakes his head. "When I met their mother," he waves a thumb at the three men, "we had a regular period of dating. I proposed and got married in the normal way. Why has every Pickle since then been full of drama?"

"I blame romance novels," Greta says. "Everybody has to have a big story."

All of us turn to her with an elongated, "Gretaaaaaa."

She throws up her hands. "What! Have you ever read a Julia Kent novel where they just date and marry? What about Pippa Grant? There's always a goat. Or weird cheese!"

Max wraps his elbow around her head and messes up her hair.

"Maxworth Packwood, let me go!" Her arms go wild, trying to push her muscled, oversized cousin off her.

"Not until you say 'I believe in love' ten times fast," he says.

Leo leans in. "Is your family always like this?"

I shrug. "Pretty much."

The helicopter shuts off, revealing another sound — the whine of small engines.

Max releases Greta, and we all turn. A whole fleet of four-wheelers, golf carts, and small cars traverses the hills.

"Here they come," Lili says. "Time to face the music."

Octavia jumps on Leo's back. "I see Mother and Father. And Grisholm. And a pile of guards. Oh, and Sid."

"No bride, though, right?" I squeeze Leo's hand.

"Nobody in white," Octavia says. "And no minister. They aren't bringing the wedding to you."

My head snaps to Leo. "Would they have done that?"

"Unlikely. But be ready to make a run for the helicopter."

Max slaps Leo's shoulder. "We got your back, bro. I can take at least four guards."

"Simmer down," Uncle Sherman says. "Let's hear what they have to say."

I half expect someone to roll out a red carpet in front of the King and Queen, but they step off the four-wheeler and pick their way through the long grass to where we stand in the sun.

"I told you we should have come here first," the Queen says. "And I told you we should have located Sunny rather than installed that other woman in the tower."

The King doesn't answer, his lips tightly pressed. His

face is red and blotchy, as if he's had to endure this sort of reprimand all afternoon.

They stop a few feet from us, but nobody bows or curtsies. We have the upper hand, and we know it.

"Leopold the Second," the Queen says, and her tone tells me this is her equivalent of first and middle names to indicate trouble. "Those theatrics have cost our family a great deal of distress. You could have saved us much embarrassment and expense if you'd stepped forward and spoken your mind."

Leo's body stiffens. "When exactly would I have done that, Mother? During my guarded escort to the underground rooms? Or perhaps while being forced to entertain women who should never have been in my company in the first place?"

The Queen whirls to the King. "I thought he wanted to meet them. You expressly told me that the Helenista woman had caught his fancy."

The King wisely remains silent.

But she's not done. "We have a despondent bride, an angry ambassador who has already resigned, a befuddled staff, and now, a confused and shaken country."

Leo's grip on me gets tighter. "Mother, if that's all you care about even now, then I wish you good luck. I abdicate my crown." He turns to me. "You up for showing me how to make an acceptable sandwich? It sounds like I need a job."

I don't get a chance to answer because Lili and Octavia rush forward.

"I'm out, too," Octavia says. "I'm twenty-two and

haven't been allowed to so much as date. Sunny, are there any eligible men in your town?"

"So many," I answer automatically, but my head is pounding with the implications of what they're saying.

The Queen turns to Lili. "And you? Are you also abdicating your title?"

"Why not?" Lili says. "You olds need to figure your shit out."

"Lilianne Elizabeth Montgomery the First!"

Oooh, that's a mouthful.

Lili isn't having it. "Mother, we're adults by law."

"Not by royal decree," Father bellows. "You do not come of age until you marry or turn thirty."

So, technically, even Leo is still a kid. His birthday is two weeks away.

"Am I kidnapping a minor?" I give Leo a shove.

"Hopefully." He presses a kiss into my hair.

The guards have all assembled in a line behind the royal couple. Grisholm walks around them. "Might I suggest a solution?"

Great. I can't imagine what this might be.

"Go ahead," the King says.

"Let them marry. Right here. It's the seventh day. We're within the law, as it is." His gaze rests on me. "It's what they want."

"Is it?" the Queen asks. "What you want?"

I squeeze Leo's arm. "Yes."

"Absolutely," he says.

"Good." Grisholm rubs his hands together. "I assumed it would be so. I've already engaged the revelers."

What does he mean?

But soon it becomes apparent. There is the bray of donkeys. And music.

"I want to see!" Octavia walks up to Max. "Lift me up."

He lifts her to sit on his extra-wide shoulder. "It's carts!" she says. "Lots and lots of carts!" She waves her hands at them. "And a band. And people waving white ribbons. Oh, it's a lot of people."

Soon I make out the singing. It's the song I first heard from the tower, the townspeople dancing with the donkeys on the square. As they grow closer, the sound becomes louder and the words more distinct.

Long live Avalonia, the paradise of the hills. Where donkeys bray and people say that heaven's in the fields.

I glance down at my royal wedding T-shirt and red pants. Not what I thought I'd be wearing to my ceremony. The other bride got my dress.

I shouldn't have worried. The moment the towns-people arrive, my T-shirt is covered with a gorgeous hand-woven summer shawl in bright white with sparkling silver strands. The children weave wildflowers into a skirt, and a kind woman gifts me her own beautiful head wreath made from white roses and ribbons.

Max takes the helicopter back to fetch the rest of the family. Grisholm sends guards on golf carts to rescue Grammy and my parents from the traffic jam.

Word seems to get out that the wedding is happening in the fields, and as swift preparations are made, more and more of Avalonia's citizenry arrives on the hillside.

Handmade dishes are set out on blankets. The contents

of everyone's coolers are spread into a feast. The wedding cakes that were passed out on the square with Helenista's initials are smashed and rolled into cake balls dipped in chocolate melted from candy bars held over candles. Musicians set up in the shelter of the trees, and the bunting from the square is stretched along the branches.

The herders, back on duty, lead their charges to the edges of the crowd, where children continue to weave flower wreaths to wrap around their necks. More palace staff appears, including Vellemond, who I'm angling to get promoted after he helped me at the abbey, and, eventually, even Rosenthal shows.

Leo skips the formal jacket, leaving the pale gold vest he had made to match my name.

A bouquet is made from the wildflowers, but before it's passed to me, Rosenthal rushes forward and snatches it away. "This has hyacinths in it! Don't you know the future Queen is allergic to hyacinths?"

He knows where his bread is buttered.

A new bouquet is quickly prepared, all peonies and pansies and daffodils.

Grammy and my parents arrive. She takes both of my cheeks in her hands. "You made it," she says. I know she doesn't mean the wedding. I made it out of the place I had been for years, caught up in my failures. And she gave me the final push.

The helicopter lands, and Jude gets out with little Caden, followed by the others.

We're a ragtag bunch in shorts and T-shirts, chosen for vacation travel.

But we're here. All of us.

We're about to move to the top of the hill when we realize we don't have the minister.

"Who can marry us?" Leo asks. The crowd rumbles with talk, wondering if there is another member of the clergy in their midst.

But it's the King who steps forward. "I am the head of state. There is no contract, social or otherwise, beyond my power to execute in Avalonia's borders."

Rosenthal passes the King a book. "So it looks more official." It's the only detail of the new royal wedding he's been able to control.

It's not a Bible. I bend my head to catch the title on the spine. *How to Make Friends and Influence People.*

Leo sees it too. He leans close to my ear. "I'm pretty sure he's never read it."

"And yet, he carries it around?" I stifle a giggle.

Lili rushes over. "You need something borrowed. It's an American tradition, right?" She holds up a strip of her dress and ties it around the bouquet.

"And something new," Grammy says. "I made this for you to carry today." She presses a handkerchief into my hands.

It's white with a lace edge. Green leaves surround the words *love grows here.*

She's right. It does. And will keep doing so as Leo and I get to know each other even more. "Thank you."

"You need something blue," Mom says. She pulls off the aquamarine ring that I've seen on her finger ever since I was old enough to hold her hand. She never takes it off. "You seem short a ring. This was my grandmother's engagement ring. It's yours."

I hold it for a moment. It's hard to imagine her finger without this ring. I hold her close. "Thank you."

I give the ring to Caden. He'll be the ring bearer after all. He looks at it curiously, then immediately drops it in the grass.

"Caden!" Greta cries. She digs in the grass in a panic until she locates the ring. She puts Caden on her hip and holds the ring herself. "I think we'll do this job together."

The sun is setting when we walk to the hilltop. From this vantage point, I take in how many people are out there. Far more than would have fit in the abbey.

It seems right. I understand the worries about security, but I like that my royal wedding will be attended by the townspeople, the guards, and the herders.

Everyone falls quiet, and the King's voice booms, carrying across the valley. "Citizens of Avalonia, we are gathered here today for the royal wedding of Prince Leopold the Second, heir to the throne of Avalonia, and Sunny Marie Packwood."

Gosh. He knows my name. No Sunholia or Sunandia nonsense.

Leo and I grasp hands, unable to take our eyes off each other. I've never seen a smile so big, nor have I ever heard his voice so earnest when he repeats the vows.

"I, Leopold the Second, take you, Sunny Marie Pack-wood, to be my lawfully wedded wife. To have and to hold, from this day forward, as long as we both shall live. May we reign long over Avalonia."

My voice shakes when it's my turn. "I, Sunny Marie Packwood, take you, Prince Leopold the Second, to be my lawfully wedded husband. To have and to hold, from this day forward, as long as we both shall live. May we reign long over Avalonia."

The King nods. "Do we have the ring?"

Both Greta's hand and Caden's pudgy fingers extend the ring out to Leo.

When his father draws in a breath to continue the vows, Leo shakes his head. "I've got this."

"Proceed," the King says.

He slides my great-grandmother's ring on my finger. "Sunny, when I met you, I was literally crawling on the floor. Since then, you have lifted me up, and I solemnly hope that as we move through life together, I will do the same for you."

I'm trying not to cry.

"You told me once that you allowed an outsider to take away your dream of poetry. We will never allow that. While your hope is in my hands, there is nothing we won't accomplish. You are the dream I didn't know existed. And I look forward to living it for the rest of my life."

We stare at each other for long moments. Then the crowd chants, *"Kiss her, kiss her, kiss her!"*

The King says, "It's official as far as I'm concerned."

We laugh, and then Leo's lips are on mine.

I'm home. I can feel it.

Before, my home was where I grew up, with my parents and sister. Then I thought I had a home at the university, when I studied poetry, but I eventually had to walk away.

Even my little apartment was only a temporary place to live. In these hills, I know my place. To walk with my husband, my prince. To write poetry.

And probably not *Death of a Princess*.

I want others to come to me with their aspirations, writers, poets, whoever they may be. I know what it is to be crushed. To lose your way. I want them to see a future beyond the daily grind.

Mopping floors doesn't mean you can never write a powerful song or invent some new perfect thing. Chopping pickles all day doesn't exclude you from studying dance or shooting a film or blowing the most beautiful glass.

And as long as it's in my power, no one who comes to me will feel anything but hope in their dreams, no matter how far away it feels.

CHAPTER 40

Prince Leopold

Two weeks later

On the morning of my thirtieth birthday celebration, I find Sunny sitting at the desk in her poetry room. We've rearranged the chambers to make this space for her, and our bedroom is elsewhere.

I lean over her shoulder and kiss her neck. She has a preview copy of the special edition of *The Universe of Poetry* that includes the pictures of the walls as well as her full poems. "How do they look?"

"Good. I wish I could get better at my craft before this issue runs, but we'll go with what we've got."

I brush loose hair from her forehead. "They wanted to strike while the iron was hot. The visibility will help set up your poetry trust." She's already had the legal director create a fund that will help other poets take long periods away from work to focus on their writing skills.

I'm proud of her.

"I can't believe I'm finally going to be in this magazine." She flips the page. Two whole spreads of her verses.

"I can't believe it took them this long to recognize your genius."

She laughs. "Hardly. But beauty is in the eye of the beholder."

"Mmm. And I have something in my eye right now."

"You crazy man." She turns to greet my kiss.

A rap on the door interrupts us. My new butler Jacoby enters. "Your Royal Highness, the King and Queen request a private luncheon with you and the Princess before the party."

"Sure. We'll be down… in a few minutes."

Jacoby's jaw shifts, and I know he's biting his cheek to stop from smiling. He's figuring out that when we say *not now*, we have better things to do for the moment.

He gives a nod and quickly exits the room.

I pull Sunny from the chair. "So we've broken in most of the rooms in our wing, but never with your published poetry on the desk." I lift her up to sit beside the pages. "What do you think?"

"I think it's damn hot."

"You can do better than that."

She laughs. "It's *fucking* hot."

"There's that language I was looking for. We can't have you going all prim princess on me."

"No chance of that." She leans forward and bites my neck, a fiery little predilection we discovered on our honeymoon. I like it.

I bury my face in her hair. "Are you obeying my royal decree?" We have a list of them, just between us. She's been weaving them into a collection of naughty limericks.

"The one about any skirt longer than my knees?"

"That's the one."

"I wrote the rhyme for it."

I pull her to the edge of the desk and find the hem of the long, full skirt she's wearing. "Let's hear it."

"A prince chose a skirt for his bride."

I slip my hands beneath the skirt to find her knees. "I did choose this one."

"Long enough to go well past her thigh."

My thumbs slide up the inside of hers.

"She knew he was peckish."

"I'm always hungry for you."

"In need of his fetish."

And I am. My hands keep moving up her legs.

"And tossed her cute panties aside."

I reach the top of her thighs and press my fingers inside her, unhindered by satin or lace. "It's good when you obey your sovereign."

"What are you going to do with your naked princess?"

I'm already unbuckling my pants.

"I think you already know."

"I better."

She gasps when I enter her, jerking her body forward onto mine. I unbutton the front of her floral blouse. She's blossoming here, both with her dreams and our craving for each other.

As I lower my mouth to a breast and listen to her cries

as our bodies fit together, I have no doubt that my years of searching brought me to her.

At the last moment I could have found my princess, a New York chase at the end of my bachelorhood led me straight to the love I will hold on to for all of my life.

Epilogue: Sunny

Six months later

I want to tell Octavia and Lili the news first, so I cross the palace to their wing, Emilio at a reasonable distance behind.

Lili is in her room. "Where's your sister?" I ask.

"Watching the guards from the tower, probably. It's all she ever does."

Interesting. "Let's go up. I have something to tell both of you."

Lili uncurls herself from the chair.

I haven't been in the tower since the days before the wedding. It's soiled to me after the other bride was there, but as we enter the bedroom, I find I don't think on that at all. I see Leo everywhere, crawling through the window, tangled in the sheets.

"She must be in the sitting room," Lili says. "I swear she's been here every day since the new contingent arrived."

We cross to the other room, and Lili's right. Octavia's not at the window facing the square, but the side window, which looks out upon the great lawn inside the castle walls. Below, four lines of guards are doing pushups.

They have their shirts off.

"I see the appeal," I say, startling Octavia. She really was in the zone.

"Oh. Hey. Yeah."

I can't help but laugh. "It's all right. They're the first group under thirty, right?" It's one of the changes we made after traveling with an aging brigade who did not have fun attending dance clubs and other loud, busy nightlife spots Leo was dying to take me to.

Lili plunks down on the seat beside her, aiming her cell phone down. "Thirst traps. Totally great for my feed."

Octavia watches the men a moment longer. I sit on a chair away from the window, remembering how we glittered Lili's shoes the night I met them.

That time seems so long ago. I run my fingers over the rings on my other hand. The blue wedding ring my mother gave me. The additional band provided by the family, ten outrageous diamonds that fit against the sapphire perfectly.

And the original betrothal ring, which is a tradition to wear for the first year of marriage before it's placed in the vault to await the next Crown Prince.

The pale, shimmery dresses are gone, other than for official dinners. I have a whole new wardrobe, mostly suggested by Rosenthal, who finally realized we had the same taste for bright colors and theatrical ensembles.

A whistle blows below, and Octavia closes the window with a sigh. "They'll be inside for the next few hours."

She's got it bad. "You know their schedule."

"She's been helping serve their lunches," Lili says. "Father hasn't caught her yet."

"Is there one in particular?" I ask.

"Oh, no, of course not." But Octavia's words and the blush on her cheeks say different things.

I push, just a little. "What's his name?"

She shakes her head. "It's nothing."

Lili and I meet gazes. She shrugs. "I've been trying to get it out of her since they got here."

"There's no one," Octavia insists. "Because it doesn't matter. Guards aren't allowed near us. Even at the lunch I have to stand on the back side of the table."

Lili picks up a pillow. "Grab one and drag him into the pantry. That would be so hot." She clutches the pillow to her in a passionate embrace.

Octavia snatches it away. "Stop it. You two came up here for something, I assume. Not just to spy on me."

I hold up my hands. "No spying here."

"I'm always spying," Lili says.

I wait until they stop jostling each other. I should speak to Leo about taking them traveling. They should get out more, see more things, meet more people. It's a priority now that his tour as Crown Prince is over, although there will definitely be a break in our travel eventually.

"So, your brother and I have news."

"You're not moving to New York, are you?" Octavia glances at her sister. "We've been terribly worried about you two doing that and leaving us alone again."

"Nope. Not moving there. But a trip soon, though. Very soon. Next week, even."

"With us?" Lili looks extraordinarily hopeful.

"Absolutely with you two."

"So, is that the news?" Octavia asks. "We're all going to New York?"

"No. There's more." I subconsciously press my hand to my belly.

"Oh my God!" Lili shouts. "You're pregnant!"

I nod.

"Oh my God! Oh my God!" Both sisters jump up and lock arms, turning in happy circles.

Octavia is the first to approach my chair. "Are you feeling okay? Do you throw up a lot? When is the baby due? Should you really go to New York?"

I laugh. "Feeling fine. I've only thrown up a few times. Baby is due in September. And it's fine to travel this early. I've decided to tell my family in person. And you two are coming!"

Lili turns in circles. "Imagine the footage I can get there! And we could go to parties. And meet people!" She shakes Octavia's shoulders. "This is going to be great!"

"Do Mother and Father know?" Octavia asks. She keeps looking at my belly in my red pantsuit.

"We're telling them at dinner. We thought it would be fun to let you know first."

"We knew first! We knew first!" Lili continues her circles until she collapses on the window bench.

Leo's head pops into the room. "The guards said you all were up here."

I hold out my hand to him. "We are."

"Do they know?"

"They do."

Lili runs across the room, crashing into Leo's belly. "I'm going to be the best auntie. I'm going to buy her toys and make sure she listens to the important bands and teach her how to work around the YouTube block in the palace."

Leo laughs. "You do that. Even if it's a boy."

"Ugh, boys. I guess that will be okay."

Octavia stays seated by me. "Sunny says we're going to New York next week to tell her family in person. All of us!"

"I like that plan."

He kneels next to me, and his sisters park themselves on the floor.

It's better than maids or ladies-in-waiting. It's family. Mine. Leo's. All of ours.

I have it in spades.

And the best times for this royal family are still ahead.

Love the Pickle family? Each of Sunny's three cousins have a love story! Get started with Jason's secret boss romance with Nova in Big Pickle or watch big, tough Max fall for his best friend's sister in Hot Pickle.

Never miss a Pickle book by signing up for the text or email alert for new releases!

BOOKS BY JJ KNIGHT

Romantic Comedies

Big Pickle

Hot Pickle

Spicy Pickle

Royal Pickle

Tasty Mango

Second Chance Santa

Single Dad on Top

The Accidental Harem

MMA Fighters

Uncaged Love Series

Fight for Her Series

Reckless Attraction

Get emails or texts from JJ about her new releases:

JJ Knight's list

About J J Knight

JJ Knight is one of the pen names of six-time *USA Today* bestselling author Deanna Roy. She lives in Austin, Texas, with her family.

To choose your next read from one of her fifty books, visit the web site **Read Laugh Swoon** to pick by book boyfriend, story line, heat level and more!

facebook.com/jjknightauthor

twitter.com/deannaroy

instagram.com/deannaroyauthor

bookbub.com/profile/jj-knight

tiktok.com/@deannaroy.author